The Unknown Arthur

Forgotten Tales of the Round Table

John Matthews

Illustrated by Mark Robertson

BLANDFORD

A BLANDFORD BOOK

First published in the UK 1995 by Blandford
A Cassell Imprint
Cassell plc, Wellington House
125 Strand, London WC2R 0BB

Distributed in the United States by
Sterling Publishing Co., Inc. 387 Park Avenue South,
New York, NY 10016–8810

Distributed in Australia by
Capricorn Link (Australia) Pty Ltd
2/13 Carrington Road,
Castle Hill, NSW 2154

**A Cataloguing-in-Publication Data entry for this title
is available from the British Library**

ISBN 0–7137–2476–5

Typeset by Keystroke, Jacaranda Lodge,
Wolverhampton

Printed and bound in Great Britain by Bath Press

Contents

The Round Table

For no man wist who was best
nor in arms the doughtiest –
did he ordain the Round Table
that men tell of, many fables.
None sit within, none sit without,
but all ever round about;
none sat first, none sat last,
but peer by peer ever cast,
none sat high, none sat low,
but all evenly for to know;
none was sat at the end
but all around, and all were hende;*
none wist who of them most was,
for they set all in compass.
All at once down they sitten,
at once rose, when they had eaten;
all were served of a service.
evenly all of an assize.

Robert Manning of Brunne (1288–1338)

* gentle

Introduction

The Lost Tales of Arthur and His Knights

THE legends of King Arthur and his knights – termed the Matter of Britain, to distinguish them from the Matter of France, the legends of Charlemagne – remain for many the most singular literary phenomenon of the Middle Ages. Surfacing from a melting-pot of folk tradition and myth in the eleventh century, stories and songs, poems and dramas relating to Arthur became over the next 500 years the most familiar, most often requested material of song-makers and story-tellers. Histories (called chronicles) or collections of tales such as the *Historia Regum Britanniae* (*History of the Kings of Britain*) by Geoffrey of Monmouth, the massive Old French *Vulgate Cycle*, collected and set down by monks of the Cisterian order, and the wonderful collection of tales known as *Le Morte D'Arthur* (*The Death of Arthur*) by the renegade English knight Sir Thomas Malory existed in dozens of manuscript copies – a rare thing at a time when all books had to be painstakingly written out by hand and an indication of their obvious popularity.

Such was the fame of Arthur that in the 1170s the historian Alanus de Insulis was able to write:

What place is there within the bounds of the empire of Christendom to which the winged praise of Arthur the Briton has not extended? Who is there, I ask, who does not speak of Arthur the Briton, since he is but little less known to the peoples of Asia than to the Britons, as we are informed by our palmers who return from the countries of the East? The Eastern peoples speak of him as do the Western, though separated by the breadth of the whole earth. Egypt speaks of him, and the Bosphorus is not silent. Rome, queen of cities, sings his deeds, and his wars are not unknown to her former rival, Carthage. Antioch, Armenia and Palestine celebrate his feats.

Elsewhere, the same author bears witness to the passion with which native peoples clung to the stories of Arthur, and to the belief that he was not dead but sleeping within some hill or tumulus until the need of his people should call him back. In this case, Alanus noted:

Go to the realm of Armorica, which is in lesser Britain [Brittany], and preach about the market-places and villages that Arthur the Briton is dead as other men are dead, and facts themselves will show how true is Merlin's prophecy, which says that the ending of Arthur shall be doubtful. Hardly will you escape unscathed, without being whelmed by curses or crushed by the stones of your hearers.

The truth behind the great epics is somewhat different. In reality there are probably three Arthurs, in addition to the king of medieval tradition. They are:

1 Artorius, the Roman *Dux* or 'Duke' of Britain, a leader rather than a king, who united the Britons in their struggle against the Saxons some time in the fifth century. His reputation caused him to be subsumed by

2 Arth, the Bear God, an ancient, shadowy, Celtic deity who is possibly remembered in the name of the constellation of Lyra – in Wales known as Telyn Idris, the Harp of Arthur – who in turn metamorphosed into

3 Arthyr, a half-legendary Celtic king with a band of wondrous warriors with names like Glewelwyd Mighty-Grasp and Gwri Interpreter of Tongues and others who had skills that enabled them to hear, say, an ant scratching itself fifty miles away, or who had strange anatomies which enabled them, say, to stretch up to the top of a tall tree and see the enemy coming, or take shelter from the rain under an enormous bottom lip!

All of these were drawn upon by Arthur's first major chronicler, Geoffrey of Monmouth, whose *History of the Kings of Britain* became a twelfth-century best-seller. In the time between the end of the historical Arthurian period – the late fifth and early sixth centuries, as far as we can judge – there had been a mass exodus of people from Britain into Brittany and Gaul. And, of course, they took their stories with them. Now these same tales returned in the repertoire of the bards and story-tellers attached to the Norman court. By the middle of the eleventh century, the stories of King Arthur and his knights of the Round Table were firmly re-established in both Britain and France, but they had been transformed into courtly romances, dressed in the costumes and following the ways of the eleventh century.

Beneath the elaborate façade of these tellings – many of them of the highest artistic quality – lay something much older: a collection of mythic tales, told at the hearthside by flickering firelight in the halls of ancient Celtic kings. Here the first stories were told, and in the telling grew into a vast cycle of adventure, passion and magic. Arthur was joined by others whose names have become familiar to all who love the enchanted realms: Merlin, Gawain, Lancelot, Guinevere, Tristan, Iseult.

Looking deeper, behind Malory's mail-clad knights and their silken ladies, we find a whole world of myth and wonder. In collections such as the Welsh *Mabinogion*, collected and written down in the early Middle Ages but containing material from a much earlier time, we find many of the seeds which later blossomed into the splendour and panoply of *Le Morte D'Arthur* or the intricate poems of Chrétien de Troyes.

In an even more ancient text, the *Preiddeu Annwn* (*Spoils of the In-world*), which dates from the ninth century, Arthur leads a wild band of warriors – among whom one may detect the presence of Lancelot, though under another name – in a voyage to the Celtic Otherworld, there to find and bring back the magical 'Cauldron of Annwn'. This object, one of several which had the power to bring the dead back to life, among other things, is our earliest version of the Grail. By Malory's time the quest for this magical vessel, now identified with the cup of the Last Supper, had become the subject of visionary writings of all kinds – an extraordinary pageant mirroring humanity's search for the greatest truths.

Such was Arthur's renown that, when William Caxton set up his printing press in Westminster, one of the first books he produced (in 1485) was Sir Thomas Malory's *Morte D'Arthur*. In the foreword to that famous edition, he writes:

many noble and divers gentlemen of this realm of England came and demanded me, many and ofttimes, wherefore I [had not] made and imprinted the noble history of the Sangreal, and of the most renowned Christian and worthy, King Arthur, which ought most to be remembered among us English men tofore all other Christian kings.

Thus prompted, Caxton went on to produce the book which, more than any other, established the fame of Arthur in Britain. Not only was Malory one of the finest prose stylists ever to write in English, but he tells a superb story with pace and flare. His ear for dialogue and his unerring ability to delete the prolix and dull from his sources make his book as exciting a read today as it was 500 years ago.

Inevitably, though, when drawing together the parts of such a vast subject matter, Malory left out as much or more than he put in. There is no account of Sir Gawain's encounter with the Green Knight, as found in the great fourteenth-century poem of that name, or indeed of Gawain's marriage with the hideous Dame Ragnall (see pages 99–106), Arthur's encounter with Gorlagon (see pages 41–51) or his fantastic adventures with the parrot (see pages 138–59).

Interest in Arthurian subjects did not end with the Middle Ages. Despite a brief decline in the sixteenth and seventeenth centuries, the stories were not forgotten. Such luminaries as the Spanish novelist Miguel de Cervantes and the great English poet John Milton both toyed with Arthurian themes – Cervantes including Merlin in his picaresque novel *Don Quixote* and Milton considering an Arthurian epic before he turned to the biblical story of the Fall. Michael Drayton, in *Poly-Olbion*, his extraordinary poetical meditation on the history and land of Britain, traced the presence of Arthur and his companions in 100 different sites and stories.

In these ages, for the most part, Arthur was a purely mythical figure, and it was only in the eighteenth century that a new breed of antiquaries – proto-historians – began to examine the historical and archaeological evidence for the existence of a real Arthur. Learned men like William Camden and William Stukeley, really more folklorists than actual historians, noted local legends of Arthur at places like Cadbury Camp in Somerset, believed to be the actual site of the fabled Camelot, and of course the multifarious legends and stories which concentrated around the town of Glastonbury, also in Somerset (the Summer Lands of Celtic myth), to where the most sacred relic in Christendom, the Holy Grail, was said to have been carried by Joseph of Arimathea. The stories of the Grail, the cup used by Christ at the Last Supper and into which some of his blood fell at the Crucifixion, added an entirely new dimension to the original warrior ethos of the Arthurian tales – they were for ever after stories of spiritual quest as well as of high chivalric adventure.

From the middle of the nineteenth century onwards, when the Poet Laureate Alfred, Lord Tennyson published his massive *Idylls of the King* and achieved a success seldom equalled by poets before or since, a vast stream of works centring on one or other aspect of the Arthurian tales has continued to pour forth. Whether the poets wrote of Merlin, or the Grail quest, or the loves of Arthur and Guinevere, and Tristan and Iseult, they kept the Arthurian dream alive and made it for ever a part of the literature of the land.

In our own time this has been no less the case. With the upsurge of interest in fantasy literature and the mythopoeic approach promoted by the writings of J.R.R. Tolkien, new novels, plays, poems and movies with Arthurian themes have continued to appear regularly every year. Story-tellers the world over continue to add to and embellish the original medieval tales.

Along with this explosion of material has gone a rich revival of medieval scholarship which has begun to bear fruit in the shape of new translations and critical studies. Unfortunately, many of these remain obscure, the territory of the medievalist or the passionately committed Arthurian; which is a shame, since it robs the general reader of much that is entertaining, exhilarating and profound. Modern editions of Malory abound (at least five are in print as I write), while numerous translations of the poems of the great French writer Chrétien de Troyes are readily available. This is, however, only a very small part of the story. Literally dozens of texts exist – some alas still untranslated into English – which are seldom if ever referred to in the more popular books about Arthur. They are no less exciting or fascinating than Malory, Chrétien or even the better known – though seldom read – authors such as Wolfram von Eschenbach (whose *Parzifal* was the basis for Richard Wagner's great opera of the same name) and Gottfried von Strassburg, whose extraordinary erotic poem concerning the love of Tristan and Iseult remains little known outside the realms of medieval literature classes. Alongside these great works are a smaller collection of texts by less familiar authors. Who today, for example, has heard of Guillaume Leclerc (author of *Fergus of Galloway*) or Renaut de Bage, who wrote *The Fair Unknown*, or Heldris of Cornwall, author of the *Romance of Silence*, who is perhaps the first feminist writer? Those who have never sought out these obscure authors and their even more obscure titles have missed a good deal. They will not know about the girl-child Avenable, nick-named 'Silence', who was brought up as a man and later captured Merlin: or about the knight Lanval, who met and married a faery woman, and the trouble this brought him; or, indeed, about how Sir Gawain and Queen Guinevere met a grisly ghost by the shore of the haunted lake Tarn Wathelyn.

All these episodes, and much more besides, are contained in the stories retold here. I hope that everyone who reads this book will be not only pleasantly surprised at the unfamiliar richness of the stories which await them but also encouraged to seek out the original, full-length versions of the texts, many of which are far more accessible than might at first be thought, and certainly deserve reading now every bit as much as they did when they were originally written.

The versions printed here are not translations in any exact sense of the word, but rather are retellings of the original stories in modern prose. However, I have generally resisted the temptation to 'improve' on the originals by rationalizing the plots or motivation, even though these may seem at times bizarre or odd to us now. I felt that the stories deserved to be read as far as possible as they were written, and have opted instead for explanatory introductions to each story, with very occasionally an expansion or abridgement of detail to make the less familiar themes and ideas clearer.

In working through these stories, I have found there to be a number of common themes –

chivalry, of course; romantic love; the bravery of the errant knights who pit themselves against all kinds of danger. But by far the most potent and powerful theme is the continued encounters between Arthur and his knights and beings of the Otherworld. It is almost as though there were some kind of warfare going on, a rift between the worlds which prompts otherworldliness to invade. Again and again we find scenarios which reflect this. It seems that almost every time either the king or one of his knights leaves the safety of the walls of Camelot or Caerleon or Carlisle, the Otherworld awaits him – often just around the corner. If, on the other hand, they do not venture forth, the otherworldly beings are just as likely to force an entry themselves – offering games, quests or challenges which none of the fabled fellowship can risk refusing for fear of damaging his reputation as a brave and fearless man.

It is through such inspired story-telling that we learn details of not only the rich and varied medieval life and spirituality of the time but also the dreams that haunted the minds of their makers – men and women who were certainly a great deal closer to the world of subtle reality than most of us today. It is this inner life which continues to inhabit the Arthurian tradition and means that it continues to exercise such a powerful fascination over us today.

To all who enjoy a good story, then, and who would like to know more about King Arthur and his times than just the old familiar tales of Lancelot, Gawain, Merlin and the rest, this volume is dedicated. May you all find as much pleasure and delight in reading it as I did in writing it!

John Matthews, Oxford

1

The Vows of King Arthur and His Knights

THE tale known as *The Avowing of King Arthur, Sir Gawain, Sir Kay and Baldwin of Britain* exists in a single manuscript, the Liverpool Ireland MS, now in Geneva. This dates from some time after 1450, though the poem itself was probably written earlier. Like *The Adventure at Tarn Wathelyn* (see pages 107–13) and the more familiar *Wedding of Sir Gawain and Dame Ragnall* (see pages 99–106), it is written in a Middle English dialect which suggests that it was composed by a poet living in the West Midlands. It is some 1,148 lines in length and full of lively description and passages of action which still read well today.

The story it tells is really several tales bound together by the device of the multiple vow. This theme is well known throughout medieval tradition and appears in several other Arthurian tales, including *The Wedding of Sir Gawain and Dame Ragnall*, *The Carl of Carlisle* and the famous *Sir Gawain and the Green Knight*. All these illustrate, in their own way, the importance of the vow, which was not taken lightly and was seldom, if ever, reneged upon.

The theme of Arthur's pursuit of the boar goes back to Celtic myth, where, in the old Welsh tale of *Culhwch and Olwen* not only Arthur but also his entire band of heroes pursue the mighty Twrch Trwyth, a boar of such mythic stature that it destroys half the country before it is finally brought to bay. In the story as given here, there is a wonderfully realistic account of the battle between the king and the boar which could have been written only by someone who had taken part in such hunts. The boar was certainly a worthy opponent at the time when the poem was written, since boars were larger and fiercer than their current descendants, weighing in at around 300 pounds and often measuring up to four feet in height. The seeming exaggeration in this poem, with the beast described as 'taller than a horse' might, then, not be so far from the truth.

The knight encountered by Kay and Gawain, who is named Menealfe in this story, may represent a lingering echo of a more otherworldly characteristic the story once had before it was written down by its rather pious author. Menealfe can mean 'Elf-man', or even, as suggested by Nirmal Dass (see below), derive from classical Greek, meaning 'he incurs the wrath'. If the former is true, the knight has certainly lost any of the supernatural qualities such a name might lead us to expect.

The three knights who accompany Arthur include the familiar Gawain and Kay and the less well-known Baldwin, who actually carries the weight of the story. He appears elsewhere in another Middle English poem, *Sir Gawain and the Carl of Carlisle*, where he is referred to as 'Bishop Baldwin'. As Louis Hall (see below) points out: 'In this last tale the bishop acts like a knight, but here the knight talks like a bishop.'

The *exempla* (literally 'examples') given by Baldwin are hard to swallow in this day and age – especially the first, in which Baldwin seems to be saying that if women are kept busy, they remain submissive, but if they are allowed too much freedom or idleness, they may well get up to evil! Not many readers would stomach this kind of sexist remark today, but we have to remember that in the Middle Ages customs were different and women were, by and large, depicted as second-class citizens (and even, by the Church, as tools of the devil).

Perhaps the only way to interpret the tale for a modern audience is to see Baldwin's remarks as an ironic comment on the lives and mores of his peers. Indeed, none of the knights, save Baldwin himself, comes off very well in this story. Arthur is shown as an irreverent prankster, Kay as a boastful coward and Gawain, though he conducts himself well enough, is little more than a cipher of knightly excellence. Baldwin, by comparison, towers over the rest. He is a more rounded character, with humour, wisdom and manly courage. Perhaps his earlier portrayal as a bishop had something to do with this, since despite the changes which characters regularly undergo in the Arthurian legends, they frequently carry over aspects of their earlier incarnations into later texts. Baldwin's other stories are more universal and actually carry a powerful charge of wisdom.

However one feels about any of this, the tale moves along briskly and ends in a well-rounded way. It is a story rooted very much in this world, with a minimum of magical detail of the kind usually found in Arthurian texts. As a story of four boastful men, it can amuse us; as a piece of the pattern which is the Arthurian mythos, it is exciting and rich in detail.

Editions include W. H. French and C. B. Hale, *Middle English Metrical Romances* (New York, Russell and Russell, 1930) and, more recently, Roger Dahood, *The Avowing of King Arthur* (New York, Garland Press, 1984). There is also an excellent verse translation by Nirmal Dass (New York, University Press of America, 1987). I have used mostly French and Hale, augmented by Louis B. Hall's excellent prose rendition in his *The Knightly Tales of Sir Gawain* (Chicago, Nelson Hall, 1976).

NE DAY KING ARTHUR HELD COURT at Carlisle, and there a huntsman came to him and told him how a grim boar stalked the forest nearby. 'Never did I see such a one before. I have broken more spears and arrows on his hide than I care to remember, and he has killed a number of my hounds. He is truly vast in size and strength; big as a bull, black as a bear, tall as a horse. His tusks tear up whole trees and he leaves a trail of dust behind him like an army.'

'If this is true,' Arthur said, 'we shall look into the matter. I would see this monster for myself.'

The king gave orders that no one else was to go after the boar save himself and three knights whom he chose from among his best men. They were Sir Gawain, Sir Kay and Baldwin of Britain. These four, together with Arthur's chief huntsman and master of hounds, set out to track the dreadful beast to its lair.

First they loosed the tracker dogs, then the hounds, and soon enough the music of the chase echoed through the forest. Yet when the great boar was cornered at last, it turned upon the hounds and ripped them to pieces with its terrible tusks.

When King Arthur and his knights arrived, the huntsman awaited them. 'There is the beast,' he said grimly. 'Be advised and leave him alone, for I swear he will slay you all if you venture near him.'

Therewith the huntsman turned for home, since all his hounds were dead, and there was no more work for him to do. But Arthur looked to where the boar could be heard, snorting and rooting in his den, and said, 'Sirs, I will make a vow before you all. Even though my huntsman was not hardy enough to attempt it, I will bring the beast down by myself and prepare him for the feast. Now, I command you, do you each make a vow of your own!'

Gawain, ever ready to accept a challenge, said, 'I will watch at Tarn Wathelyn all night', for he remembered, doubtless, the apparition which had haunted him there before.*

Kay said roughly, 'I will ride through this forest from now until this time tomorrow and kill anyone who stands in my way or challenges me to combat.'

All three now looked at Baldwin, who laughed and said, 'I'll not be different. I vow that never in all my life will I be jealous of my wife, or suspicious of any pretty girl; nor will I refuse food to anyone that asks for it, or fear any threat of death from any man.'

Having made their vows, the four men parted and each went his own way: Arthur turning towards the boar's den, Gawain towards the tarn and Kay into the forest. Baldwin, however, returned to Carlisle and went to bed.

---

* See *The Adventure at Tarn Wathelyn*, pages 107–113.

Now let us speak first of the king, as is right. He sent his own hounds into the thicket around the boar's den. But the fearsome beast soon routed them and Arthur was forced to call them off. Then he heard the beast coming towards him, rooting up trees and stones as he came. The king leapt upon his horse and seized his spear and prepared to meet the creature. No one knew what his charge was like, since no one had ever survived it.

When the creature came in sight, King Arthur quailed. Red-eyed it was and horribly bristly. It charged with its mouth wide open and flecks of foam flew from its jaws. Its tusks were at least three feet long and its hide was so thick and hard that when Arthur used his spear to fend it off, the wood splintered and the beast smashed straight into him.

The king fell winded from his horse, which was killed outright by the blow. Arthur himself received such a wound that he was to feel it the rest of his life. He struggled upright, leaning against the side of his dead mount for support, and, uttering a prayer to St Margaret, drew his sword and raised his shield.

When the boar struck him a second time, the shield shattered at once and the king was knocked over again. The beast smelled like a kiln or a hot kitchen, and its breath so overwhelmed him that he was almost overcome by the stench. He leaned against a tree and strove to collect his strength. This time, as the boar approached, Arthur was able to dodge to one side and he struck the creature so hard that it staggered. Quick to press his advantage, the king charged and struck again. His sword point went into the beast's throat and it fell to the earth. There the king dispatched it with a great blow to its neck, then he cut off its huge head and stuck it on a pole and set about butchering the body with all the skill of a professional venerer.

Until this was done, he would not rest, but when he had completed his bloody work and strips of meat hung drying from the branches of a great oak, he knelt briefly and gave thanks for his delivery. Then, weary and hurt, and with no one to attend him, King Arthur fell into a deep sleep.

Now let us turn to Sir Kay. As night began to fall, he rode in the forest and heard the sound of two horses approaching. Drawing aside from the path, he waited in the cover of the trees until he saw who came there. In front rode a girl weeping bitterly, followed by a grim-faced knight who drove her on. As she came abreast, Kay heard her cry out to be set free from this villainous knight. At that he rode forward, calling out to the knight to release the girl or turn and fight.

The other answered, 'I will be glad to accept your challenge, if you think you are ready for it.'

'Tell me first who you are,' demanded Kay.

'I am Sir Menealfe of the Mountain,' replied the knight. 'I won this lady in a tournament at Liddle Mort, just north of Carlisle.'

'Then prepare to lose her to me!' cried Kay, and the two dressed their shields and, laying their spears in rest, charged together.

Menealfe was the stronger of the two, as he proved by knocking Kay clean out of the saddle. He was so shaken and winded by this that he could not even get up at once, and, taking this as a sign of surrender, Menealfe declared him prisoner.

When he could speak again, Kay said, 'Sir, nearby is Sir Gawain, who awaits my coming. If you go to him at once, he will certainly ransom me.'

'I will be glad to do so,' replied Sir Menealfe at once. 'Let us go.'

They rode the short distance to the edge of Tarn Wathelyn, and there Gawain challenged them.

'It is I,' called out Kay. 'I made a vow I could not keep and as a result I am this knight's prisoner. Will you be so good as to ransom me?'

'Gladly,' said Gawain. 'What should I give?'

'Will you run a course with this knight?'

'Why not,' answered Gawain, 'If he is willing . . .'

'That I am, and gladly,' said Menealfe, and the two knights prepared to do battle.

Both were strong and powerful, but Gawain was the more skilled in the joust and his first spear laid out his opponent on the earth. Kay rejoiced then, mocking his fallen captor. But Gawain helped up his adversary, pulled off his helmet and let the air get to his face. Menealfe spoke quietly to him. 'Sir, you have ransomed this knight, who is so loath to let matters rest there. If you will allow me to rest for a while, I should be glad to joust with you again for this lady, who is my rightful prize.'

'I would be glad to do so,' said Gawain. And when Menealfe was rested, the two took fresh spears and mounted their horses and rode together again. Once again Gawain was victorious and Sir Menealfe was laid low with a wound to the head.

'Ha!' cried Kay. 'Now you have lost everything, for all your boastful talk.'

'Good fortune never lasts for ever,' said Gawain reprovingly. He went to help the fallen man to his feet, though indeed Kay's words caused him more hurt than his wounds.

'If we were alone,' he said to Kay, 'I would make you eat those words.'

'But we are not,' said Sir Kay haughtily, 'and you have lost everything.'

'God forbid we should speak so to a good knight who is fallen,' said Gawain. 'I pray you not to take Sir Kay's words ill. When you are stronger, ride with this girl to Arthur's court at Carlisle. Greet the queen for me and tell her that her knight, Sir Gawain, sends you. Let her decide the disposition of this matter. You will find, I am sure, that she will ransom this lovely girl in an appropriate manner.'

Sir Menealfe swore on the hilt of his sword that he would do as Sir Gawain asked and give safe passage to the girl on the road to Carlisle.

As they spoke, day was already beginning to dawn and they heard the notes of King Arthur's hunting horn. At once they all started out through the forest to find the king. They came to the place where the strips of boar's meat hung on the tree and the fearsome head was set up on a pole, and there they found the king, stiff and sore from his wounds and a night in the forest and still without a horse to ride, even though he was the king. So they gave him the girl's mount and set her up behind Sir Menealfe and the whole party set out for Carlisle.

As they rode, the king asked for an account of his two knights' adventures.

'I kept watch as I promised,' began Sir Kay, 'but this knight won me and then Sir Gawain won me back, and this girl as well, and took Sir Menealfe prisoner.'

The girl herself laughed aloud at this and began praising Sir Gawain.

'What is the ransom set to be?' asked Arthur.

'In truth I know not,' replied Menealfe. 'This brave knight would send me to the queen. She it is who will have the accounting of my life.'

'Now God be praised!' exclaimed Arthur. 'Do you ever fail in your quest, Sir Gawain? It seems to me you are always successful.'

Soon they reached Carlisle, and Sir Menealfe went before the queen and told her all that had occurred and pleaded his cause. Guinevere, praising Sir Gawain, gave as her judgement that the knight should swear allegiance to Arthur, and be a knight of the Round Table and serve him well in this way; and that the girl should become one of her ladies until such time as she was ready to marry.

Meanwhile, Kay spoke to the king. 'My lord, it seems to me that we three have all fulfilled our vows, but that we have still to hear from Baldwin. His vow seemed far greater than ours, but it is still to be proven.'

'By my faith, you are right,' said Arthur. 'I would indeed like to know how this vow can be fulfilled.'

'If you give me leave,' said Kay slyly, 'I will find a way to test at least some part of Baldwin's vow.'

'Very well' Arthur said. 'But only on the condition that you do him no great harm, nor bring shame to him.'

To this Kay promised, then he went and sought out five other knights, all cronies of his, and explained to them that Baldwin had sworn to overthrow anyone he met on the road who would challenge him. 'Let us,' said Kay, 'ride together and abreast so that he cannot pass. I know well where we shall find him.'

So they were agreed and rode in a body, side by side, upon the road which led to Baldwin's castle. It was raining hard and they all drew cloaks over their armour to keep it dry and to hide their identity. In this way they rode until they saw Baldwin approaching from the opposite direction, armed and eager like a man ready and willing to do battle.

Kay called out to him. 'Either stay or run, for you must fight us all if you want to pass this way.'

'Though you were twice as many you would not make me flee,' answered Baldwin. 'Now stand aside, for I am on my way to speak to the king and nothing will stop me.'

'You may take any other route you wish,' answered Kay, 'and no one the wiser. But you shall not pass here unless you fight us all together.' Then the six knights threw back their cloaks and showed themselves armed and ready.

'Very well,' said Baldwin, raising his shield and choosing a spear from those that rested by his saddle-bow. 'But don't say I failed to warn you. For I intend to continue on this way despite you!'

Then he charged them and knocked Sir Kay down first, and then, just as quickly, four others without even breaking his spear. Then he stood over Sir Kay, who had been helped up, and said, 'Is this enough for you?'

'Go where you want,' answered Kay groggily.

So Baldwin rode on until he reached Carlisle and went and stood before Arthur. 'Did you see or hear anything untoward in the forest?' asked the king.

Baldwin looked thoughtful, then shook his head. 'Sire, I heard and saw only the wind in the trees and the song of birds as I came this way.'

Then they went in to hear Mass and by the time they emerged, Kay and his fellows had arrived back at the court. Arthur took the seneschal aside and asked him how he had fared.

'Sire,' said Kay, 'Baldwin is indeed a mighty knight. Nothing could make him turn aside. I and five others have the bruises to prove it.'

This made Arthur smile, but he determined to test Baldwin himself this time and called to him his minstrel. 'I bid you go to the castle of Baldwin of Britain and stay there forty days. See whether any man is turned away from his door in that time or if anyone is refused meat who asks for it.'

So, while Baldwin remained with Arthur, the minstrel made his way as fast as he might to Baldwin's castle and there found ready admittance.

There were many guests already at table that evening and among them the minstrel found that no one was refused anything. He was free also to wander where he might, among both high- and low-born folk, and to take food or wine from any table there. Finally he went to the high table, where Baldwin's lady and her most noble guests sat, and was made welcome there also. Saying that he came from the southlands, he entertained all there with news from distant places and was rewarded with rich viands, wine and comfortable lodging – in which he remained for another week, until Baldwin himself returned, bringing King Arthur and Queen Guinevere to dine with him.

Such a royal procession of dishes and fine wines then came to them from the kitchens that even Arthur was moved to exclaim that he had never feasted so well. 'Well, sire,' Baldwin replied, 'God has a good plough and sends enough for us all. Why should we stint ourselves?'

'Now, indeed, I am having so good a time here that I will stay another day and night,' said Arthur, 'and I bid you to go and win us a fresh deer for the table. Take your hounds and huntsmen and see what good fortune attends you.'

To this Baldwin willingly agreed, but the moment he had set forth Arthur summoned his own huntsman and bade him go out and drive the game away from the place so that Baldwin was sure to be hard-pressed to capture anything. Then, when the hunting party had left, the king waited until darkness began to fall and called one of his knights to attend him. Then he went to the door of the chamber where the lady of the house slept with her maids.

The king knocked loudly. 'Open up!' he cried.

'Why must I do so?' asked the lady.

'Because I command it. I have come here for some secret sport.'

'Surely you have your own lady here,' replied Baldwin's wife, 'just as I have my own lord to love me?'

'Open up,' said Arthur again. 'I give you my word that no harm will come to you.'

After a moment one of the lady's maids opened the door, and the king went inside and sat on the end of the bed. 'Madam,' he said, 'this fellow of mine must lie beside you all night in this bed. But do not be alarmed,' he added quickly, seeing the lady start and blush, 'for this is no more than a bet to settle an argument.'

To the knight he said brusquely, 'Come on, man, get undressed and get into bed with this lady – but see that you do not touch her, on pain of death. Don't even stir or turn towards her.'

Hurriedly the knight obeyed and when he was beneath the covers King Arthur called for lights and a chessboard, and one of the girls to play with him. And thus they sat all night, until the morning dawned and they heard the sounds of the hunt returning.

Presently Baldwin entered the chamber, where he saw the king sitting by his wife's bedside while the knight lay beside her.

'Come in, sir,' said Arthur. 'How fared you at the hunt?'

'Well, my lord, I thank you,' said Baldwin.

'I see you looking at this knight,' said the king. 'I missed him last night and eventually found him here. I decided to await your return to ask you what action you wanted taken against him.'

'Why, none at all,' answered Baldwin, smiling at his wife. 'I will tell you why. Unless she wished it, or was so commanded, no man would come into this room. Also we have been together many winters and she has never done me harm before. Therefore I am certain there is no evil intended here.'

'So you are not angered by this?' demanded Arthur.

'Not at all,' said Baldwin. He looked calmly at the king. 'I would tell you a story, my lord, so that you may better understand why this causes me no pain.'

'Very well,' said Arthur, and Baldwin sat upon the edge of the bed and began to speak.

'During your father's youth, when his father, King Constantine, still ruled over Britain, it befell that the king gathered a host to fight against the Saracens in Spain. I had the honour of fighting in that war as a young knight, and I well remember how thoroughly we defeated the sultan and his men. I had the fortune to be noticed by the king, whom it pleased to reward me by giving me command over a number of men and giving me the lordship of a castle in that land.

'Now, it happened that there were only three serving women to care for our needs and, as is the way of things, one was more lovely than the others, for which reason her companions grew jealous and decided to kill her. This they did, and were dragged before me in fear of their lives. I asked them to give me reasons why I should not condemn them to death there and then, and they both fell down and begged for their lives, promising that they would do as much work as they *and* their companion had done before. "And," they said, "we shall see to it that none of you lack for anything, day or night."

'Well, they kept their promise, fulfilling their duties by day and entertaining us at night also. Until it befell that one of the two, who was prettier than the other, became jealous of her companion and, one night, cut her throat.

'Several of my fellows came to me and asked whether they should not kill the woman at once. But I counselled them to bring her before me and see what she would say. This they did and, as before, she promised to do as much work as any one woman could and to satisfy us at night according to our needs.

'So it fell out. By day she worked for us and at night offered us her body.

From this I learned that if women of this kind are left to follow their own course, they may well do evil, but if they are given the opportunity to devote themselves to others, without threats, and with plenty of goodwill, they will follow a better way of life. Therefore I shall never be jealous or suspicious of anything that happens because of a beautiful woman, for they are just as full of goodness as they are of evil. In any case,' Baldwin added, 'everything here on earth comes to an end in time.'

'You speak well,' said King Arthur. 'Therefore I will tell you what really happened here.' And he related all that had taken place the night before and how he had remained there all through the hours of darkness. Then he said, 'Sir, you have truly kept all your vows. But I would know more of your reasoning. Why do you not fear for your own death and make all welcome who come to your door. For as far as I can tell, your gates are always open.'

'I will be glad to tell you,' Baldwin said. 'In the same castle where the adventure I just spoke about took place, it happened that we were besieged. One day we decided to make a sortie and to try to take prisoners for ransom. One of our fellows was so fearful of the death which might come to him that he stayed behind, hiding in a barrel. While we were outside fighting, a projectile from a catapult came like a bolt of lightning and smashed the barrel to pieces. When we returned, we found his head completely severed from his body. From this I learned that death is not something one can avoid – it is natural and best welcomed when it comes.'

'These are fair words indeed,' said Arthur thoughtfully. 'But tell me why you never turn anyone away from your door that comes asking for food and shelter.'

'That is soon explained,' said Baldwin. 'At the time of the siege that I spoke of just now, our supplies ran very low and we were fearful that we should starve. Then a messenger came from the enemy and demanded that we give up everything we had and surrender ourselves to his master. I gave thought to this and then called the steward to prepare the very best of everything we had to eat – the best wine, bread, meat and fish that had been preserved against our last days. All this the sultan's messenger watched, and then, as he took his leave, we gave him a splendid flagon of wine and other gifts.

'When the messenger was gone, all the men in the castle complained to me that I had given away our last supplies. They were angry and despairing, but I knew what would happen and I was right. The messenger went back to his master and told him to give up the siege. "For though we have pressed these infidels for so long, they are as fresh as ever, and make merry as though it were a feast-day." And, because in truth the Saracens had disguised the fact that their own supplies were running low, they took counsel together and decided to raise the siege. Next day, they were gone.'

Baldwin finished his recital and smiled at the king. 'And so you see that I have never ceased to give all that I have, in the knowledge that there will always be sufficient. Nor have I ever been wrong in this belief.'

Then King Arthur embraced the older knight and said, 'Truly, there is no falsehood in you. All that you vowed you have honoured. Let it be recorded that you are foremost in worthiness among all my knights of the Round Table.'

And so it was done. And King Arthur said to Baldwin, turning to his wife, 'If you are wise, as I deem you must be, you will take this fairest of ladies to your heart. For a deep love lies within her and in her sight, as well as mine, you have fulfilled all your knightly vows.'

2

The Fair Unknown

THE story of the Fair Unknown appears in several versions and in more than one language. In English the text is called *Libeus Desconius*, in French it becomes *Le Bel Inconnu*. The story it tells, of the adventures of the famous son of a famous father who must prove his abilities whilst labouring under an alias or nickname, is a frequent theme in Arthurian legend. One of the most famous is Sir Thomas Malory's *Tale of Sir Gareth*, which forms an extended and largely separate episode within the pages of *Le Morte D'Arthur*. Malory almost certainly knew one of the versions of the Fair Unknown story, though he made several changes to it and gave it an overall coherence which its fellows lack.

The version I have followed here is *Le Bel Inconnu* by Renaut de Bage or Renals de Biauju, of whom nothing much is known beyond the few clues he gives in the text itself. He may have been a member of the influential Bage family, and if this identification holds up, the romance was probably written some time between 1191 and 1250. We cannot be more precise than this.

The story betrays the influence of Chrétien de Troyes, as well as the *Lai du Lanval* of Marie de France and the first and second *Continuations* of the French *Perceval*. References to famous knights of the Round Table such as Gawain, Lancelot, Sagramor, Kay, Yvain and others betray Renaut's wide reading, and the romance is dotted with exquisite detail of the costumes and customs of the twelfth and early thirteenth centuries. The author never fails to spend as long as possible (without holding up the action) on descriptions of buildings, clothing, food and song. The scene where the Fair Unknown reaches his goal, the enchanted city of the Golden Isle, and there encounters the enchanted *jongleurs* (singers), produces an array of nearly every musical instrument in current usage at the time, and there is indeed a strong musical influence running through the whole work.

Renaut was clearly a follower of the courtly love tradition, which placed women on pedestals and extolled the virtues of adultery. His frequent pleas to the figure of Love herself make it clear that he saw himself as a lover in the courtly fashion. The curious and, some would say, unsatisfactory ending of the romance, in which Renaut refuses to tell us anything more about his hero until he has held his own (lost or rejecting) lover naked in his arms again, suggests a personal story underlying the one which is being told.

In particular the portrait of the lady White Hands (perhaps named after Tristan's ill-starred wife) is interesting, since she clearly began life as a faery woman, and has been adapted to become a mysterious woman well versed in magic and the seven liberal arts – an education which would have been denied to most women at the time Renaut was writing. The fact that she knows her fate but does nothing to prevent it may seem unsatisfactory to modern readers, but is very much in keeping with the lore and custom of the time, when otherworldly women are seen as being unconcerned with mortal pursuits.

The realm of the Isle d'Or (Isle of Gold), over which she rules, is itself clearly an otherworldly dwelling. The palisade of sharpened stakes, bearing the heads of slain heroes, and the custom of the challenger who must replace the reigning champion if he succeeds in defeating him are enough to show this. Both are common themes in Arthurian stories, and always indicate the presence of supernatural events or places. Likewise, the episode of the Terrible Kiss (the *Fier Basir*, as it is called in the original romances) appears in several texts. Generally, the serpent would have had the head or face of a beautiful woman, but Renaut chooses to make it a serpent pure and simple – though no less fearsome for that.

Other notable episodes are those in which the Fair Unknown hesitates to enter the chamber of the lady White Hands, and, then, when he does, is presented with a number of fearsome tests – a raging torrent, toppling walls – which turn out to be illusions – all of which helps to reinforce the otherworldly nature of the story.

The Fair Unknown is a long work, numbering 6,266 lines. I have resisted the temptation to omit some of the adventures, because they all prove to have been foreseen and to have a bearing on later events. The teller's skill in keeping the listener alert for such a long time bears witness to his ability as a poet – though most readers would find him dull and jingly by today's standards. But his delight in the story and the way he plays with the literary conventions of the time – attributing the same features to more than one of his fair heroines in a deliberate attempt to illustrate his hero's confusion – show him to have been both well read and no slouch at his craft.

There have been three editions of the text, all of them in French and all generally superseded by the recent publication by Karen Fosco, admirably translated by Coleen P. Donagher (New York and London, Garland Press, 1992). I have used this edition throughout, with occasional reference to the introduction and notes by Williams G. Perrie in his revised edition of 1939 (Oxford, Fox, Jones, 1915).

NE YEAR IN THE MONTH OF AUGUST King Arthur held court at Caerleon. Most of the great knights were present, too many to list. In the evening they sat down to supper, and you may be sure it was the best meat and drink to be had in all the land! While they were eating, a young man rode his horse right into the hall and up to the dais where King Arthur, the queen and several of the knights were sitting.

'Sir, be welcome,' King Arthur said. 'Dismount and join us.'

'I thank you, most noble Lord,' replied the youth, 'but before I do so I crave a boon. Since this is Arthur's court, I know that I will not be refused – whatever it may be and whatever comes of it.'

'So long as it gives offence to no one, I shall grant it,' Arthur said. 'Now pray dismount and be welcome among us.'

Squires rushed forward to hold the youth's horse and to help him unarm. Many admired his fine armour and weapons, and the shield he carried, which was azure and bore upon it a lion of ermine. A place was found for him at the table and fresh food and drink set before him and water in which to wash his hands.

When he was seated, King Arthur sent his butler, Sir Bedivere, to ask the youth's name and parentage. But when Bedivere returned, it was to say that the youth had no name that he knew, but that he had always been called 'Fair Son' by his mother, and that as to his parents he knew only one, and that was she. Of his father's name or rank he knew nothing.

Then King Arthur looked to where the youth sat and said, 'Since you have no name and we must call you something, I shall give you a name. Let it be *Li Biaus Desconeus*' (which is to say, in the English tongue, 'The Fair Unknown').

As they were speaking there came two more people into the hall. In front came a maiden fair as a summer flower, riding upon a horse the colour of the clouds. Behind her, urging on the horse, came a dwarf, who for all his small stature had a face of great nobleness and beauty. Reining in her mount before the king, the maiden spoke.

'King Arthur, I am here to ask for your help for my lady, the daughter of King Guingras. She is held captive against her will, and the only way that she can be rescued is for a single knight, who must be the best and bravest of all your fellowship, to endure the adventure of the Fearsome Kiss.'

All this poured forth in a great rush of words, and when the maiden fell silent all the court was silent also. King Arthur looked around, seeking a face among the knights whom he might chose to send on this adventure. Before he could find anyone to name, the youth whom he had but now named the Fair Unknown leapt up.

'Sire,' he cried, 'now do I claim my boon, which is that you allow me to undertake this task.'

King Arthur frowned. 'This is too great a task for one so young and inexperienced,' he said.

'Sire, you gave your word to me that you would grant any boon I asked save that it did no disgrace to anyone. I ask for nothing more than that you honour your word.'

'So be it,' said the king. 'But first, come near, that I may make you a knight of the Round Table, for only thus may you undertake this adventure.'

As the Fair Unknown approached the king, the maiden, who had been silent thus far, now cried aloud. 'King Arthur! I asked for the *best* knight of your fellowship – not the worst. I see that I came hither in vain, and that I must return to my lady and tell her that there is no help coming from King Arthur! Come, Tidogolain!' And before the king could find words, she turned her horse and rode out of the hall, the dwarf trotting at her heels.

'Well,' said King Arthur to the Fair Unknown, 'do you still wish to pursue this course?'

'I will well, sire,' the youth answered.

'Then I declare before all that you are this day made knight of the Round Table.'

Thus the Fair Unknown was knighted, and before he set forth in pursuit of the maiden, Sir Gawain came forward and offered to arm him, for there was something about the youth that he admired, seeing something of his own high courage in him. As well as arms and weapons, Gawain entrusted to him one of his own squires, a clever young lad named Robert.

Thus armed and accoutred the Fair Unknown rode swiftly away from Caerleon in search of the maiden and the dwarf. Soon enough he espied them on the road and hastened to overtake them. The maiden's welcome was far from encouraging.

'What! Is that you, boy?' she said. 'Run home at once before you get hurt. I need a real knight to help my lady, not a beardless boy who was only knighted today.'

'My lady,' answered the Fair Unknown, 'the task has been given to me by my lord, King Arthur. I must follow you and attempt the adventure.'

To his surprise the dwarf Tidogolain spoke up.

'Lady, I think you should let the boy try his luck. After all, even a newly minted knight is better than no one at all.'

But despite his words the maiden continued to pour scorn on the Fair Unknown, though there was nothing she could do to stop him riding with her.

And so they journeyed until they came to a place that was known far and wide as the Perilous Ford. It had an evil reputation and most people avoided it. But the maiden's road lay this way, and the Fair Unknown must needs follow her.

As they approached the ford they saw a rough hut on the far side of the water, outside which leaned a shield that was one half gold and the other silver. In the entrance sat a tall knight playing chess with two youths. His name was Blioberis, and he was as proud and evil-hearted as he was strong. When he saw the Fair Unknown approaching with the maiden and the dwarf, he at once sprang up and the two youths began arming him. The squire, Robert, brought the arms that Gawain had given to the Fair Unknown and likewise prepared his master for battle.

Seeing this, the maiden turned to her unwanted companion. 'You had best be going home now,' she said. 'This is a most fierce and terrible knight and he will certainly kill you.'

But the Fair Unknown ignored her words and rode to the edge of the water. 'Sir,' he called out to the other knight, 'will you let us pass? I am on an urgent mission for King Arthur on behalf of this maiden's mistress.'

'I have held this ford for seven years,' Blioberis snorted. 'I am not about to give it up to a mere child.'

'Then you are no more than a brigand,' replied the Fair Unknown, and called out to Robert for a spear.

The two rode together and met with a crash in the middle of the ford. Both were unhorsed, but while the Fair Unknown escaped unhurt, his spear went directly to its target, opening a deep wound in Blioberis's side. The two knights drew their swords and went at it for some while longer, but Blioberis soon grew weak from loss of blood, and finally he fell down on his knees and begged for his life.

The Fair Unknown agreed to spare him, but made him promise that as soon as he was fit to ride, he would go directly to Arthur and place himself at the mercy of the king.

To this Blioberis agreed, and as Robert helped unarm his master, the dwarf was heard to remark to no one in particular that the young knight had certainly acquitted himself well, and that it was really a very good thing that he was with them.

The maiden merely shrugged her shoulders and again suggested to the young knight that he should return home. And again, just as firmly, he declined.

And so they rode on, leaving the wounded Blioberis in the care of his attendants. But, when the Fair Unknown was scarcely out of sight, the proud knight began thinking of how he might be avenged for the disgrace he had suffered. His thoughts turned to three companions with whom he had lately spent time, and who were expected back at the ford any time. These three were Elin the Fair, the Lord of Graie; the Strong Knight of Saire; and William of Salebrant.

That night they returned and, finding Blioberis lying wounded in his hut, asked what had occurred. Blioberis told them the whole story, and begged them to pursue the unknown knight and avenge him. 'Kill or capture him, I care not. Only thus may I be freed from the promise I made to him.'

That night the Fair Unknown, the maiden and their servants camped in a meadow, and there the young knight learned that his proud and unresponsive charge was named Helie. Beyond this they spoke little and soon settled down for the night. Later, when the moon had risen, casting its cool light over the land, the Fair Unknown woke suddenly to hear a voice from the depths of the forest crying out for help.

Helie and the others were woken also and the young knight asked if they heard it too. The maiden at once dismissed the cries as a something to be ignored. 'If you were thinking of going to answer that call, you would be advised not to. There will be adventures enough on the road ahead.'

The Fair Unknown answered courteously. 'Permit me to go,' he said. 'It is my duty as a knight of the Round Table to answer all cries for help.'

'Go then, if you want,' answered Helie, tossing her head. 'I certainly care nothing for what you do. You have followed me against my wishes, and now you are leaving me here against my advice.'

The Fair Unknown called out to Robert to saddle his horse and fetch his armour. Then, once he was properly accoutred, he set off through the forest in the direction from which the cries had seemed to come. The maiden, not liking to be left alone in the forest, elected to come too, though she warned the knight that ill would come of his foolhardiness.

Soon they came to a clearing, and there were two huge, loathsome giants camped beside a fire over which they were cooking a wild pig. One of the two was turning a spit and watching his companion, who was crouched over the body of a woman. They were arguing, in their ugly, barbarous voices, over who should have her first, while the woman herself lay half dead with fear, her cries dwindled to mere whimpers as she watched her terrible captors preparing to rape her.

The maiden Helie whispered to the Fair Unknown to hasten away from that place as quickly as possible. 'I know of these evil creatures,' she said. 'They have laid waste the entire neighbourhood. Their appetites know no bounds.'

The Fair Unknown was not even listening. Sizing up the situation in a glance, he spurred his mount into the clearing and skewered the giant nearest the woman with a single thrust of his spear, tossing him aside into the fire. The second giant was up and waving a huge club and roaring in a moment, but before he could strike, the young knight thrust again with his spear wounding him deeply; then, drawing his sword, he cut the giant's head in two with a single blow.

The whole thing was over in a moment, and Tidogolain clapped his hands with delight. 'See, my lady,' he cried, 'see how well the young knight deports himself. I think perhaps you were wrong about him all the time.'

Looking sheepish and crestfallen, Helie craved the young knight's pardon, which he accepted with a silent nod of the head, turning his attention to the maiden he had rescued from the giants. Weeping with relief, she thanked him profusely and told them that her name was Clarie and that she was the sister of Sir Sagramore, a redoubtable knight of the Round Table. She had been sitting in her father's garden that morning when the giants had broken in and seized her.

Robert, meanwhile, had been exploring and had found a cave nearby which had been the giant's den. Within were all the goods and viands they had stolen from the surrounding area, including food and wine and even table-cloths. Helped by Tidogolain, the squire soon had a marvellous feast prepared and you may be sure that all the company dined well that night.

But this was not the end of their adventures for that day. As they were preparing to settle down once more, and as Robert was fetching fresh grass for their mounts, he saw coming towards them three armed knights, who from their bearing seemed anything but friendly. Hastening back to his master, Robert told him of their approach and the Fair Unknown at once sprang up, all unarmed, and, drawing his sword, prepared to defend the two women and the servants.

He might have fallen to the spears of the three knights, who were indeed the friends of the defeated Blioberis, had not Helie herself come forward and called upon them to stop. She reminded them of their knightly vows and begged them to give the Fair Unknown time to arm himself.

She herself helped Robert to buckle on his armour, and as she did so reminded him again of her own lady, whose life he was pledged to save. The Fair Unknown swore that nothing would prevent him from carrying out his task, then he turned to face his new adversaries.

The first to come against him was William of Salebrant, who soon regretted it, as the Fair Unknown's spear passed through shield and hauberk and struck him dead from his horse's back.

With a cry, Lord Elin of Graie attacked. The Fair Unknown unhorsed him and left him mangled on the ground, nursing a broken arm.

Third and last came the Lord of Saire, by far the strongest of the three. When he met the Fair Unknown, their shields split and their lances shivered and they were both unhorsed. With swords they fought on, until at length the Fair Unknown beat down his opponent and, pulling off his helm, placed the tip of his sword at his neck. The Lord of Saire begged for mercy, and the Fair Unknown granted it, bidding him put himself at Arthur's mercy and tell him all that had taken place.

Thus it was agreed, and next day, after burying the dead knight, the others departed for Camelot, taking the maiden Clarie with them in their care.

When the Fair Unknown was rested he, Helie, Robert and Tidogolain rode on their way towards the Desolate City, where Helie's mistress was held captive. The forest still stretched all around them, though the way was wide.

As they rode, a stag of sixteen points burst from the trees and ran across their path, followed by a pack of greyhounds and brachets. One of the latter lagged behind the rest, limping. It was all white save for one black ear and a black spot on its left flank. When she saw it, Helie stopped and got down from her horse. She picked up the dog and pulled out the thorn she saw sticking from its paw. Then, with no warning, she suddenly leapt back on to her mount and, spurring it, rode off at a furious pace, with the dog still held beneath her arm, crying that she meant to take it to her mistress.

While the rest of the party were staring in astonishment, a hunter rode out of the trees and set off in pursuit of Helie, easily overtaking her. As the Fair Unknown caught up with them he heard the man demand the return of the dog. Helie refused. The Fair Unknown added his pleas, but Helie remained unmoved.

For a moment it looked as though the huntsman would use force, but with a dark look at the young knight he rode away, muttering as he went that they had not heard the last of this.

The huntsman, who was known as the Proud Knight of the Glade, rode straight home to his castle and got his armour and weapons. Then he rode like thunder to overtake the Fair Unknown and his charge, who, though she refused to explain her actions concerning the dog, had agreed to ride once again with her companions. As soon as he saw them, the Huntsman shouted out, 'You there! It was unwise of you to allow my dog to be stolen by this woman! Now you shall pay dearly for it!'

So saying, he charged full-tilt at the Fair Unknown, who scarcely had time to raise spear and shield before his adversary was upon him.

The fight that ensued was long and hard. Both were strong, fit men and well matched. They fought until both were exhausted, finally belabouring each other with their broken spear-butts, and, when these splintered, dropping them and drawing their swords. When at last they were too exhausted even to lift their weapons, and still neither had the advantage of the other, they threw aside their swords and wrestled with each other, even though they were in full armour!

At length, the Fair Unknown had the advantage, pulling the huntsman down and sitting astride his chest. Then he seized his sword from where it lay close by and, forcing off his adversary's helm, would have cut off his head had not the latter begged for mercy.

This the Fair Unknown granted, though, as was his habit, he made the Proud Knight promise to make his way to Arthur's court and tell all that had occurred. Then the company went on their way, leaving the huntsman to return, bruised and battered, to his home.

As daylight was ending they emerged at last from the forest and saw ahead of them the castle of Becleus, a rich and well-fortified place – really more of a city than a castle. A river ran past it, with much traffic plying to and fro. Rich meadowlands lay on either side of the water, on which cattle grazed and windmills turned their wide sails in the wind.

There on the road they met with a beautiful woman, riding a fine horse. She was clad in silk with a cloak trimmed with swansdown, but tears coursed down her cheeks and she wept bitterly.

'What is amiss with you, lady?' asked the Fair Unknown.

'Alas, I have lost the one most dear to me,' she replied.

'How so?'

'In that castle,' she answered, trembling, 'there is a custom that cost my lover his life. A beautiful sparrowhawk stands on a golden perch. It is offered to any maiden whose knight is strong enough to win in battle against the lord of the castle. My knight tried, but failed to win. All he got was his death!'

'Then,' said the Fair Unknown, 'I shall undertake to win the hawk for you. In so doing, I may avenge the death of your knight.'

Then the maiden, whose name was Margerie, wept afresh, though this time from hope, and the whole party continued together to the gates of the castle, where they entered unchallenged.

The people who stood in the streets cried aloud when they saw the stern young knight, with his dented steel and notched shield – the marks of his many battles upon him. There was much speculation as to his purpose, and concerning the two fair women who accompanied him – one of whom, Margerie, they recognized from her recent visit.

They rode onward until they reached the bailey of the castle. There they saw the hawk, fastened to its golden perch, and there, at request of the Fair Unknown, Margerie took up the bird on her gloved hand.

At once, as though at some unseen signal, the lord of the castle emerged and rode towards them. His mount was a spirited grey and his armour and shield were of silver, adorned with red roses, which also decorated his horse's trappings. Even his helm had a wreath of fresh roses around it. He seemed more like bridegroom than a warrior, dressed so, but there was no mistaking his intentions, since he carried a clutch of spears at his saddle and a great sword by his side.

With him rode his lady, who was called Rose Espanie, meaning, in the English tongue, 'Rose in Bloom'. To the surprise of all there, she was neither young nor fair, but seemed ugly and wrinkled – a strange contrast to her lord, who was in the prime of life.

To Margerie he called out, 'Set down that bird, madam, for you know you have no right to it.'

Then the Fair Unknown spoke up. 'I am here to prove by the strength of my body this lady's right to own this prize. I am called the Fair Unknown and I serve this lady and the noble King Arthur.'

'I am Griflet le fils le Do. I serve no man save myself and this lady. Let us see whether you can match your words with deeds!'

Therewith the two knights dressed their shields and met in combat. They fought grimly for a time, but it was not long before the Fair Unknown had the better of his opponent, felling him to the earth with a mighty blow which rendered him unconscious.

When he recovered, Griflet willingly conceded the right of the maiden Margerie to take the sparrowhawk and, as he and the Fair Unknown embraced as worthy opponents, promised to ride to Arthur's court and tell all that had occurred.

Next morning they set out once more upon the road, Griflet having promised to escort Margerie home to her brother's castle. He, it transpired, was king of the neighbouring land, and when Helie learned that his name was Agolant, she cried aloud with astonishment, for this king was her father's cousin, and thus she and Margerie were related by blood. The two women embraced and Helie gave up the little dog which the Fair Unknown had won for her to her new-found cousin, who departed at the crossing of the ways with both hawk and hound, under Griflet's protection. Thus was her own lord's slayer made her protector!

The company continued upon their way until their road led them at last to the sea. There, on a part of the cliffs which became an island when the tide rose, stood a great and noble palace called the City of the Golden Isle. It seemed to them all that it must have been constructed with the aid of magic, for its walls were of white marble and its roof of silver bedecked with mosaic, and it had 100 towers of red marble surrounding it. The Fair Unknown was about to turn in that direction when Helie spoke up. 'This is a dreadful place. Within it lives a damsel of great beauty called the Maiden of the White Hands. She is schooled in the seven liberal arts, knows the mystery of the stars, and the ways of enchantment. For five years she has been besieged by a knight named Malgier the Gray. Every suitor who has tried to approach her he has killed.'

'Then let us approach and see if we can achieve this adventure,' said the Fair Unknown.

Helie shook her head at him angrily. 'Remember that it is *my* lady whom you are sent to rescue. It will not help her if you fall to this knight's strength. Also, there is another thing that you should know. Each time one of the suitors is killed, the maiden of the city commands the victor to hold the bridge for seven years. Malgier has succeeded for five years. This is not done without great power and skill.'

But the Fair Unknown would not be turned aside. He had already turned his horse in the direction of the city, and refused to turn back.

As they approached they saw a causeway that stretched from the entrance to the city over the place where the sea rushed in and out with every tide. To one side of the end nearest them stood a tent surrounded by a palisade of sharpened stakes. A dreadful decoration was upon these stakes – human heads, altogether 143 – all that remained of the knights slain by Malgier the Gray. Even as they approached, they could see him, already accoutred, preparing to mount and ride to meet them. His shield bore upon it the emblem of two white hands – his way of showing how secure he felt in his suit to the lady of the Golden Isle.

As the two knights prepared to do battle, the walls of the city were lined with its citizens, everyone come to see either Malgier or the Fair Unknown fall. In the tallest of the red towers the Maiden of the White Hands watched also.

The combatants hurtled together with such might that both flew from their mounts and lay on the earth stunned. They soon recovered, however, and with drawn swords fell to with great vigour. This way and that the battle went, until at last the Fair Unknown struck a blow which sent Malgier's helm flying. He followed this up with a blow that split the other knight's head in twain.

Thunderous cheers echoed from the walls of the city and, as the gates opened, the people rushed forth to joyfully lift the young knight upon their shoulders and carry him within. There the Maiden of the White Hands waited, smiling – for in truth she had hated Malgier and wished fervently for his death. To the Fair Unknown she seemed like the most beautiful sight he had ever seen – her beauty took away his breath and left him speechless. She, in turn, liked the look of him, and thanked him most profusely, promising him wealth, lands and – herself! She also promised that the custom of the causeway battle would cease henceforward. The Fair Unknown thanked her politely, more than a little overcome with this turn of events.

He scarcely had time to think, however, as arrangements went forward for a great celebratory feast. Helie and Robert, together with Tidogolain the dwarf, were given quarters in the city, while the Fair Unknown himself was given the fairest chamber and fresh clothing.

In no time at all the feast commenced. The young hero was placed at the head of the table, with the maiden White Hands on one side and Helie on the other. As the evening progressed, Helie managed to speak privately to the Fair Unknown, telling him that White Hands had sent for all her lords, telling them that she intended to take her young rescuer as husband.

'But what if I refuse?' he asked, visibly shaken by this turn of events.

'Then doubtless you will either be captured or be killed. In which case,' she added, 'you will be ill-equipped to carry out your true task – to help rescue my lady.'

'What, then, should I do?' asked the Fair Unknown.

'There is only one course open to you,' Helie replied. 'You must leave here secretly. I have lodgings in the city, as you know. Robert will have a horse ready and waiting before daylight dawns. I, together with Tidogolain, will await you near the chapel that lies just beyond the gate. Tell anyone that asks that you intend to go there to give thanks for your victory.'

To this the Fair Unknown agreed, and soon after the celebration ended. Helie was escorted back to her lodgings, while the Fair Unknown was shown to his own fair chamber, where a bed of great comfort and splendour had been prepared.

There, as he lay abed, thinking over the events of the past few days, the Fair Unknown became aware that the door to his chamber had opened, and that the maiden White Hands had entered. Through half-closed eyes he saw in the dim light that her hair was unbound and that she had on only a cloak pulled over her shift. He caught a glimpse of her slender white legs and small bare feet.

Softly she approached and stood looking down at him. 'Is he asleep?' she breathed.

'No, lady,' he replied, opening his eyes.

Smiling, White Hands sat upon the edge of the bed. They talked for a while and she laid her head upon the pillow next to his. Gently, the Fair Unknown reached for her, bending his lips to hers. But White Hands drew away quickly. 'No!' she cried. 'There shall be no love-play between us until we are wed!'

With these words she quickly left the room, leaving the Fair Unknown angry and dismayed. For by this time he was more than a little in love with the lady and to be thus close, only to be turned away, was almost more than he could bear! Now he was thankful that he had decided to flee the place, where before he had been filled with regret.

Next morning all went as planned. Soon the Isle of Gold was far behind them, and Helie all but sang for joy, for soon they would reach the Desolate City. Only one more obstacle lay before them, and this Helie already dreaded, knowing by now how the Fair Unknown would turn always towards danger.

Thus, when less than a day later they sighted the walls of another city, she was already prepared for his question. Yet he surprised her, for after riding in unusual silence for some time, he asked if it was a good place to stay.

'It is not,' replied Helie. 'The lord of this city is called Lampart. He fights anyone who comes here and if he wins – which seems to be always – the loser is driven from the city by the people, who throw rubbish at him in a shameful way.'

For the first time since escaping the Isle of Gold, the Fair Unknown brightened. 'Such an evil custom should not be allowed to continue. Let us go there at once.'

Nothing Helie could say would dissuade him. They rode unchallenged into the city, but once they were within its walls people everywhere began to laugh and point to them – some even began gathering dirt from the streets in readiness for what, to them, was an inevitable outcome.

They found Lampart sitting in the sun outside his great hall. Grey-haired and powerful, he was engaged in a game of chess and, as the companions entered, triumphantly checkmated his opponent.

He rose to meet the Fair Unknown and his party and greeted them courteously. 'Welcome, sir knight; my lady, welcome to you. If you seek lodging here this night, I shall be pleased to offer it to you. But first you must joust with me. If you win, then all shall be well. If, however, you lose, you shall depart at once and receive no good escort from this city.'

'That is well with me,' said the Fair Unknown grimly, and called to Robert to arm him.

The joust took place inside a great hall, where lists had been set up and a magnificent carpet laid upon the floor. The two combatants armed themselves with care – Robert attending his master, while Lampart, seated in a chair which stood upon the image of a grey leopard woven into the carpet, was attired in splendid armour which was much at variance with the young knight's battered harness.

Once they were ready, the two mounted and rode towards each other with their spears in rest. The first course both spears shattered, and though both men were rocked in their saddles neither had the advantage. The second course was the same, but on the third encounter the Fair Unknown unhorsed his opponent fairly, landing him on the earth with a crash. Lampart rose and, putting off his helmet, courteously offered lodging to the party.

Helie now came forward and greeted him warmly. Then she turned to the Fair Unknown. 'Sir, this knight is my lady's seneschal, the finest knight in our land. By defeating him you have indeed proved – if proof were necessary – that you are ably fitted to attempt her rescue.' Then she turned again to Lampart and told him something of their adventures, admitting that at first she had spoken harshly to the Fair Unknown. 'Since when he has proven himself over and again to be a strong and worthy knight, one who, I dare say, has the blood of true nobility in him, for all that he chooses to hide both name and rank.'

That night the company were royally entertained and in the morning prepared to depart for the Desolate City. Lampart insisted on giving the Fair Unknown fresh arms and on riding with the companions to within sight of the walls. As they rode, he spoke quietly with Helie, while the Fair Unknown rode in silence, secretly fearful of his ability to overcome the danger which lay before him. Until now he had felt no such fear, but as the end of his journey approached he began to doubt his own strength, and only with difficulty hid his desire to turn aside.

Nor was this helped by the appearance of the Desolate City, for when they came at length to a place which overlooked it, it appeared ruinous, with broken towers and fractured walls. Here Helie and Lampart prepared to turn back. But first they helped arm the Fair Unknown in his new armour, and all the while Helie wept openly, and even the seneschal had tears in his eyes.

'It is time for you to go on alone,' said Helie. 'In the heart of the city you will find a hall still standing. It is made from white marble and is of an ancient design. It has many windows. In each one you will see a *jongleur* standing, each with a different instrument. Greet them all with these words: "May God curse you!" If you survive this far you may enter the hall. There you should await whatever comes. But be warned, do not enter any of the side chambers you will see leading off from the hall.'

The Fair Unknown promised this and, having bade farewell to his companions, rode on alone. As he approached the city, he saw where two rivers ran past its fractured walls. Over one of these a bridge still stood intact, though it led only to a broken gate. The whole place seemed empty and utterly desolate, rightly earning its name, though once it must have been splendid beyond dream.

Reining in before the broken gates, the Fair Unknown crossed himself and then went forward through tumbled walls and shattered pavements. In a while he saw what he knew must be the palace, its white walls sparkling in the sun. There, just as Helie had told him, were dozens of *jongleurs*, dressed in a mad assortment of patchwork clothing, each and every one carrying a different instrument. Among those he saw were the harp, the rota, the bagpipe, hurdy-gurdy, fiddle, shawm, lute, horn, tambourine and tabor, cornemuse, psaltern, pipes and trumpets.

As the Fair Unknown approached, they began to sing. 'May God bless King Arthur's knight, sent hither to help the lady of this place!'

This made the knight at once puzzled and wary. But he remembered the instructions which Helie had given him and, drawing his sword, he cried, 'God's curse upon you!' and rode swiftly into the hall.

One of the *jongleurs* leapt down and slammed the door behind him. Within the hall was brightly lit by many candles, and in the centre stood a seven-legged table. The Fair Unknown reined in his mount and sat waiting. Then a knight with a green shield appeared from a side chamber and attacked him. Two or three blows with his sword proved enough to drive the fellow off, and in his eagerness the Fair Unknown pursued him to the very door of the chamber from which he had emerged. At the last moment the young knight paused, remembering Helie's words to him, and as he did so he saw two great axe-blades descending towards him. He backed quickly away and the chamber door banged shut. Retreating into the hall again, he called upon God to protect him as the lights were doused and the place became as dark as night.

After a moment a few of the candles were lit again by one of the *jongleurs*, and as the Fair Unknown prepared himself a second knight appeared from a further door. This one was dressed entirely in black armour and rode on a horse which sprouted a horn from its brow. Smoke and flames issued from its nostrils as if it were a dragon!

The two champions came together with a mighty crash and both were unhorsed. Drawing their swords, they fought on – never was there such a battle since Tristan fought the Morholt. But at the last the Fair Unknown, wounded and exhausted by his long fight, gained the upper hand – he stuck a blow with all the force of his arm and the black knight's head went spinning. As the body fell to the floor, a plume of black and sulphurous smoke arose from it, and the body became putrid.

At this the *jongleurs* reappeared and doused all the candles, then departed, slamming shut both doors and windows, so that the hall became dark and the very walls seemed to shake.

In terror, the Fair Unknown stumbled across the hall until he felt the edge of the table beneath his hands. This he clung to as if it were a piece of spindrift in a merciless sea. He found himself thinking of the maiden White Hands, and regretting his precipitous departure.

Slowly his senses adjusted to the dimness, and he found that he could see – though only a little. He made out the shape of a huge cupboard set against the wall behind the table and, as he looked, the door to this began slowly to crack open.

A strange red light shone through, and by its glow he saw a most terrible thing. A serpent, its body as thick in places as a cask of wine, emerged and advanced towards him. Its fearsome and terrible head towered over him, its tongue darting forth, dripping with venom. Grasping his sword, the Fair Unknown prepared to face it, but as he raised his shield the serpent stopped and bowed its head almost to the floor. The Fair Unknown hesitated, and as he did so once again the serpent slithered nearer. Again he raised his sword, and again it stopped and bowed low.

Bewildered, the Fair Unknown stared at the creature, and as he did so he met its eyes. They were fierce and mesmeric, but oddly human. Then, as he stood irresolute, the creature drew suddenly closer and, before he could do anything to prevent it, shot forth its head and tongue and touched his lips.

The Fair Unknown drew back in horror, but the serpent was already withdrawing. The door of the cupboard closed upon it and a silence fell even deeper than before. Bewildered and fearful, the Fair Unknown waited in the darkness.

Then, into the silence, came a voice which spoke clearly. 'Son of my lord Sir Gawain, no other knight could have done what you have done, no one but you could have endured the Terrible Kiss – only perhaps your father himself. Only you could deliver the lady from the danger which beset her. King Arthur named you the Fair Unknown. I tell you now that your true name is Guinglain. You are the son of Gawain and Blanchmal the Fay. She it was who armed you and sent you to King Arthur, and she who placed upon you a spell which caused you to forget who you were . . . You have done well! Rest now.'

The voice ceased, and the Fair Unknown, who was Guinglain in truth, fell into a deep sleep, his head and arms resting on the table.

When he awoke the day was well advanced and there, awaiting him, was a lady more beautiful than any he had ever seen – save only White Hands. She wore a dress of the faery colour and her hair was as bright as the brightest gold.

'Greetings, Sir Guinglain. I am she whom you were sent to rescue. My name is Esmeree the Blonde, daughter of King Guingras.'

'I am glad to see you so well' said Guinglain.

'That is thanks to you, sir knight. I have waited long for your coming. Only three months after my father died, two enchanters came to this land. They made everyone go mad and destroyed the city. Then, when I would not marry the eldest, whose name was Mabonagrain, they laid upon me the shape of the serpent you saw last night. Only he who was brave enough to endure its kiss could save me. You have succeeded and have won me. Indeed, sir knight, I am yours now.'

Guinglain bowed his head. 'Let us return to King Arthur. Only he may say whom I may marry, for he is my cousin.' But in truth, as he spoke, he was thinking of White Hands.

At that moment Helie, followed by Lampart and the others, arrived and all were filled with joy, Helie and Esmeree to see each other, Lampart to see his lady restored, and both Robert and Tidogolain to see their master and mistress happy. Now they made to help Guinglain to unarm and saw at once that he was sorely wounded in many places. The two women at once sent for water to wash and cleanse his wounds, and then they called upon the others to carry him to a chamber, where he was laid in a great bed and where he soon fell into a deep sleep.

In the days that followed the work of the two enchanters was gradually undone. First the people, who no longer wandered madly in the wild lands around the city, returned; then came the bishops and clergy, who blessed the walls with holy water so that the illusion that had been cast upon them vanished and it was seen that they were in truth not broken at all. Then the celebrations began for the restoration both of Esmeree the Blonde and her city.

All this while Guinglain lay resting, recuperating from his many wounds, reflecting on his adventures and remembering the life he had known before ever he set out for Arthur's court. And there at length came Lampart, with other nobles and a bishop of the place, to request formally that he take their lady to wife.

Just as formally Guinglain replied that he could wed no lady without the permission of King Arthur, and suggested that Esmeree herself should travel to the king to thank him for sending his knight to rescue her. This was agreed, and in a matter of days the lady set out with a fine entourage, leaving Guinglain still resting, placed in the tender care of her doctors.

But as he lay in bed in the great palace, Guinglain had thoughts for no one but White Hands, and at night he dreamed of her entering his chamber with hair unbound, clad only in her shift, just as she had in truth done in her own castle. And thus he determined to return thither, and to ask her forgiveness for his sudden departure, and to give his reasons for it.

Rising from his bed despite the protests of the doctors, Guinglain set out and soon overtook Esmeree and her party. There he excused himself from riding with them by saying that he had other urgent business to conclude. And if Esmeree was saddened by this, or puzzled in turn, she said nothing of it, but gave him her leave to go.

Guinglain rode full-tilt to the Golden Isle. As he neared the city, he encountered a hunting party and his heart leapt when he saw that White Hands was among the riders. Greatly daring, he rode up to her and there and then, haltingly, confessed his love for her. White Hands looked coldly upon him and demanded to know who he was.

Guinglain gasped. 'I am Guinglain, that was known as the Fair Unknown! Do you not remember me?'

But White Hands' expression did not change. 'Yes, I remember you! You are the one who crept away when no one was looking – doubtless to the arms of some other lady. Be sure of one thing, I shall never allow you to have such a hold over my heart again. Now begone from my sight!'

'Then I shall die in your land,' Guinglain said, 'for no other place is as holy to me as this place over which you rule.'

So saying, he watched as the bright-clad hunting party rode on, leaving him in their dust. With sorrow weighing heavy upon him, he made his way slowly to the city and sought lodging in an inn in the town that gave him a good view of the castle where he knew White Hands to be.

Weeks passed and gradually Guinglain gave away all his goods to pay for his room. Finally, even his fine arms and armour were gone, after which he took to his bed – too weak and sorrowful to get up.

Then, a few days later, a maiden arrived at the inn with fresh clothing and an invitation to visit White Hands. Trembling with joy, Guinglain washed and dressed and hurried after the maiden. She took him to a beautiful garden, filled with the song of birds, where White Hands awaited him. She bade him sit beside her, and took his hands in hers.

'Sir, how are you?'

'I have not fared well,' answered Guinglain truthfully. 'These last weeks have been unkind to me. But I am made better by the sight of you.'

'Sir, what proof have I that if I were to let you once more assume that place you once held in my affection, you would not run off again?'

Guinglain hung his head in shame. 'Lady, the truth of the matter is that I had to leave to honour the promise I made both to my king and to the lady who had sent to Arthur for aid. I feared that you would not permit me to go. I know now that this was wrong, and I beg your forgiveness.'

White Hands looked at him and in her heart knew that she loved him as much as he loved her. Only memories of his secret departure kept her from holding him close. Instead she spoke sternly.

'Sir Guinglain, I must think upon these things. Meanwhile, you may stay in my castle.'

Guinglain's heart leapt at these words, but he kept his eyes lowered and merely thanked White Hands for her generosity.

Soon after they went in to dinner, and when they had eaten the splendid repast laid out for them, Guinglain was shown to the same richly decorated room as before. There, White Hands bade him good-night with these words: 'My chamber is just across the way, sir knight, and I shall sleep with the door open to see that you do not run off again! However, see that you do not enter unless you are invited!'

Guinglain lay down in a turmoil of confusion. Again and again he thought of the words White Hands had uttered. What did they mean? Her look had seemed to say to him that he should come to her that night, yet her words belied him. Several times he got up and went to the door of his own chamber, looking across to where he knew White Hands lay. Each time he lay down again, and tossed and turned some more.

At last the desire to find out how the lady truly felt towards him grew too much, and he left his chamber and started towards hers. At once it seemed to him that he stood upon a narrow plank bridge over a roaring stream of black water. As he stood in bewilderment and fear, the bridge began to shake, and next moment he found himself clinging to the edge above the churning water. At that he cried out – waking both himself and others. He found himself clinging to a hawk's perch in the hall of the castle!

Shamed, he made his way back to his chamber and once more tried to sleep. Again, he could not, and in a while rose again and made his way towards White Hands' room. This time, as he stepped across the threshold, it seemed that the walls began shaking and were about to fall upon him. He leapt back, crying out – and woke in his bed with a pillow over his head!

Thoroughly miserable, Guinglain lay down again, still debating. Then a sound alerted him to where a maiden entered his room with a candle. She approached his bed and smilingly beckoned him to follow her. At first he thought her another dream, but she urged him to rise, and when he did so led him to White Hands' chamber. Right up to the bed she led him and then retired, leaving the two alone. Softly White Hands placed her hand in his and led him beneath the covers. There the two made merry and were fulfilled of the love each felt for the other.

Later, as they lay side by side, Guinglain laughed aloud at the thought of his two earlier forays, and when White Hands asked to know why he laughed, he told her of his dreams. Now it was her turn to smile. Then she told him that these were no dreams, but her own working of magic, in which, along with many other arts, her father had bade her to be educated. Then she confessed that she had always known that Guinglain would come, and that he would leave her and return again. Indeed, the whole of his great adventure had been her doing. She had visited him as a child in his mother's home, preparing the way even then. She it was who had sent Helie to Arthur's court to ask him for a knight. She had even instructed her to carry off the little dog. It was her voice that announced his true name after he had braved the serpent's kiss. 'And so you see, my love, I have been awaiting you for a long time.'

'Well, now I am here, I shall never leave again,' said Guinglain.

'See that you remember those words,' said White Hands seriously. 'For if you ever forget me, you shall just as surely lose me.'

'That could never be,' Guinglain replied, and the two turned again to loving.

Next day White Hands summoned all her lords and barons and declared her happiness to them all. Even as she did so, Esmeree the Blonde and her followers were getting closer to Camelot. On the road they encountered four knights: Blioberis, the Lord of Saire, the Proud Knight of the Glade and Griflet le fils le Do – all of whom had been defeated by Guinglain. Esmeree declared that she was the very lady the young knight had been on his way to rescue and told them his true name.

Soon after they reached Camelot, where Arthur received them all graciously and heard of the adventures of the Fair Unknown – also learning at last his true identity. There Esmeree formally asked for Guinglain's hand in marriage, and Arthur promised to consider the request, while wondering aloud how they were to locate Guinglain. One of his knights suggested they hold a great tournament, which was sure to attract knights from all over the land. To this Arthur agreed, and a date was set one month hence on the plain below the Castle of Maidens. Tristan was to lead one side in the lists and the King of Montescler the other.

The month soon passed and far off on the Isle of Gold Guinglain heard of the great tournament. He longed to go and to tell Arthur of all that had occurred. Yet when he spoke of this to White Hands and begged leave to go, she would not hear of it. 'I have read in the stars that if once you leave this place, you will never again return to me.'

'That could never happen!' cried Guinglain with passion.

'Nevertheless, you shall not go by my leave, since you evidently do not love me enough to forgo this one small pleasure! The decision is yours alone to make.'

Hotly denying these accusations, Guinglain declared his intention of going to the tournament and of returning soon. That night he fell asleep beside White Hands and woke next day in the forest, horse and arms at his side and Robert the squire sleeping nearby. Angered by what he saw as his lady's doubt of his faithfulness, Guinglain set forth at once for the Castle of Maidens, arriving there three days later.

There was already gathered a great company of knights, including those whom Guinglain had defeated during his adventure. He chose to fight with Tristan on the side of the Cornish knights and, though he kept his identity secret, he carried the same shield that he had born on first arriving at Arthur's court – which bore an ermine lion on an azure field.

That day the tournament began and Guinglain distinguished himself with such might that by the end of the day everyone was talking of his prowess and King Anguishance of Ireland invited him to dine in his tent. Next day he did even better, defeating knight after knight until it was clear to all that he was the outright winner of the tournament.

Arthur, feeling in his heart that he knew the identity of the stranger, summoned him to join the royal party on the road to London, and there welcomed him as his nephew! Gawain too was present, and father and son were united amid great rejoicing.

Arriving in London, they found Esmeree the Blonde awaiting them. She greeted Guinglain with delight and Arthur proposed they be married as soon as matters could be arranged. Both Arthur and Gawain begged Guinglain to accept, and to this, as last, he gave his assent.

Next morning a great and splendid party set off for Esmeree's land. Arthur himself had agreed to attend the wedding, and he rode with them. In the lady's land the wedding was celebrated in great splendour and Guinglain was crowned king of that place.

It is said that he lived a long and happy life, and was well remembered as a good lord and a brave and true knight of the Round Table. He never returned to the Isle of Gold, nor did he ever see White Hands again. As she had predicted, he had forgotten her, and if there was magic at work in this I know it not and therefore will not speak of it at all.

3

Arthur and Gorlagon

ARTHUR and Gorlagon is one of several surviving Arthurian romances written in Latin in the thirteenth and fourteenth centuries, others being *The Story of Meriadoc, King of Cambria* (see pages 68–89) and *The Rise of Gawain, Nephew of Arthur*. All these tales have a 'realistic' quality which puts them at variance with the more exotic works of the romance writers. Nothing is known of the author of this little story, which is none the less a powerful tale in its own right.

It is certainly a grim piece, half morality tale and half horror story, with a shock ending worthy of a modern spinner of such tales. It is also a good deal less equivocal about the savagery of medieval life than most tales of its kind. Thus the wolf does not hesitate to kill the children of his former queen; while Gorlagon's punishment for his own faithless wife is barbaric in the extreme. Yet this reflects the true state of affairs at the time, when the situation of women was anything but happy, and they were frequently regarded as potentially evil by nature. Arthur's quest, prompted by Guinevere's response to his apparently innocent kiss, suggests a darker theme, while the end is far from conclusive, since the obvious answer provided by Gorlagon's story is that all women are treacherous and deserve to be punished accordingly. Like the story of *The Vows of King Arthur and His Knights* (see pages 9–19), this presents a heavily misogynistic view – though other tales, such as *The Wedding of Sir Gawain and Dame Ragnall* (see pages 99–106), where a similar question is asked, show another side of the coin.

The origins of the story are not hard to trace. It belongs to a series of 'werewolf' stories which include the Celtic folk-tale of *Morraha*, and two medieval tales, *Melion* and *Bisclavaret*. Both these last-named stories belong to the genre of the 'Lai' (story) and possess strong evidence of Breton (hence also Celtic) origin. The original folk-tale was in all probability far simpler, containing only one evil queen, one brother, and probably omitting the episode of the hidden child and the false accusation against the wolf, which derive from the Welsh story of Gelert, where a faithful dog is wrongfully accused of killing a child.

The three brothers, who appear to know nothing of each other until the end of the story, all bear names which can be traced back to the Welsh word for 'werewolf'. In both the Breton versions the role of the queen is different. She is usually a faery woman, or goddess, who, having married a mortal, seeks to return to her own country and does so by discovering her husband's secret and turning him into a wolf. Apparently the anonymous Latin author heard the story and found within it a vehicle for his personal misogyny. As Alfred Nutt remarks in his notes to the story, 'The free self-centred goddess, regally prodigal of her love, jealously guarding her independence, become a capricious or faithless woman.'

I have added a final paragraph to the tale, which it seemed to require, and which I hope does not detract from the original intention of the author. Whether he intended to write more, perhaps to add some worthy comment concerning the subsequent betrayal of Arthur by Guinevere, we cannot know. It is reasonable to suppose that his audience would have been familiar enough with the Arthurian mythos to draw their own conclusions.

In the text Kay and Gawain are referred to by their Latin names, Caius and Walwain. I have opted for the more usual spellings for the sake of harmony.

Arthur and Gorlagon is found in a late fourteenth-century manuscript, Rawlinson B.49, in the Bodleian Library, Oxford. It was edited by Professor G.L. Kittredge in *Harvard Studies and Notes in Philology and Literature*, Vol. viii, 1903. It was translated by F.A. Milne with notes by A. Nutt in *Folk-Lore*, Vol. 15, 1904, pp. 40–67. I have made use of this version in preparing my own retelling.

T THE FEAST OF PENTECOST ONE YEAR King Arthur kept the festival at the City of the Legions. He invited nobles and knights from all over the land to meet there and celebrate in fine style, with a great banquet to which all were bidden. Courses too numerous to name were served, and wines in abundance. As the evening wore on, Arthur suddenly turned to the queen and, in an excess of joy, embraced and kissed her in front of all the court.

Guinevere blushed furiously and asked the king why he chose this place and time to show such affection.

Arthur replied, 'Because among all the riches and delights of this place I have nothing as sweet as you.'

To which the queen answered, 'Then, if you love me so much, you must feel that you know my heart and mind as well or better than any other?'

'Indeed, I do!' said Arthur.

'Then you are wrong, my lord. For if you truly knew me you would not make such a claim. Indeed, I would say that you know nothing of women's natures.'

King Arthur looked askance, for this had been said in the hearing of everyone present. But he smiled gently enough, and said, 'My love and my queen. If it is true that I know nothing of your heart and mind, then I take heaven as my witness that I shall not rest until I do so!'

When the banquet was ended and the guests were all departed, Arthur called to him his seneschal, Sir Kay, and said, 'Kay, I want you and Gawain to fetch your horses, and a third for myself. We are going on a mission. But it is to be kept secret from everyone. Only we three shall know where we are bound.'

Only when the three men were well on the road did Arthur tell them that, as a result of his dispute with Guinevere, he intended visiting a certain lord named Gargol, who was famed for his wisdom, and trying to discover something of the nature of womankind. 'For though I doubt I am the first to try, yet I believe it is possible to discover some truth about them!'

The three rode on together for a day and a night – for Arthur would not rest until they came in sight of a castle built into the side of a wooded mountain. Arthur sent Kay ahead to discover to whom this belonged, and the seneschal soon returned with news that it was the chief castle of the very lord of whom they were in search.

Bidding his fellows to make haste, Arthur spurred his mount right up to the castle, and seeing the doors set wide and hearing the sounds of feasting coming from within, he rode right into the hall, where the lord Gargol sat at dinner.

The nobleman looked up at where Arthur sat on his horse and demanded to know who he was that entered in such urgency.

'I am Arthur, king of all Britain. I come in search of an answer to a question that concerns me deeply.'

'And what is that?'

'I seek to know what are the heart, the nature and the ways of women, for I have heard that you are well versed in such matters.'

This is a very weighty question,' said Gargol. 'My lord, do you get down and eat with us, and rest here this night, for I see that you are tired from your journey hither. Give me a while to think upon your question, and I will try to answer you in the morning.'

Denying that he was in any wise fatigued, Arthur consented to eat, and placed himself opposite Gargol, while Kay and Gawain were seated upon either side.

That night they rested and were royally entertained. But next morning when Arthur reminded Gargol of his promise the lord shook his head. 'My lord, if I may say so, you show your lack of wisdom by asking this question. I believe that no man can answer it.'

'Yet I must have an answer,' said Arthur firmly.

'Well, if you will not give it up, then I suggest you go a little further, into the next country, and visit my brother, Torleil. He is older than I, and wiser. Perhaps he can help you find an answer.'

With this the king had to be content, and with Kay and Gawain at his side, he rode for the rest of the day until they came to the city of Torleil, who welcomed them. When he heard who his guests were, the lord invited them to sit down and eat with him, and once again, when Arthur at first refused, and explained his reasons, persuaded him to wait until morning for an answer to his question.

Yet when morning came, Torleil confessed himself as unable to answer as his brother had been. 'Though, if you must seek further, I recommend that you visit my eldest brother, Gorlagon, who lives in the next valley. He is far wiser than I and I believe he may be able to assist you.'

With this Arthur had to be content, though by now his patience was all but worn away. The three men set out at once and after a day's ride arrived at Gorlagon's castle, where, as on both previous occasions, they found the lord at supper. When he learned the identities of his guests, and the nature of the king's question, he shook his head.

'This is indeed a weighty question, my lord. Sit with us, and take food and drink, and on the morrow I will attempt an answer.'

But this time Arthur would not be moved. He swore that not a morsel of food or drink would pass his lips until he had heard what Gorlagon had to say on the matter.

The old lord sighed. 'Well, since you will drive me so hard, I will give you an answer, though I doubt it will serve you well. But at least sit down, you and your men, and eat while you listen. But let me say this,' he added, 'that when I have told you my story, you may well feel you are little the wiser.'

'Tell on,' Arthur said, 'but speak no more of my eating.'

'Very well, but at least let your companions eat.'

Arthur nodded, and allowed himself to be conducted to a seat at the table. Then, as Kay and Gawain satisfied their hunger and thirst, Gorlagon told the tale which I will tell now.

'There was once a king, famed for his truth and justice. He had built for him a garden of surpassing beauty and richness, and there he planted all kinds of trees and shrubs, fruits and spices which grew in abundance. Now, among the other trees which grew there was a slender sapling which had sprung from the ground on the day of the king's birth, and was exactly the same height as he.

'Now it was said of this tree that if anyone were to cut it down and, striking his head with the slenderest part of it, say, "Be a wolf and have the understanding of a wolf," he would at once take on the form of that animal. And for this reason the king set a guard around the tree, and had a wall built around the garden. No one was permitted to enter it save the king himself, and a trusted guardian who was his close friend. Every day he used to visit the tree at least three times – nor would he eat so much as a morsel of food before he had done so, even though it sometimes meant fasting for a whole day. He alone knew the reason for this, but kept a close mouth about it.

'Now this king had a very beautiful wife, and it chanced that her love for him was less than he believed, for she had a young lover. And such was her passion for him that she determined to arrange some way that he might lawfully enjoy her favours. And observing how the king entered his garden every day alone, and spent some time there, she became curious.

'That night, the king returned home late from hunting, but before he would eat or rest he went into the garden, as was his wont. And when at last they sat down to eat supper together, the queen smiled a false smile and asked why her lord always went alone to his garden, even though he was tired at the end of a long day's hunting.

'Quietly the king answered that he had nothing to say to her on the matter, which did not concern her, and at this the queen cried out that he must be going there to meet with a mistress. Then she said that she would eat no food until he had told her. Then she went to her bed and feigned sickness for three days and nights.

'At the end of this time the king grew fearful for her life, and began to beg her to get up and take some food, saying that the thing she asked was a secret he dared not share with anyone, but that he was as faithful to her now as he had ever been. "Then," cried she, "you ought to have no secrets from me, not if you love me as much as you say you do!"

'In a great turmoil, and feeling the depth of his love for his queen, the king at last gave in and told her the truth about the sapling, having first extracted from her an oath that she would tell no one.

'Of course, she had no intention of honouring this promise, since she saw this as a means to bring about the crime she had long contemplated. As soon as the king went out next day, she went immediately to the garden and, taking an axe, she cut down the tree and concealed the topmost part of it in her long sleeve. Then, when her husband returned home, she made a point of going to meet him.

'There on the threshold she made as if to throw her arms about him, and then, before he could do anything to prevent it, she struck him about the head with the sapling and cried, "Be a wolf!" But when she came to say, "And have the understanding of a wolf", in her excitement she said, "Have the understanding of a man!"

'And so it was. The king fled in the shape of a wolf, pursued by hounds which the evil queen set upon him. But his humanity remained unimpaired.'

Gorlagon stopped and looked at King Arthur, who was totally engrossed in the story, and said, 'My lord, I ask again that you take some food. For this is a long tale, and even though you will be little the wiser for hearing it, still you should not starve in the hearing.'

But Arthur shook his head. 'I like what I hear. Continue. I will eat later.'

So Gorlagon, shaking his head the while, began again.

'The queen, having chased away her rightful lord, now invited her lover to take his place, relinquishing all authority to him. Shortly thereafter she married the younger man and in due course had by him two sons. The wolf meanwhile wandered in the woods, and during this time allied himself with a she-wolf, who bore him two cubs. And all this time he thought about the treachery of his queen and how he might be revenged upon her.

'Now nearby at the periphery of the woods there was a fortified house where the queen and her new lord used often to repair from the business of the world. And there one day the two wolves and their cubs came visiting. It happened that the two young boys who were the offspring of the queen were left unattended, playing in the courtyard of the house. When he saw them the wolf knew only anger and bitterness, and in his fury he rushed upon them and tore them to pieces.

'When the queen's servants heard this they came and chased away the wolves, though by then it was too late to save the children. The queen was overcome with sorrow and gave orders for a close watch to be kept in case the beasts should ever return. And return they did, sneaking into the region of the house some months later. There the man-wolf saw two of the queen's young cousins, who had been left playing unattended, and once again he rushed in upon the unsuspecting children and disembowelled them, leaving them to die a dreadful death.

'Hearing the screams, the servants assembled and this time succeeded in capturing the two young wolves, whom they hanged at once. But the man-wolf, being more cunning in the ways of men, slipped away and escaped.'

Again Gorlagon paused and looked at King Arthur. 'Do you wish me to continue?' he asked. The king simply nodded, leaning forward in his chair to listen intently to every word the old lord uttered.

'The wolf, maddened by the death of his cubs, began to wreak such vengeance against the local flocks and herds that his name became a byword for fear, and soon the people of that land mounted a huge hunt to capture and kill him. The wolf, fearful for his safety, fled to the neighbouring land. But there too he was hunted, since word of his deeds had gone before him. Finally he fled yet further from his homeland, into the country ruled by a young king whose nature was gentle and whose fame for wisdom had spread far and wide. There he wreaked such havoc, not only against sheep and cattle but against human life also, that the king announced a day in which he would set out and hunt the beast down once and for all.

'Now it happened that the wolf was out hunting that night and, chancing to be lurking beneath the window of a certain house, overheard someone within speaking of the great hunt and also of the kindness and wisdom of the king. The wolf, hearing this, fled back to the cave where he had his den and fell to wondering what he should do.

'In the morning the great hunt assembled, and advanced into the woods with a mighty pack of hounds. But the wolf, using his human skills, evaded discovery and lay in wait for the king himself.

'Soon he saw the young monarch walking near, accompanied only by two close friends. The wolf ran out of the bushes where he had been hiding and, approaching the king, knelt at his feet and fawned upon him as would a human supplicant. The two young noblemen, fearing for the king's life, for they had never seen such a large wolf before, cried out, "Master! See, here is the very animal we seek. Let us slay him at once!"

'But the king, moved by the actions of the beast, held his hand. "There is something strange about this creature," he said. "I swear he is almost human."

'The wolf at once pawed and whined loudly, licking the king's hands like a huge dog.

'Despite the doubts of his companions, the king blew his horn to recall the rest of the hunt and instructed them to return home. Not without many fearful glances at the wolf, they obeyed, and the king and his companions set out to return to the castle, accompanied by the beast. As they passed through the forest suddenly a huge stag appeared in the way before them, and the king looked to the wolf and said, "Let us see what you can do, my fine fellow", and commanded him to bring down the stag.

'The wolf, who knew well the ways of such beasts, at once sprang after the stag, and in a short time had captured and killed it. Then he dragged the body back to the king and laid it at his feet.

'"Now I swear you are a noble creature and ought not to be killed," said the king. "It is clear to me that you understand the nature of service, and that you mean me no harm. Therefore let us go home and you shall live with me in my house."'

Gorlagon ceased his recital again and looked at Arthur, but the king only signalled brusquely that he should continue.

'The wolf remained with the king, accompanying him everywhere, sharing his food and sleeping at night next to the king's bed. Then the day came when the king was forced to go on a journey to visit a neighbouring monarch, and since the journey was to take ten days, he asked his queen to take care of the wolf in his absence. But the queen had grown to hate the wolf, being jealous of the bond between the beast and its master, and she begged him not to ask this of her, since she was afraid that the wolf would turn on her once the king was gone. This he denied, for he had seen nothing but gentleness in the creature since its coming. But he promised to have a golden chain forged with which the wolf would be fastened to his bed.

'This was done, and the king departed, leaving the wolf in the queen's care. But as soon as he was gone, she fastened the chain to the bed and kept the beast prisoner there both day and night, even though the king had given instructions that it was only to be so chained at night.

'But worse was to come. The queen, like the man-wolf's own faithless wife, loved another, a servant of the king, and once her husband was gone from the court, she arranged to meet with him in the royal bedroom. There, they fell to kissing and fondling each other, until the wolf, angered beyond bearing by this betrayal of his master, and the memory it stirred within him for his own state, grew beside himself and began to howl and rage against the chain. Eventually the chain gave way, and the wolf fell upon the faithless servant and savaged him thoroughly. But the queen he did not attack, merely glaring at her with reddened eyes.

'Alerted by the noise, the queen's women came running, and she, terrified lest the king should learn of her perfidy, invented a story. She said that the wolf had attacked the young prince, and that when her servant had come running to protect her it had then attacked him. Then, as the servant was taken away to have his wounds dressed, fearful of the king's imminent return, and of his discovery of the truth, the queen took the little prince, together with his nurse, and locked them in a room deep in the foundations of the castle.

'At that moment the king was heard returning. He was met by his wife, with her hair shorn, her cheeks scratched and blood all over her clothing. "Alas!" she cried, "See what that evil beast you call friend has done to me!" And she told the whole evil tale of the wolf's attack upon their son, her servant and then herself.

'The king was both astonished and in agony over the death of his son, but at that moment the wolf, hearing his voice, rushed out from the corner in which it had been hiding, and fell upon him with such evident joy and peacefulness that the poor king was even more bewildered.

'Then the wolf, taking the corner of his cloak in its teeth, began to pull him, at the same time growling and rolling its eyes in such a manner that the king, who was used to its ways, had no doubt that it wanted him to follow.

'Despite the queen's cries that it would turn on him and kill him, the king followed the beast into the depths of the castle and there, before a small door, the wolf stopped and scrabbled with its paws against the timbers. Curious, the king ordered the key to the door to be brought, but even as his servants searched, the wolf drew back and with great force flung himself against the door, breaking it open. Within was the king's little son and his nurse.

'"Something is amiss here," said the king, and went at once to the room where the wounded servant was lying. When the wolf saw him, it was all the king could do to prevent him attacking the man again, but when questioned the servant would only repeat the story told by the queen.

'"But you are wrong," said the king, "for my son is alive and well. Therefore you are lying and I would know the truth." Then he let loose the grip he had upon the wolf's collar, and the beast leapt upon the wounded man and threatened to tear out his throat, until the man screamed and began to babble of the truth.

'Well, what more need be said? The man confessed all, and both he and the queen were impeached and imprisoned. The king, his anger growing greater as he learned the truth, called his lords and demanded them to make a judgement. Both the queen and the servant who had been her lover were condemned, she to be torn apart by horses, he to be flayed and hanged.

'After these events, the king gave much thought to the extraordinary qualities displayed by the wolf. He even summoned several wise men from within his realm and discussed it with them. "For I do not believe," he insisted, "that any ordinary creature could display such rare intelligence. It is almost as if he were a man who had somehow been given the semblance of a wolf."

'At this, the wolf displayed such great joy and recognition of the king's words that all were amazed. Then the monarch declared that he would do all that he might to discover the truth of this matter, and decreed that the wolf should lead a party, of which the king himself would be one, until such time as they might reach the lands from which the wolf came.

'All this came to pass as the king wished. He set out with a small party of his noblest followers, led by the wolf, who took the way eagerly until he reached the shore of the sea – for by this route he could more quickly return to his own land than by the longer way he had come to the king's country before. And when the king saw this he gave orders that his fleet be made ready.'

Gorlagon paused and looked at Arthur. 'Will you still not take some food or wine with us?' he asked.

Arthur shook his head. 'The wolf is waiting to cross the sea. I am afraid he may drown before this story continues!'

Gorlagon sighed and continued.

'Well, the king ordered his fleet prepared, and gathered a small but powerful force of soldiers to man it. Then he set sail and in less than a day they made landfall in the wolf's original country. He was the first to leap to the shore, where he stood waiting eagerly for the king to disembark.

'The king now led a small party inland to a nearby town where, under cover of darkness, they listened to the talk of the people. It did not take long to discover the truth: how the old king had been turned into a wolf by his evil queen, who had swiftly remarried. The new king had turned out to be an evil and overweening monarch, so that the whole land groaned under the yoke of his oppressive reign.

'The king had heard enough. Returning to his ships, he swiftly mustered his soldiers and marched against the man-wolf's rival. In a series of swift and unexpected forays, he decimated the army of the bad king and captured both he and the queen.'

Gorlagon paused. Before he could speak, Arthur said, 'You are like a harper who constantly interposes extra phrases before the conclusion of a song! Go on, I beg you.'

Gorlagon continued.

'The king quickly called an assembly of the nobles of the wolf-lord's land and had the queen brought before them. "Now see where your evil ways have brought you!" he cried, and there before the assembled company he told the story that I have just told you, omitting nothing. Then he said, "Now, perfidious woman, I will ask you this question only once, and I expect you to answer. Where is the sapling with which you turned your good and noble lord into a wolf?"

'The queen made no response at first, but under threat of torture said that she believed it to have been destroyed in a fire. The king refused to believe this, and ordered her put to the question. A few days later she confessed to the hiding place of the sapling, and the king ordered it brought to him. Then he struck the wolf lightly on the head, saying, "Be a man and have the understanding of a man."

'There, in the sight of everyone, the wolf was transformed back into his true shape. People said that he was even more regal and handsome than before, for his ordeal had undoubtedly transformed him in many different ways. The two kings embraced, laughing and crying together, then the king who was a wolf reclaimed his sovereignty and prepared to give his judgement upon those who had wronged him.

'The evil king he ordered to be put to death, but the queen he spared, only divorcing her. The young king who had helped him regain his place and his human form he rewarded with all the richness in his power, and they swore undying fellowship before the young king returned to his own land.'

Gorlagon paused. 'There, my lord, you have heard all my story. Thus is my answer concerning the heart and mind and ways of women. Think and then ask yourself if you are any the wiser for it.' Then he smiled and said, 'Now I ask you again to eat and sup with us, for we both deserve something – you for hearing the tale, and I for telling it!'

'There is yet one more thing I would ask' said Arthur. 'Who is the woman who sits opposite you, and who has before her a dish containing a human head, which she kisses every time you smile, and who wept whenever you kissed your wife during the telling of this tale?'

'I would refuse to answer that if the answer were not known to every-one at this table. This woman is indeed the very same one who wrought such evil against her lord – that is to say, against myself, for I it was who was the wolf, and it was my two brothers, the very same whom you visited, to whose lands I travelled in search of help. And the youngest of them is Torleil, who is the same as he who took me in and who helped me find my true self again.'

Gorlagon paused and sighed heavily. 'As for the head in the dish, that is the embalmed remains of this woman's lover, who became king in my place for a time, and died for it. In sparing her life, I decreed that she should have it always before her, and that when I kissed the wife I married after her, she should kiss the remains in token of her evil acts.'

Then King Arthur turned his attention to the food and wine that were set before him, and he ate in silence, speaking no more, nor looking once at the woman whose terrible fate was displayed before him.

Next morning Arthur, Gawain and Kay set off back home, and in nine days they were there. But what Arthur told the queen concerning his journey this story does not tell, nor if he saw any truth or wisdom in the tale of Gorlagon.

4

Guingamor and Guerrehes

THE story told here actually derives from two separate texts. One is the Breton *Lai of Guingamor*, dating from *circa* 1185, and the other is part of the *First Continuation* to the Old French romance of the Grail by Chrétien de Troyes. Attributed to Gautier de Danans and dating from *circa* 1190–1200, this attempts to extend and complete the story left unfinished by Chrétien at his death. In connecting the two stories, I am following the lead of Professor Dell R. Skeels, whose translation of the two stories was published in *The Anthropologist Looks at Myth* (Austin, Texas, and London, University of Texas Press, 1966).

Originally, the two stories were probably part of a longer tale, told by one of the many wandering Breton *conteurs* who preserved and disseminated so much of Arthurian literature. At some point, the second part, concerning Guerrehes, became detached, to resurface again in the longer *Second Continuation* – itself an episodic work with little real connection to Chrétien's original poem. Yet the tales require a knowledge of each other to explain their motivation and indeed to make sense of their complex symbolic frame of reference. The Guerrehes story, in particular, makes little real sense without the existence of the Guingamor story, which really sets the scene and establishes the relationship between the human and otherworldly characters.

In the first half of the story, Guingamor pursues the mythical white boar, which leads him, ultimately, into the Otherworld. This has been duly noted for its similarity with the

hunting of the great boar Twrch Trwyth in the old Welsh Arthurian story *Culhwch and Olwen*, in which Arthur and his heroes assist the young Culhwch to win the hand of a giant's daughter, and in the process hunt the great boar across most of Wales.

In fact, this is only one of several borrowings from more ancient traditional material concerning the relationship of mortals and the people of faery. The last part of Guingamor's name, like that of King Brangamor in the latter half of the tale, derives from the French word *mort* (death) and it is evident, as Dr Skeels has pointed out, that the latter 'has inherited, both in name and actuality, mortality or death from his father, Guingamor'. And, as he adds, 'It is the task of Guerrehes to remove the infection of death from his father.' This much is evident, though unstated, in the work itself. At the end, the mysterious faery woman from the island tells King Arthur that 'a miracle will happen in his court' once the body of the dead king is returned. Since Guingamor himself, though impossibly aged from his 300-year sojourn in the Otherworld, is apparently able to father a child on his faery mistress, and must therefore have been restored after his return there, it is not beyond the bounds of possibility that the 'miracle' would constitute the restoration to life of the dead King Brangamor.

In telling this story I have resorted, more than usual, to a degree of 'restoration'. This is purely to strengthen the ties between the two halves of the tale, which are less satisfactorily connected in the original texts. For example, I have suggested that the king to whom the charcoal-burner relates the story of Guingamor was in fact Arthur, since this seems more than likely from the internal evidence of the stories, though he is not named at all in the original text of *Guingamor*. Other than this, however, I have allowed the tale to speak for itself, since the text is, anyway, remarkably modern-sounding, with the characters, though not always clearly motivated, behaving in a way consistent with the story itself.

Like many of the tales retold in this book, *Guingamor and Guerrehes* is very clearly Celtic in origin. The description of the Otherworld, with its magical fountain, its strange castles and the miniature knight who gives Guerrehes so much sorrow, all derive ultimately from Celtic sources. The presence of two names containing the prefix 'Bran' strengthens this further, since Bran began life as a Celtic deity and his story influences the whole of Arthurian literature and tradition to a marked degree (see Helain Newstead, *Bran the Blessed in Arthurian Literature*, New York, Columbia University Press, 1939, for a full analysis).

There are obvious parallels between this story and the Grail myth, to which only the Guerrehes story is attached by reason of its presence within the *First Continuation*. In particular we might instance the whole matter of the spearhead, which is clearly a magical talisman of some kind, which must be first removed from the wound in the dead knight's chest and then driven into the breast of the evil knight in an exact imitation of the earlier blow. This recalls the Dolorous Stroke in the Grail story, where the Grail king, Pelleam, is wounded in the genitals by a spear which is one of the 'Hallows', the four sacred objects which are part of the Grail mystery. Given that the original wounded king was himself Bran the Blessed, together with the fact that Pelleam can be cured only by the same spear that wounded him, we can see several striking parallels between the Guerrehes story and the Grail myth.

The hero of the Guerrehes story is called Gaheres in the *Morte D'Arthur* and is one of the four brothers who form the Orkney clan – Gawain, Gareth and Agravain being the other three. He is a somewhat shadowy figure both in Malory and in the longer *Vulgate Cycle* from which Malory drew his story; here he has a far more pronounced role. The similarity between the names Guingamor and Guinglain (see *The Fair Unknown*, pages 20–40), who is Gawain's son by a faery woman, suggests that at some point the story may have been related to the elder brother, though no trace of this remains extant.

Guingamor was edited by Gaston Paris in *Romania*, Vol. VIII, 1897, pp. 50–9, and *Guerrehes* by William Roach and Robert Ivy in Vol. II of *The Continuations of the Old French Perceval of Chrétien de Troyes* (Philadelphia, University of Pennsylvania Press, 1950). I have used Professor Skeel's translation to complete my own version, and have consulted Roach and Ivy for the background to the texts.

I

N BRITTANY THERE WAS ONCE A POWERFUL king who ruled over wide lands. He had a nephew named Guingamor whom he loved well and who was most popular among the people of that land. And since the king himself could not have children, he decided to make the youth his heir.

One day the king went to the woods to amuse himself hunting. Guingamor remained behind since he had just been bled and was still feeling weak, and once the king had departed he retired to his lodgings to rest. Later, he returned to the castle, where he met the seneschal and the two men decided to play draughts.

Now it chanced that the queen passed that way on her way to the chapel. She paused for a while to watch the men playing, and a beam of sunlight fell across Guingamor's face, causing the queen to view him with new eyes. At that moment she began to feel great love for him and, returning at once to her chamber, sent one of her serving maids to ask Guingamor to come to her. Excusing himself from the game, he accompanied the maid at once.

When he arrived in her rooms the queen made him sit down with her. Then she said, with great weight, 'Guingamor, you are young, valiant and handsome. It is scarcely surprising that someone should fall in love with you. I have heard that someone has done just that. She is courtly and beautiful, and I know of no other who is so worthy in all this realm. She loves you greatly and would, I dare say, become your mistress.'

'Lady,' answered Guingamor in puzzlement. 'I know of no such person, and I believe I would find it hard to love someone whom I had neither seen nor spoken to. Besides,' he added, 'I do not wish to begin an affair this year.'

The queen answered, 'My love, do not refuse me. I love you from the bottom of my heart and will always do so!'

Guingamor, startled, was silent for a time. Then he said, 'Lady, I know that I ought to love you, as the wife of my liege lord and uncle.'

'I do not speak of that kind of love,' the Queen replied, 'but of another sort. I would be your mistress if you will. You are handsome and I am still young. We can be happy together, I know.'

At that Guingamor blushed and felt greatly ashamed. 'Madam, that can never be,' he answered, and made to leave the room. Desperately the queen caught him in her arms and attempted to kiss him. Then, as Guingamor pulled away, the queen snatched at the edge of his cloak, so that he was forced to pull away from her. The clasps which held it broke, and Guingamor left the garment in the queen's hands.

Hurriedly he returned to where the seneschal still sat at the game-board, where he tried to hide his distracted feelings and continue the game. The queen, meanwhile, grew fearful, having revealed so much of her innermost feelings. Also, she realized that she still had Guingamor's cloak, and at once bade her maidservant carry it to him. So intent was Guingamor in keeping his thoughts in order that he scarcely noticed when the girl stood by him and then draped it about his shoulders.

Not long after the king returned, full of the day's sport. All through dinner the knights who had been with him talked and boasted of their success in the hunt, and all the while the queen shot covert glances at Guingamor. Then, during a lull in conversation, she began to talk about the great white boar that haunted the woods nearby. 'What a pity it is,' she said, 'that none of you here – though you boast so much about your prowess in the field – has the courage to hunt that dreadful beast.' As she spoke she looked straight at Guingamor.

The king frowned. 'My dear, you know that I do not like any mention of that creature to be made in my hearing. I have lost too many knights to that terrible beast.'

After this the party soon broke up, and everyone retired to bed. But Guingamor forgot nothing the queen had said. Instead of retiring, he knocked on the door of the king's chamber. On being invited to enter, he knelt at his uncle's feet and begged to be granted a favour.

'You know there is nothing I would not give you,' the king said, smiling.

'Then, uncle, I ask that you give me the bloodhound, the brachet and your own best horse, and give me leave to go and hunt the white boar.'

Now the king was dismayed and saddened. He wished profoundly that he had never been asked this thing. Still, he begged his nephew to reconsider.

'Sire, nothing will persuade me not to go,' said Guingamor. 'If you will not lend me what I have asked for, I shall go anyway.'

At this moment the queen entered the room, and when she heard what Guingamor had requested, she lent her own words to his, pleading with the king to grant his wish, for in this way she hoped to be rid of the youth, and thus of her fears for what he might one day say concerning her protestations of love.

At length the king gave his consent, and Guingamor hurried away to spend a sleepless night in his lodgings. In the morning he rose with the dawn and sent for the king's hunting horse, his bloodhound and brachet, which were duly brought to him. A group of huntsmen with two packs of hounds was gathered. The king himself, and all his knights and their ladies, as well as most of the population of the city, turned out to see him depart. Many wept openly, for they expected never to see him again.

They trailed the boar easily enough to its lair, and Guingamor sent the bloodhound in to drive the beast away. Then Guingamor sounded his horn, and let loose one of the packs, bringing the others on but not yet giving them the signal to pursue the boar.

The pursuit was long and wearisome, and soon the rest of the hunt fell behind. But Guingamor kept on, driving the king's horse onward. The first pack of hounds grew exhausted and began to fall back, whereupon Guingamor released the second pack, and then the brachet, and then set himself to blowing the horn as best he might to guide and encourage the pack.

After a time they entered a dense part of the forest, and for a time Guingamor could no longer hear the barking of the dogs. He feared that he had lost them, and began to think what the king would say when he returned empty-handed. Then he came to a high hill and rode to the summit, from where he could see much of the forest.

It was a clear day and the sun shone down on the trees, turning them green and golden. On all sides birds sang, though Guingamor had no ear for them. However, as he sat his horse and strained to catch a glimpse of movement in the forest, he heard the yelping of the brachet and then saw the boar itself, closely pursued by the dog, appear and pass him on the way to higher ground.

Eagerly Guingamor spurred his horse down from the hill and went full-tilt after his quarry. He rejoiced that he might succeed where no other had done, and imagined what the king would say – aye, and the queen – when he returned with the boar's head on his spear.

Fast as he rode, he could not seem to overtake the two beasts. The ground rose steadily, and he found himself leaving the woodlands behind and entering a part of the country he did not recognize. Then, before him, he saw rising from a meadow starred with flowers a most beautiful castle. Its walls were of green marble and its towers, where they rose above the walls, seemed to be of silver, flashing in the sun. A wide gateway opened in the wall near where he sat on his horse and gazed in wonder. They were of ivory inlaid with gold and seemed to have no clasp or fastening of any kind. Guingamor determined to enter the place, certain that he would find a guardian of some kind within who might have seen the boar or the dog. Besides which, he was curious to know more of this place, the whereabouts of which he had never before suspected.

He rode boldly into the castle and looked about him. He could see no one moving anywhere, and when he dismounted and went inside the most beautiful palace he found within, it was again deserted. Everywhere he looked he saw plates and goblets and furniture of solid gold, but not a living being.

Wondering greatly at this, Guingamor mounted his horse again and rode back out to the meadow. He listened but could hear no sound of the brachet or the boar. He began to regret his impulse to enter the castle at all, and without a backward look rode on until he entered the forest again. There he thought he heard the barking of the brachet, and spurred his mount in that direction, blowing his horn the while as strongly as he might.

The way led again into more open ground, and there he found a fountain that rose beneath a single great tree. The fountain was most beautifully and elegantly carved, and the gravel around it seemed to be made of silver and gold. But nothing was more beautiful to his eyes than the maiden who was bathing herself in the fountain, while another combed her hair and washed her feet and hands. Her limbs were long and smooth, her breasts slight, and her hair a cloud of gold.

As he checked his horse, openly staring at her naked beauty, Guingamor saw that her clothes were laid out to one side. On an impulse he gathered them up and placed them high up in the fork of the tree, thinking that he might capture the boar and return in time to find the maiden still there – for he was sure she would not leave without her clothes.

But the maiden had seen him and now she called out.

'Guingamor, leave me my clothes. You would surely not wish it to be said that you had stolen a maiden's clothes in the depths of the woods. Come here and talk to me. You have ridden far today without success. Stay with me a while and all will be well.'

Shamefaced, Guingamor gave her back her clothing. Then he excused himself, saying that he must continue his search for the boar and the brachet. The maiden smiled and offered him her hand. 'I promise you you will search for ever and not find either of them without my help. But if you stay with me for three days, I will undertake that you shall have both the boar and your dog at the end of that time. Then you may go home. This I promise.'

At this Guingamor dismounted and stood by while the maiden dressed herself. The serving woman busied herself with preparing a mule for herself and a white palfrey for her mistress. Then the three of them set out back towards the castle which Guingamor had already explored. As they went he kept stealing glances at the maiden, and the more he looked the more he liked what he saw. His heart began to pound and his palms sweated. Finally he could keep silent no longer and confessed that he felt a great love for her and that if she reciprocated his feeling he would never so much as look at another woman.

The maiden smiled at Guingamor and replied that she did indeed feel such feelings for him. There and then the knight leaned over to her from the saddle and they kissed and embraced with passion.

The serving maid hastened on ahead of them, and by the time they reached the castle it was all a-bustle with servants running hither and thither preparing food and drink for the couple, while minstrels tuned their instruments in the galleries and a band of knights and squires came forth to greet them. Guingamor saw with astonishment that these were the very men who, over the years, had gone forth from his uncle's land in search of the white boar. They were all most happy and welcomed him with delight.

They dined well that night and Guingamor was put to rest in a great bed where, later on, the maiden of the fountain joined him. Three days and three nights they spent together thus, and then on the third day Guingamor declared reluctantly that he must return to his uncle. 'And I ask that I be given the brachet and the head of the white boar, as you promised, my lady. As soon as I have returned home and shown my prize, I shall come back here.'

The maiden looked at him oddly. 'Sir,' she said, 'I will give you the things as I promised. But there is something you must know. Though only three days have passed here, in the world from which you came 300 have gone by. All those whom you knew are long since dead, and I dare say you will not even find anyone who remembers your name.'

'My lady and my love, I cannot believe that what you say is true!' cried Guingamor.

'Nevertheless, it is so,' said she.

'Then I must go forth and see the truth of this for myself. Do you give me leave to depart, and I promise to return at once when I have satisfied myself.'

'Very well,' said the lady, 'but I warn you that once you leave the borders of this land – there by the river where we first met – you must neither eat nor drink anything, no matter how hungry or thirsty you are. If you do so, you will never be able to return here.'

Guingamor gave his word on this, and the lady had his mount, ready saddled, brought out. With it came the dog, which he took back, holding it by the leash, and the carcass of the boar, the head of which he took and placed on the end of his spear. Then he set out, the lady riding by his side until they reached the riverside, where a boat awaited him. There he took leave of his mistress and crossed the swift water to the other side.

There he found the forest much deeper and more entangled than he remembered it, and many other things seemed changed also. He wandered there for most of the morning until he came upon a clearing where a charcoal-burner was at work. Guingamor asked for news of the king, and after some thought the man replied that he had heard tell in old stories of such a monarch, but that he was long dead, close on 300 years ago. Guingamor asked if he had heard anything of a nephew of this old king, and the charcoal-burner, thinking deeper, said that he had heard something about a nephew, but he had gone into the forest to hunt and had never returned.

'I am that nephew,' said Guingamor, pale and trembling, and there and then he told the man the whole story, and showed him the boar's head. 'I bid you take this trophy of mine, and show it to anyone you meet, and tell them my story. For I must return now whence I came.'

So saying, Guingamor turned his horse about and rode back through the forest the way he had come. By now it was well past midday and as the afternoon sun rose higher in the sky, he began to experience terrible thirst and hunger, until he believed he would go mad. Then beside the road he saw an apple tree laden down with fruit and, forgetting the lady's warning, he took three of the apples and ate them hungrily.

As soon as he had done so, he began to feel the weight of his years. His body and limbs grew wasted and he no longer had the strength to sit on his horse. He fell down there by the roadside and could not even lift a finger to help himself.

There the charcoal-burner found him, having followed him out of curiosity for his strange story. He found Guingamor so wasted and frail that he seemed unlikely to live out the day. Then he saw two damsels riding towards him who, when they came abreast, dismounted and began to reproach the knight for failing to obey his lady's commands. Then right tenderly they helped him to mount his horse and, supporting him on either side, made their way towards the river. There the charcoal-burner saw them cross in the boat which had brought the knight across earlier.

The peasant returned home and showed the boar's head to everyone and told them of the knight's story, at which all marvelled greatly. Later the head was taken to King Arthur, who was the ruler of that land. There it was preserved by him for as long as might be. And the king gave orders for the story to be set down in writing so that it might not be forgotten. But this was not the end of the story.

II

N A HOT NIGHT YEARS AFTER, King Arthur lay sleepless in his bed. The sky was overcast and thunder rolled along the horizon and lightning split the sky. The king summoned two of his chamberlains and asked them to bring him a silken cloak and light boots and breeches. Then he called for torches and went out to a lodge overlooking the sea from where he was wont to watch the play of the wind and the waves, and from where, at need, he could descend through a gateway and thence by a path to the edge of the sea.

The king sat for a time looking out at the storm, and in a while he saw it pass, leaving the horizon clear. And there he observed, toward the horizon, a light like a star that seemed to grow larger as he watched.

'What do you see out there?' he demanded of one of the servants.

'My lord, it seems like a strange light. What can it be?'

As they looked, the light grew brighter, till it cast a glow over the surface of the sea, and they could see that it was a barge, freshly painted, draped with a rich, dark pall of silk. There seemed to be no one alive on the barge, but most astonishing of all was a great swan, its neck enclosed in a golden collar to which chains were attached, and which enabled it to pull the craft.

As the barge drew level with the place from which the king and his servants watched, the swan stopped, and then began to cry and beat the sea with its wings. Astonished, Arthur went out through the little gate and took the path down to the shore, where the barge had come to rest. There he stepped aboard, finding the craft curtained with rich hangings, and with two great candles burning, one at each end of the deck. In the midst of the boat was a shelter, which the king entered. There he found the body of a knight lying under a cloth of richest brocaded silk, trimmed with ermine. From the breast of the dead man protruded the haft of a great spear.

Gently the king drew back the coverlet and inspected the body. Never had he seen so strong and handsome a person! His clothing was richer than the king's own, and at his belt was a purse richly embroidered with gold thread. This the king opened and inside found a letter which he read.

'King. The corpse which lies here requests, before death comes upon it, that you allow it to lie undisturbed in your hall until such time as one may come who will draw out the spearhead from this flesh. May he who draws it forth successfully have as evil a fate as Guerrehes had in the orchard if he fails to take just revenge upon the one who struck the blow. Let him strike the villain in the same place with this same spearhead. If this is done you shall know all there is to know concerning this corpse. If the spear is not withdrawn before the year be out, then have it interred with such honour as you think fit. Meanwhile, know that the body is well embalmed and will be preserved for as long as may be needed.'

When Arthur had read this, he replaced the letter in the purse and drew the coverlet up as before. Then he called to his servants to take the body and lay it in the midst of the castle, in the great hall. 'And let be known,' he said, 'all that has taken place this night.'

While his commands were carried out the king returned to the window and once again looked out on the sea. There he saw the swan trumpet with joy and once more beat the sea with its wings. Then it turned about and drew the barge back out upon the water, and the two candles, which had not ceased from burning, were extinguished, and with them the light went from the sea and darkness returned. And as the king stood there marvelling greatly, he heard the voice of the swan raised in lamenting, until it faded at last from his ears. Then the king returned to his bed and lay for a long while thinking upon all that he had seen until he fell asleep at last.

In the morning the first to rise was Sir Gawain. He roused several of his brothers-in-arms and they set out to celebrate Mass in the great hall. When they entered they were astonished to see the knight lying there on a table before the altar. At first they thought he was asleep, then the spied the spearhead in his breast and marvelled even more.

'Who is this?' demanded Gawain. 'Does anyone here know him?'

But all the knights looked closely at the dead knight's face and none could recognize him.

Word soon spread throughout the city, and people began to crowd into the hall to see the dead knight. Gawain, meanwhile, went to rouse the king, but he said nothing of the body in the hall, and Arthur himself chose to hold his counsel on the matter. In the hall he drew back the mantle and exclaimed over the beauty and fineness of the corpse. Then he drew forth the letter. Everyone crowded near to hear what it might say.

'My lords,' said King Arthur, 'this man who lies here before us had a great faith that he would be avenged by one of the knights of the Round Table.' He then read the letter out loud for all to hear.

Tor, the son of Ares, said, 'This is a great mystery. How can we know who killed him or how when nothing of this is told in the letter?'

'Aye,' said Gawain, 'where should we even begin to look?'

'As to that,' said King Arthur, 'we must wait and see.'

The king ordered a fine coffin to be made to contain the body, which was thereafter to rest in state before the altar until such time as one came forward to attempt the mystery of the knight's death.

Gawain, meanwhile, sought out his brother Guerrehes, for he was certain that in some way he must be concerned in the mystery, since his name had been mentioned in the letter. Guerrehes, who had not been present in the great hall, and knew nothing of the coming of the barge with the dead knight, was at first reluctant to speak of the adventure in which he had been shamed – indeed, he marvelled that Gawain could know anything of what had occurred. But the latter would not explain anything of his knowledge until he had heard Guerrehes's own story.

It seemed that Guerrehes had set out in search of adventure one day and that he had ridden for three days without meeting anyone. Then he came into an area of rich grassland, through which a broad river flowed. Following this for a time, he came in sight of a walled city of great beauty, its walls of red marble and white limestone, carved all over with the shapes of beasts. Now Guerrehes was very hungry by this time, and hurried to enter the city. Inside, the streets were deserted, and he rode right up to the castle at the centre of the city without seeing a soul. Entering into the splendid building, he found this too to be deserted. He passed through the great hall and into a chamber in which were four beds richly adorned with gold and ivory and covered in costly bedspreads. He sat down upon one to remove his helm, for the heat was irksome.

Wandering on, Guerrehes found himself in an even larger chamber, in which were two beds, more richly apparelled than the first. Beyond this lay a third room, decorated with gold, in which a single bed of unparalleled richness stood. The room had a window and, looking out of this, Guerrehes saw an orchard filled with fruit trees bearing a rich load of apples. In the centre of the green lawn two silken pavilions were set up, and as he looked Guerrehes saw a hideously ugly dwarf pass from one to the other, bearing a silver bowl and a towel.

Guerrehes at once climbed out of the window and dropped to the lawn below. Then he hurried over to the pavilions and looked within the first. There he saw a most fair and beautiful woman sitting in a silver chair. She was crumbling bread into a silver bowl held by the ugly dwarf. It contained milk and almonds, with which she was attempting to feed a strongly built knight who lay on a bed with a bloodstained bandage bound about him.

'God's greeting to all here,' said Guerrehes.

The wounded man glared at him. 'Get out of here!' he cried, and struggled to sit up, knocking the bowl of milk from the dwarf's hands so that it spilled upon the floor. The effort of moving caused his wound to break open again, and he fell back with a groan.

'I am sorry,' stammered Guerrehes. 'I had no notion my presence would cause such distress.'

'God's mercy!' exclaimed the wounded knight, 'I shall die if you do not go hence!'

'Fear not,' said the dwarf. 'You shall be avenged when the Little Knight comes.'

All this time the damsel said no word at all, but simply stared at Guerrehes. Now there entered the pavilion a small knight on a small horse. He was no more than two feet high, yet he was no dwarf, being perfectly proportioned and wearing a suit of armour to match his size. Without even speaking a word, he drew his sword and struck Guerrehes hard across the shoulders. 'I will have your head for this!' he cried.

The wounded knight added, 'Do not let him go from here unshamed. He showed great arrogance in entering here, where he is not wanted.'

Guerrehes went quickly outside and he found that his horse and shield and helmet had been brought there, and awaited him. He hastened to put on the helmet, then took up the shield and mounted. Towering over the little knight, he declared his intention of leaving at once, and peaceably. But the Little Knight would not have it. 'Not until you have jousted with me, arrogant fool!' he shouted.

Astonished by this, Guerrehes set his spear in rest and charged at his small opponent. To his amazement, however, when his lance struck home on the centre of the Little Knight's saddle-bow, it shattered; while he himself went flying from his horse's back at what seemed the merest tap of the other's spear.

He lay winded, and the Little Knight at once dismounted and came and set his foot upon Guerrehes's neck. The weight of the small foot felt as though it were crushing the life from him, and when the small one demanded his submission, Guerrehes extended his hands and gasped out the words of surrender.

'Now learn the custom of this place,' said the small knight, placing his hands on his hips. 'All whom I overcome – and they are many – are given three choices. The first is to become a weaver, to make and sew costly linens and draperies. To learn to make brocade curtains for my master's beds. The second is to fight me again – and, if you are victorious, leave here without further trouble. The third choice is to lose your head. You have a year to think about this. At the end of which time you must return here to me and give your answer. Do you understand, varlet?'

Numbly Guerrehes nodded his head. The small knight nodded in satisfaction. 'Good. You were much too precipitous entering this orchard the way you did. Now you can leave the same way as you came, through the window!'

Guerrehes climbed back the way he had come and was astonished to find the room beyond filled with maidens making lace and ribbons and purses of leather. With one accord they began to laugh at him and to call out insults. Hurriedly the knight made his way into the next room – the one with the two beds – and this he found to be full of squires and damsels who were all busy at making things. They too mocked him, crying, 'Craven! Coward! The Little Knight beat you soundly! So much for your size and strength!'

Face crimson, Guerrehes hurried into the third room, where he found a number of knights playing chess and backgammon. Again they hurled insults at him, comparing his great size to that of the Little Knight and mocking him for being so easily overthrown.

Never had Guerrehes felt such shame. But this was as nothing compared to what still awaited him. In the hall of the castle, now filled with knights and ladies and their retainers, he was noticed at once, and everyone there cried out that this was the miserable fellow who could not even defend himself against the least of men.

Hiding his grief as best he might, Guerrehes escaped to the courtyard, where he found his horse waiting. Mounting swiftly, he trotted out through the gates, meeting no one. Thus he thought to have escaped further vilification, but the streets of the town were now filled with people, and even they seemed to have heard of his misfortune. They pelted him with stones and offal and fish guts, crying all the while, 'Behold the craven knight!' until Guerrehes thought he would scream.

Finally he was beyond the walls of the vile city and, setting spurs to his horse, set himself to put as much distance between himself and its walls as he might. He rode by way of fields and woods, avoiding roads or trackways where he might encounter people who knew of his shame. For two more days he rode, scarcely pausing to rest and not at all to eat. Then, as the country grew more familiar, he chanced to meet a group of soldiers from Arthur's court. All greeted him in friendly fashion, and no word was made of his defeat by the Little Knight.

Thus reassured Guerrehes rode on until he reached Caerleon, where a few days later Gawain sought him out and demanded to know the truth of his recent adventure.

At first Guerrehes refused to answer, saying that the letter lied, and that it must refer to another man named Guerrehes. But when Gawain pressed him, he finally gave in and told the whole of his sad and sorry tale. At the end of it Gawain said, 'I believe we should go together and look upon the corpse. For this is a mystery which is best attempted at once, lest it fester and grow within you, brother.'

So not without some reluctance, Guerrehes accompanied Gawain to the hall, and there along with several other knights who were present looked upon the corpse. After a while, he said angrily, 'I do not know this man.' And he added, 'Varlet, may this warhead never come out!' But even as he spoke his hand brushed against the broken shaft of the spear and, a splinter having lodged in his finger, of a sudden the spearhead leapt from the body.

The knights stared in wonder and Sir Gawain was heard to say, 'Brother, it seems to me you are overhasty in this matter.' Sir Yvain, who was standing there and had seen everything, said, 'What is done is done. There is no sense in complaining about it.'

The knights looked closely at the spearhead, which was as fine and bright as the day it had been cast, and bore neither stain nor darkening from the blood of the dead knight. Finally they gave it to Guerrehes, who said grimly that he would honour the words of the letter, which bound him to avenge the death of the knight whether he wished or not. Then he returned to his chambers and, having called for all his spears to be brought before him, had the one from the dead knight's body affixed to the stoutest shaft.

Now it befell that a few days after this King Arthur held a great feast at Caerleon to celebrate Easter, and on this occasion asked that Guerrehes sit near him. Throughout the evening the knight spoke little and never once laughed, and finally Kay, the seneschal, asked the king if he would grant him a boon. When Arthur gave his assent, the seneschal said that he wanted to hear why Guerrehes was so solemn and sad, and that the king should bid him tell the reason to the whole court. At first Arthur refused, but Kay reminded him of his custom to always grant a boon asked before a feast. Reluctantly, and not without stern words to the

The Vows of King Arthur and His Knights

The Fair Unknown

Arthur and Gorlagon

Guingamor and Guerrehes

seneschal, the king turned to Guerrehes and commanded him to tell the reason for his sorrowful mien. Guerrehes, flushed and angry, obeyed and told again the whole story as he had told it to Gawain. Finally he said, 'Now that you know of my shame, and since I am bound to honour the request of the dead knight to avenge him, I shall remain here no longer.' And he asked of Arthur that he be given leave to depart. Arthur willingly gave his consent and without more ado Guerrehes left the hall and called for his horse and weapons set forth from Caerleon.

His journey was a long one, and took him far from the court, but at length, when the day appointed for his return to the mysterious city was approaching, he met the hated Little Knight on the road. 'Well,' sneered the dwarf, 'I was just on my way to Arthur's court to remind you of your promise.'

'I need no such reminder,' answered Guerrehes shortly.

Thereafter the two rode in silence until they reached the meadowlands and the city of red marble. There, in redemption of his promise, Guerrehes chose to fight the Little Knight again. And this time, whether by skill or luck or magic, who can say, he was the victor, and killed the small man without compunction and in fair combat.

Then the lord of the castle, he whom Guerrehes had last seen in the silken pavilion, was so angered at the death of his diminutive champion that he himself declared that he would fight Guerrehes, and accordingly called for his arms and weapons.

When the two met, Guerrehes chose the spear with the head from the dead knight, and with his first blow, though he was himself unhorsed, he ran the spear deep into his opponent's breast. Leaping up, Guerrehes drew his sword and went to finish the work he had begun. But the lord was already cold, his spirit fled. So too were all the people of the castle, who the moment their master fell dead began to depart in haste.

Then, as Guerrehes stood looking down at the body of his opponent, a most beauteous maiden appeared clad in a robe of silk embroidered with silver flowers. She came and looked at the corpse, then said to Guerrehes, 'Sir, tell me the truth. Where did you get this spearhead?'

Guerrehes told her concerning the dead knight in the barge.

With a sigh, the maiden placed her hand upon his arm. 'Sir, know that this knight was my one true love, the most worthy and honourable of men. This evil lord whom you have slain was the cause of his death. You have avenged him.'

Then Guerrehes examined the dead man more closely and saw that the spearhead had entered his body in the exact same place as the dead knight from the barge, and he marvelled greatly. Yet, as he made to draw out the spearhead, the maiden prevented him. 'Let it stay where it is!

If you draw it forth now, you will be killed. As long as it remains where it is he cannot be avenged.'

'Then let it remain where it is,' agreed Guerrehes. Then the two of them spoke some more, and Guerrehes agreed to escort the maiden back to Arthur's court, that she might see her dead lover once more and see to his interment. They left the evil castle behind, and in all the town they saw not one person.

All that day they rode together, and when evening came they found themselves by the shore of the sea. There, but a short distance across the water, lay an island on which a castle stood with many lighted windows.

'Here we shall be certain of a good welcome,' said the maiden, and called out to a boatman who came to ferry them across to the island. There they were well met and ushered into a great hall in the castle. Never had Guerrehes seen such a splendid gathering. There were more knights and ladies and squires there than he had ever seen – even in Arthur's court. Nor had he ever received such a generous welcome. Everyone there treated him with the utmost honour, providing him with fresh clothing, water in which to wash and finally sitting him at a table on which the choicest foods and wines were laid.

Guerrehes was by this time exhausted from all that he had endured that day. He scarcely heard the talk of the people around him, save that afterwards it seemed they had spoken much of the sorrow they felt for their lord, King Brangamor, and of the joy of their lady, Queen Brangepart, who rejoiced for the avenging of her son.

At some point in all of this Guerrehes fell asleep. He slept deeply and dreamlessly and awoke refreshed to find himself lying in a great bed that swayed gently from side to side. He discovered that the reason for this was the motion of the barge in which the bed was set, and, rising quickly, he found that it was being pulled by a swan. This must be the very same barge that had brought the dead knight to Caerleon! His exhaustion overcame him and, lying down again on the bed, he quickly fell asleep.

Soon the barge came in sight of the cliffs where the king's lodge was set. Word soon spread of the coming of the strange craft, pulled by a swan, and when Arthur heard of this he went at once to see what manner of wonder it bore. Together with a number of knights and lords, he descended by way of the path to the shore, and there went aboard the barge. On the deck he met with a most beautiful damsel, who greeted him and then said, 'My lord, yonder beneath the curtains of that bed sleeps a noble knight. I pray you let him sleep a little longer.'

For answer the king looked beneath the curtain. Then he said, 'He will have as much time as he needs to sleep later. For now I would speak with him.'

Then King Arthur woke the sleeping Guerrehes and welcomed and embraced him, and then they all repaired to the great hall of Caerleon, where the body of the dead knight still lay, as though asleep. When the maiden looked upon him, she sighed and then wept. 'Ah, fair love!' she said, 'you were ever the best of men, and I have mourned you this long while. Now I am glad that you are avenged.'

Then she turned to King Arthur and said, 'Sire, I may not remain here for much longer. Let me but tell you the history of this noble lord. Here lies King Brangamor, the son of Sir Guingamor and a faery lady that he loved. I am sure that you have heard the story of how he hunted the white boar and how afterwards vanished away. Well, it was because he was one part mortal that he had to die in this world, but now that he is dead he may return to the place where he was born, to his queen, and to his mother. Sire, all his people mourn him, and it is right that he should return to them. Also, I may say this: that when he departs from here a miracle will take place in his court. More I cannot say, for the island over which he ruled is one of those where no mortal man may dwell.'

Then King Arthur said, 'Let it be as you wish, lady. And he gave instructions for the body and all its fine wrappings to be carried down to the barge. There the damsel took her leave of Guerrehes, and the swan turned about and went back towards the place where it had first appeared. No more was seen or heard of the strange island, nor was any more ever learned that I know of the strange events recounted here, but the king ordered these events to be set down and added to the story of Guingamor and the Lady of the Fountain, so that all there was to know might be read over and pondered upon at leisure.

5

The Story of Meriadoc

THE *Historia Meridaoci, Regis Cambriae* (*History of Meriadoc, King of Cambria*) is one of the few surviving Arthurian romances written in Latin. The most famous of these remains Geoffrey of Monmouth's *Historia Regum Britanniae* (*History of the Kings of Britain*) and *Vita Merlini* (*Life of Merlin*), which did much to set the pattern for Arthurian writing during the eleventh and twelfth centuries. *Meridaoci* and its companion piece *De Ortu Waluuanii, Nepotis Arturi* (*The Rise of Gawain, Nephew of Arthur*) are unusual in that they tell stories which appear nowhere else, whereas the narrative structure of Geofrey's work continued to be picked over throughout the remainder of the Middle Ages, generating numerous copies, versions and translations which added significantly to the corpus of Arthurian literature in general. Yet both these stories remained almost completely unknown until they were recently edited and translated by Mildred Leake Day from the unique MSS (Cotton Faustina B.VI and Bodleian Rawlinson B.149, in the British Library and the Bodleian Library respectively).

What makes them so unique as Arthurian stories is the blend of factual, historically detailed narrative with the touch of otherworldliness which is more common to the Matter of Britain. Much of the story of Meriadoc and his sister Orwen concerns the plot against their father, King Caradoc, and their subsequent upbringing in a cave by Ivor the huntsman and forester. However, after a brief episode in which Meriadoc regains his title, avenges himself on his father's killer and sets out on a career of adventure, the texture of the story becomes suddenly otherworldly in character, with mysterious castles which appear and disappear, beautiful faery ladies, and strange adventures out of time. The effect of this is to make the otherwordly adventures all the more powerful, coming as they do on the heels of a detailed description of siege warfare (much abbreviated in my retelling).

The story proceeds with great pace and panache, as Meriadoc rises to ever greater heights, only to be cast down at the very pinnacle of his career. The story of his triumphal return, his marriage and his inheritance makes for a rich and entertaining story which blends some of the best elements of Arthurian romance with a strong touch of Roman epic.

There is also, as with so many of the Arthurian tales, a strong Celtic element underlying the text. The episode in which Meriadoc's men enter the strange castle in search of shelter and are overcome by an inexplicable sense of fear which roots them to the spot is strongly reminiscent of the story of Fionn mac Cumhail, the Irish hero, who with his men enters the Hostel of the Quicken Tree and all are similarly frozen, before being attacked by an otherworldly figure not unlike the monstrous churl in the kitchen who subsequently attacks Meriadoc while he is in search of food.

I have very slightly amended the ending of the story, since in the original it stops suddenly, leaving some untidy loose threads. It seemed appropriate to bring Meriadoc home after his great adventure, even though the text simply records his illustrious descendants. I am especially grateful to Mildred Leake Day for making this text accessible. I have worked from her edition and translation exclusively (*The Story of Meriadoc,* *King of Cambria*, edited and translated by Mildred Leake Day, New York and London, Garland Press, 1988).

EFORE THE TIME OF KING ARTHUR, Britain was divided into three parts: Cambria, Albany and Logres. During the reign of Uther Pendragon, Cambria came to be ruled by two brothers. The elder was called Caradoc, and he ruled over the most part of the land; the younger was named Griffin, and he served his brother well and faithfully.

One day King Caradoc set his mind to the conquest of Ireland, which he achieved through strength of arms and a powerful army. Thereafter he took the daughter of the Irish king in marriage, and in due time she bore him twin children, a son and a daughter. But all was not well with the king, for as time passed he began to grow weak and lose the vigour of his body. Though still a young man, he began to age, and within the space of a few years was forced to hand over the governance of his kingdom to his younger brother, Griffin, while he himself ruled in name only.

For several years Griffin served faithfully, but gradually his mind began to turn to the thought of ruling alone. Evil men, concerned only with their own overweening ambition, approached him and whispered in his ear that his brother was old and senile and ought to be put away. Surely, they said, it is a shame that this great kingdom should be ruled over by a weak and foolish old man when you are strong and in your prime. You already rule in all but name. Why not make this a reality? Be rid of your brother for ever.

And though Griffin tried not to listen, when he learned that Caradoc had sent letters to another king, seeking to wed his son to the princess of Cambria, his resolve was further weakened. Then those who had spoken to him before approached him again, reminding him that the king's son was already growing towards manhood and showing great skill and strength. Surely Griffin must realize that in time he would be stripped of everything, either through the marriage of his niece to a foreign king or through the succession of Caradoc's son to the throne. Then they put forward a scheme to murder the old king as he rode hunting. They sought only Griffin's approval to act.

Then they flattered him and spoke of possible internecine strife which could only tear the kingdom apart, and at last Griffin gave his assent to the evil deed they suggested.

But it befell that the night before the king was due to ride to the hunt, he dreamed a dream in which he saw Griffin lying in wait in the forest, sharpening two arrows, which he then gave to two men. They, in turn, waited until the king was riding by and shot at him without warning.

Caradoc woke with a scream, hands pressed to his chest where the arrows had stuck. The queen, waking by his side, first reassured him, then spoke of her own fears. 'I am certain,' she said, 'that your brother is plotting to kill you. Please don't go hunting today.'

But King Caradoc refused to believe that his brother was capable of plotting against him, and with the first light he set out with a party of nobles to the hunt. There, sure enough, just as Griffin had planned, the aged king became separated from the rest of the hunt, being unable to keep up; and there the two men who had been bribed to carry out the evil deed fell upon him and carried him deeper into the forest, where they ran him through with a hunting spear, leaving it in his body so that it would look like an accident.

It was not long before the king's absence was noticed, and still less time before his body was discovered. Amid much weeping and sorrow, the body was conveyed to the castle and there, with great mourning, interred in the ground. An attempt was made to discover how the king's death had occurred, but there was no evidence to indicate who had perpetrated the deed. Griffin, who had absented himself on administrative business so that there was no possibility of his being suspected, was informed, and wept bitterly for the death of his beloved brother. Caradoc's queen, sick at heart and knowing full well that he was the victim of murder, fell ill and died within a month of her lord's passing.

Griffin now went about seizing power utterly, and his first act was to set up an investigation into his brother's death. Alarmed, the two killers approached him, reminding him of his promise to pay them well and to raise them to high office. Griffin's answer was to impeach them, and to order them hanged forthwith without trial or appeal – having first had their tongues torn out so that they could not speak of his own part in the affair.

All of Cambria was shocked by this savage act, and many began to suspect Griffin's part in the crime. Several of the most notable lords of the kingdom came together to discuss the matter, and decided that they must secure the protection of the young prince and princess, since Griffin might well decide to remove them from the succession. Two lords in particular, Sadoc and Dunewall, who were both highly respected, spoke out against Griffin, and suggested that the royal children be taken to Cornwall and the princess betrothed to Moroveus, the duke of that land, who had no wife and was loyal to Caradoc's family.

To this end the two lords went to Griffin and demanded custody of the royal children, under the pretext of preventing any possibility of unscrupulous lords seizing them and setting them up as rival claimants. Griffin, though inwardly raging, concealed his anger and asked for time to consider the request. Then, when the lords had departed, he at once sent a messenger to the man who was at that time responsible for the fostering of the children, ordering them to be brought to him at once.

Now this man was Ivor, the master of the royal hunt. The royal children, whose names were Meriadoc and Orwen, had been entrusted to him by the old king himself, and Ivor's wife, Morwen, had suckled them from the day of their birth. Neither suspected anything was amiss and at once escorted the twins to Griffin. He, foreseeing the intention of the nobles, prepared to have them killed, sending his most loyal men to do the task.

Their intent was to take the children deep into the forest of Arglud and there hang them on a certain ancient tree which had long since been used for this purpose. But when the time came, they were so moved to pity by the sweetness and gentleness of the twins that they found it was not in their hearts to kill them after all. Therefore they contrived matters so that the rope by which they were to be hanged was so thin that it would break almost at once, letting the children fall to the earth unhurt. Thus the men could swear to Griffin that they had done their work, while the royal children remained alive.

Ivor, meanwhile, had learned of the fate intended for his fosterlings. Tears running down his face, he told his wife what was to occur. 'We must find a way to save them!' she cried, and the couple at once set out for the forest, taking with them only Ivor's bow and hunting horn and his faithful dog, Dolfin.

Having reached the forest ahead of the murderers, and knowing that he was no match for them armed with only a bow, Ivor devised a plan. He shot and killed a large buck and, having slaughtered it, scattered the pieces of raw flesh all around the place where Griffin's men were bound to come. Soon, as he had known would happen, a large number of wolves began to assemble there, drawn thither by the smell of the meat. When the murderers at last arrived, they were briefly frightened off, but as Ivor and his wife watched from the shelter of some bushes, they began to return.

The forester was ready to rush out and sell his life dearly for the children, but he heard the men discussing how they would arrange matters so that they were not killed, and so held his hand. The wolves began coming thickly now, and their howling alerted the men, who began to look fearfully around them. One drew their attention to the great tree on which they had intended to hang the children. Its vast trunk had a hole on one side, and within was a hollowed-out place big enough for several men to get into. They quickly crawled inside, taking the dazed children with them, and prepared to defend themselves against the wolves.

Ivor, drawing his bow, shot several of the creatures from his hiding place, and the rest at once fell on the carcasses of their fellows and began to rend them. Under cover of this, Ivor crept closer to the great tree and began heaping dry brushwood against its bole. Then he struck flint and tinder and started a blaze. As the men within began to cry out in terror, Ivor blew a long blast on his horn, which sent the wolves scattering in panic for fear of a hunt. Then the wily huntsman called out to the men in the tree to come out, or else he would burn them all to ashes.

The would-be murderers cried out for mercy, and Ivor ordered them to send the children forth first. This done, he snatched up a sword which had been left outside and, as the men emerged, one by one, through the narrow opening, he killed them all, and left them there to be consumed by the wild beasts. Then, together with his wife, he fled to the forest of Fleventan.

Here was a secret place discovered by Ivor long ago while out hunting. It was a certain marvellous cave, deep in the rock known as the 'cliff of the eagles', from the fact that four of these great birds perpetually nested there. The cave was really a series of caves, like rooms hollowed out of the living rock. It was believed to have once belonged to the terrible Cyclops, since when it had lain undiscovered until the huntsman had chanced across it. There, for the next five years, Ivor and his wife and the two children remained in hiding. Ivor hunted daily for their needs, while Morwen cooked and sewed clothing. Thus they wanted for nothing and remained hidden from the spite of Griffin, while the two children grew swiftly in the wild, learning all they needed from their wise and skilful foster parents.

Now a day came when they were all out in the forest seeking game and kindling, when it happened that they met two knights riding through the trees. These were Sir Kay, King Arthur's seneschal, and Sir Urien, who besides being a knight of the Round Table was also king of Scotland. It was because of his desire to return home that he passed that way, Kay going with him part of the way as an escort. Ivor's wife, Morwen, and the girl, Orwen, had become separated from Ivor and Meriadoc, and it was these that the two knights chanced upon. They passed by with a greeting, and soon after Sir Kay took his leave of Urien to return to King Arthur's court. Urien rode on alone for a time, but found that he could not forget the face of the young girl he had seen in the forest. Finally he turned around and rode swiftly back to where he had first seen her. It chanced that she was still there, having travelled only a short way along the road, and without warning Urien swooped down upon her and, lifting her up into the saddle, rode off with her, taking no heed of her cries.

Sir Kay, meanwhile, encountered Ivor and Meriadoc, who were laden down with spoils of the hunt. Kay, seeing the tall, handsome youth dressed in ragged clothes, suddenly evinced a malicious plan to carry him off. He therefore charged straight at Ivor, with spear at rest, shouting furious battle-cries at the top of his voice. The huntsman, terrified by the sight of the mail-clad, shouting knight, dropped his catch and ran away into the trees, leaving Meriadoc to be snatched up and knocked unconscious by Sir Kay, who rode back towards Carlisle in high glee.

Sadly, Ivor returned to the cave alone, where he met Morwen, likewise in a state of shock and misery. There they comforted each other, bemoaning their loss and wondering what they could do to recover their lost children.

'I will not rest until I have found our daughter,' said Morwen. 'And I remember that the man who carried her off was called Urien by his fellows, and that one spoke of coming to see him in Scotland. Therefore I propose to set out to look for her in that land.'

'You are very brave, my love,' said Ivor. 'I too meant to search for Meriadoc. I am sure the knight who chased me away so fiercely was Sir Kay, the seneschal. I have been often to King Arthur's court and have seen him there on a number of occasions. I will go to the king's castle at Carlisle and seek out our lost son.'

With many tears and blessings, the two parted company and each set out upon the road in different directions. Morwen took the road to Scotland and after a long and difficult journey arrived at the home of King Urien – only to find that he had that very day taken Orwen for his wife. Morwen stood in the crowd begging for alms outside the great cathedral where the couple had been married and saw Orwen come forth, clad in a splendid gown and wearing a circlet of gold in her hair.

With tears in her eyes, Morwen watched her foster daughter walking amid the nobles of Urien's court, until it chanced that the girl caught sight of her. At once her eyes widened and she grew pale with shock. Then she fainted into the arms of the nobleman standing behind her.

Urien rushed forward in some alarm, and as soon as Orwen recovered enquired anxiously what was amiss. 'I saw a face in the crowd that I knew,' replied Orwen, sitting up, 'the face of one whose life is as dear to me as my own. It was my own dear foster mother who saved me from death and brought me up as her own.' Looking everywhere, she called out to Morwen and, when the older woman stood forth from the crowd, she fell into her arms. 'Now, my lord,' she said to Urien, 'if you love me, you will take care of this woman and honour her as you would myself.' And this the king did, ordering Morwen to be clothed in the finest silks and to be given everything she needed for her comfort.

Ivor, meanwhile, had arrived at King Arthur's court, walking boldly into the hall as the king was at supper. Many there were amazed at his appearance and even recalled the arrival of the fearsome Green Knight – for the huntsman was above average height, tall and powerful and with a thick and bushy beard. Also he was clad in a suit of clothes made from woven reeds, giving him an outlandish appearance. A long sword was belted at his side, and a bow and arrows were at his back. Over his shoulders he carried a large deer which he had shot on the way. This he now flung down at the feet of Sir Kay, having singled him out from among the entire throng. Then, before anyone could speak, a figure detached itself from the crowd of knights at the table and flung himself at Ivor. It was Meriadoc, whom the huntsman had not even recognized, so finely dressed was he, and with freshly barbered hair. The two greeted each other with tears and a fast embrace, and then the whole story came out. Kay was censured by the king for his rash act in taking Meriadoc away from his foster parents, and in recompense the seneschal offered to take Ivor into his own service as a huntsman. All was thus agreed and Ivor's only thought now was for his wife: how she had fared and what success had greeted her quest for Orwen?

He was soon to discover, for within a week Sir Kay remembered his promise to visit Urien, and himself set forth for Scotland, taking with him a retinue of servants, including Ivor. Meriadoc also went with them, having now been virtually adopted by Sir Kay. Arriving at Urien's court, a great reunion took place. Ivor and Morwen, Meriadoc and Orwen were reunited amid great rejoicing, and all elected to remain at Urien's court together.

There, both Meriadoc and his sister began to debate how they might be avenged upon King Griffin, both for his part in the death of their father and for his usurpation of their rightful inheritance. Knowing full well that he was one of the kings who held their lands in trust for King Arthur, they knew that to attack Griffin openly they required the support of the king. Therefore they journeyed to the court and laid before Arthur the whole tale of Caradoc's death and of the subsequent behaviour of their uncle. Arthur, angered by the story, at once summoned Griffin to appear before him, and to be prepared to defend himself against accusations of fratricide and other wrongdoings.

Griffin's answer was to prepare for war. Indeed, having heard rumours of his niece and nephew's escape, he had already fortified several of his castles, and now he himself retired to the mountain fastness of Snowdon, blocking every pathway and road until there was only a single narrow passage between high cliffs which would admit only a single column of men. Then he sent back a defiant answer to Arthur, which so angered and disturbed the monarch that he allied himself with King Urien and marched forthwith against Griffin.

Finding every path blocked or heavily defended, Arthur made an attempt on the narrow path, which was held by Griffin himself with a handful of men. For a week Arthur tried to break through, but was always repulsed. Meanwhile, Sadoc and Dunewall, the two lords who had helped to save Caradoc's children, raised a small army of knights to attack Griffin from behind. He, learning of this, was forced to abandon the narrow pass and retreat to the mountain fastness he had prepared against this very contingency. Thither King Arthur pursued him, and laid siege to the castle, which was so deeply entrenched in a bastion of rock that within a week the king realized that no simple assault would overcome it. Thus he began to build entrenchments, and brought up powerful siege engines with which to batter the walls.

Griffin, who was no coward, saw the way things lay and determined to give in to nothing. Week after week and month after month he sent sortie after sortie out against the fortress of King Arthur, often leading the assaults himself, and earning the grudging respect of his enemies. But in the end it was hunger that brought him low, as gradually the supplies held within the fortress dwindled away. Finally Griffin gave himself up and threw himself on the mercy of King Arthur, who convened a court and laid the matter before not only his own judgement but also that of the council who had once served King Caradoc. Here Griffin found no mercy, and in due course was beheaded for his crimes.

The kingdom of Cambria now fell to the lordship of Meriadoc. He, being as yet young and untried, declared his intention of proving himself by undertaking a knightly quest for adventure. He therefore entrusted the kingdom to his sister's husband, King Urien of Scotland, and returned with King Arthur to his court at Carlisle.

There, as the king rested from the long and arduous siege against Griffin, a certain knight, known as the Black Knight of the Black Forest, appeared and demanded that his right to ownership of the said forest be recognized. Arthur's reply was that his father, Uther Pendragon, had stocked the forest with black boars, the descendants of which roved there at will to this day, and that this gave him full entitlement. To this the Black Knight replied that his very name spoke for his own rights in the matter, but declared that, so long as his tenure was recognized, he would be glad to allow free hunting rights of the black boars at any time to King Arthur. To this the king replied that the rights were his to begin with and that he saw no need to ask permission of anyone to hunt in his own forest.

Thus the matter stood, with first one side and then the other stating a contrary case. At length King Arthur placed the whole question in the hands of the judiciary, and awaited their verdict. The Black Knight, however, deeming that the council were bound to find in the king's favour, broke in upon their deliberations and demanded that the matter be settled by strength of arm and body – his against forty of Arthur's knights. 'Send but one man every day for forty days,' said the Black Knight, 'and if I survive, let the Black Forest be recognized as mine forthwith.'

Now King Arthur liked this bold speech, and at once agreed. But in the days that followed he began to regret his decision, as, one by one, his knights returned battered and bleeding from their encounter with the Black Knight. At last the king sent for Sir Kay and spoke to him thus.

'I was never so ashamed in my life as by this defeat of my best men by this upstart knight. There are but three days left before the forty are up and we must do all that we can to save our honour. Therefore I propose thus. Today I would have you go and undertake the adventure. I know you to be both clever and resourceful, and it is my hope that you succeed where others have failed. Should you not succeed, then tomorrow it shall be my nephew Sir Gawain's turn; and following that, on the last day, I shall myself go forth and do what I can to redeem my honour and that of the fellowship of the Round Table.'

To this Kay agreed, and at once began to prepare himself for the combat, assuring everyone that he could not fail to overcome the Black Knight. Meriadoc, who had himself been knighted by Sir Kay the year before, took him on one side and begged to be allowed to take his place. 'Surely,' he said, 'this matter can do little or nothing to increase your renown – and, should you fail, which of course I do not believe you would – your shame would be great indeed!'

At first Kay refused, but as he considered the wisdom of Meriadoc's words he began to weaken in his resolve. Finally he agreed, making much of the matter, as was his wont, and impressing upon the younger man his willingness to step aside for no other reason than to give him a chance to prove himself.

Meriadoc thus set out at once for the Black Forest, and on arriving at the ford which divided the lands of Arthur from those claimed by the Black Knight, he blew a blast on his horn. At once the Black Knight appeared and, without waiting, charged full-tilt at Meriadoc, catching him as he was crossing the water. Meriadoc, levelling his spear, caught his opponent's blow squarely on his own shield and drove the tip of his lance towards the Black Knight's throat. He, in turn, parried and received the blow in the centre of his shield. Swiftly Meriadoc released the spear and, drawing his sword, reached over and grasped his opponent's helm, dragging him sideways bodily from the saddle and preparing to cut deep into his neck. The Black Knight screamed aloud and begged for mercy, which chivalrously Meriadoc granted.

'Tell me who you are,' begged the Black Knight, 'for I have never felt such strength as you possess, and surely this must come of a great lineage.'

'I see no reason to trace my ancestry at this time,' said Meriadoc. 'It is enough that I represent King Arthur, and that I have won against you. Therefore I ask if you submit to the lordship of my lord over the Black Forest.'

The Black Knight drew his sword and, holding it by the blade, presented the hilt to Meriadoc. 'Sir,' he said, 'I fully renounce any claim to this place and I honour you for your courage and strength. Will you not tell me now whose son you are and of what lineage you come?'

And so Meriadoc told all that you have heard here, from his birth and upbringing and the treachery of Griffin to this very adventure. At the end the Black Knight bowed before him and said that this was no less than he had expected. Furthermore, he swore undying allegiance to Meriadoc, promising that he would accompany him where he wished, and remain at his side as a loyal companion for as long as he was permitted. This

Meriadoc gravely accepted, before the two knights returned side by side to King Arthur's court.

There, he was received in astonishment by all, for it seemed amazing to them that an inexperienced knight could overcome one who had defeated no fewer than thirty-seven of their kin. Arthur greeted the youth warmly and offered him any reward he cared to name.

Then Meriadoc astonished everyone by asking that the Black Knight's lands, on which the whole dispute was based, be returned to him, and despite King Arthur's evident displeasure, he would accept nothing other than this. In time, Arthur acceded, and the Black Knight received full reparation of his lands in the Black Forest.

Once word of this escaped, a second knight, calling himself the Red Knight of the Red Forest, appeared and made a similar demand of the king. Meriadoc defeated him, just as he had the Black Knight, and received his fealty. Shortly thereafter, he performed the same set of deeds in response to a challenge by the White Knight of the White Forest – then, with these three sworn vassals at his side, he set out in earnest in search of adventure.

Their first goal was the land of the emperor of the Alemanni, who at that time was at war with Gundebald, the King of the Land of No Return, who had stolen away his daughter. Thus the emperor had sent word to the four corners of the earth to all knights and heroes who would fight on his side against his enemy, and it was in answer to this summons that Meriadoc, together with the Black, Red and White Knights, came to the emperor's lands. In a very short time Meriadoc proved his worth to such a degree that he was promoted to a place of high authority, commanding all the mercenaries and errant knights who, like he, had come there in answer to the emperor's call.

Soon after there came a messenger with news of a fresh attack by Gundebald, who had landed with a large army on the coast of the emperor's land. Meriadoc, at the head of a strong force, led the counter-attack. Skilfully deploying his forces, under the leadership of his three companions, Meriadoc routed the enemy so thoroughly that only a handful escaped, while all of the plunder they had taken was recovered.

Pursuing the last remnant of Gundebald's army, under the command of a general named Saguntius, Meriadoc found himself in the depths of a dense forest which, his men were quick to tell him, was widely believed to be haunted.

Despite this Meriadoc and his men rode deep in among the trees, pushing on all that day until the evening began to come on, when Meriadoc called a halt. He posted guards and settled down in the lush grass of a clearing, in the shadow of a huge oak tree. The guards were instructed to awaken the camp at first light, but it seemed they had hardly begun their watch when the day began to dawn. Rubbing their eyes blearily, they awoke Meriadoc, who was astonished that so little time seemed to have passed since he had composed himself for sleep. Nevertheless, he roused the rest of the camp and the company set out again on the road, soon reaching an open plain where Meriadoc remembered hunting with the emperor. To his astonishment, however, a great castle now rose where, but three weeks earlier, he had ridden to the hunt.

'Let us try to find out more about this place,' Meriadoc said, 'for I know not how it comes to be here so soon after I rode this way and saw it not.'

As they approached, a company of servants emerged from the castle and came to meet them, inviting them to enter and rest for a time. After a moment's hesitation, Meriadoc decided to accept the invitation, and he and his men entered the great building, which was richly decorated with the finest marble and porphyry, its walls hung with silken banners and elaborate tapestries.

They were led, by way of a great stair, to a chamber decorated with great taste and richness. There, on a marble throne, sat a lady of great beauty and nobility, who, when she caught sight of Meriadoc, rose to her feet and called to all her retainers to do likewise. 'Welcome, Meriadoc,' she said, 'I have waited a long time for this moment. Your courage and prowess have gone before you.'

Astonished, Meriadoc replied, 'Lady, I am amazed that you even know my name. But even more a cause of wonder is this palace, for I swear it was not here when I rode this way but a few weeks past.'

'Do not be surprised,' said the lady. 'I have known of you for a long time. As to this place, it is not what it seems. I assure you it has existed for a long time, since ancient times indeed. Nor is it where you think it to be, that is merely an illusion.'

More than this she would not say, but bade Meriadoc and his men be comfortable and dine with her. Servants brought many dishes, both rich and rare, and wines and sweetmeats as fine as any they had ever seen. But no one spoke at all during the meal, and servants and guests were alike silent.

After a time, Meriadoc could stand this no longer and, beckoning to the seneschal, who had been overseeing the feast, asked him what the name of the place, and its lady, might be. By way of answer, the man simply pulled a face at him. Meriadoc, puzzled, repeated his question, and this time the man stared wild-eyed at him, and, putting his hands to his head, waved them at Meriadoc and opened his mouth so wide that he seemed like a demon about to devour his prey.

Meriadoc started back, and half rose from his seat. At this the lady spoke furiously to her servant, reproving him and demanding that he cease his foolish behaviour. But by now both Meriadoc and his men were so frightened by the unnatural behaviour of their hosts that they rose as a body and hastened from the hall.

They found their horses still waiting where they had left them and, mounting, rode hurriedly from the place. It seemed to be only just past midday as they departed, but almost at once the darkness of night overtook them, and with it their horses seemed possessed of an even greater fear than they had felt themselves, so that they became unmanageable.

Rearing and plunging, their mounts charged through the forest, crashing into one another, screaming and striking out at their fellows. Completely maddened, they ran throughout the rest of the night until they were at last exhausted and either fell down or stood trembling in every limb.

When morning came, Meriadoc and his men found themselves by a rushing stream. More than half their number were lost, led who knew where by their maddened horses. Mourning their lost companions, they prepared to ride on. 'I believe we have spent some time in the Otherworld,' Meriadoc told his companions. 'Even now we cannot be sure that we are safely out of this strange place. Let us proceed with caution.'

With little notion of where they were going, the little company rode on. At noon a fierce storm blew up from nowhere, with sheets of rain and fierce bolts of jagged lightning and mighty crashes of thunder. Battered and driven half mad from the noise and the cold water which lashed at them from the heavens, they sought shelter beneath the trees and Meriadoc enquired if anyone among them recognized the country and knew if there was a place to rest until the storm passed.

One man spoke of a castle which he knew of, and which was close by, he reckoned. 'But it is a deadly place,' he added, 'and no one who enters there comes away without shame.'

More than this he would not say until another man, named Waldomer, who was the emperor's brother-in-law, pressed him hard to show them the way. Finally the man shrugged and said that he would take them there. 'But I myself will not enter that place,' he said, 'and you may be sure you will regret it before you leave.'

They followed the knight through the lashing rain, until the walls of a castle rose up before them through the murk. Waldomer, seeking Meriadoc's permission, led a party of men to investigate the place, since Meriadoc would not risk all of their party in another strange place until he was certain it was safe.

So Waldomer and his men rode through the gates of the castle, which gaped wide, and went within. They found the place entirely deserted, though in the great hall a fire burned brightly, and there were warm carpets on the floor. The stables also contained fodder for their mounts, and when he saw this Waldomer ordered them to look to their horses and then to repair to the hall. 'Everything is laid out ready for us,' he said, 'and since it seems as though we are expected, it would be foolish to turn down such excellent hospitality.'

So the knights stabled and fed their horses and then gathered about the fire in the great hall. But when they had been there only a short while, a sudden, inexplicable fear overcame them. They sat staring at the floor, afraid even to move a hand or eye, as though Death himself was stalking them and might strike at any moment.

Meriadoc, meanwhile, waited under the dripping trees. The storm grew even more intense, and the men who had stayed with him began to grumble. Finally, when no word came from the castle, Meriadoc prevailed upon the knight who had originally told them of the place to lead him and the remaining men there. This he did, though once there he elected to return to the woods alone rather than enter.

Meriadoc led the remainder of his troops within and there they found Waldomar and his men sitting, still as statues, staring at the floor.

'What is amiss here?' demanded Meriadoc.

Waldomar started visibly. 'Lord,' he said, 'we are too afraid to look one another in the face.'

'Then I command you to get up,' answered Meriadoc sternly. 'Only your fear holds you thus. Rise now and set the tables. I will search for food and drink.'

As though released from a spell, the men began sheepishly to obey. Meriadoc set off alone through the empty, echoing halls in search of victuals. Passing through several rooms, he entered a chamber where he saw a young woman sitting alone. The table before her was laden with bread and wine, and at the sight of it Meriadoc became so overcome with hunger and thirst that he snatched up an armful of bread and several skins of wine and left the room without even speaking. As he did so, he encountered a tall figure who, seeing the food and drink in his arms, demanded angrily to know who he was and what he meant by robbing the maiden's table. When Meriadoc did not answer, but rather pushed forward to pass him, the tall man struck him a blow to the temple which felled him where he stood and sent the sword which he had been holding skittering across the floor.

Staggering to his feet, and still clutching most of the bread and wine, Meriadoc fled from his adversary, only stopping when his breath failed him.

Now he found himself in a strange part of the castle, with no idea of how to get back to the hall where his men awaited him. Also his sword was gone and he had no means of defending himself. At this moment the tall servant appeared, carrying his sword and began to berate him for taking the food and drink, and for running away from an unarmed man. He then threw the sword at Meriadoc's feet and withdrew.

Meriadoc, shamefaced, picked up the sword and, still intent upon the acquisition of food, followed his nose until he reached the kitchen. There he saw a huge shaven-headed man with a grossly fat body, asleep before a fire over which was stretched a roasting spit hung with cranes. As soon as

Meriadoc entered, he awoke and, with a cry of rage, seized the spit and attacked him, striking him about the head and shoulders until Meriadoc fell groaning to the earth.

Angry as well as hurt by this unprovoked attack, Meriadoc sprang up and, seizing his opponent round the waist, flung him down. Then, seeing where a well opened in the floor close by, he dragged the huge man to it and, with a great heave, flung him down into the watery depths.

This done, Meriadoc gathered up as much food as he could carry and found his way back, not without some difficulty, to where his men still waited, gathered into a tight knot, and looking all the while over their shoulders.

The sight of the food and drink revived them considerably, and they fell to with a will. Hardly had they eaten above a few mouthfuls when an enormous man, carrying what looked like a whole roof beam, came crashing into the hall, roaring out that they had stolen his master's food. Before anyone could react, he had felled more than a dozen of Meriadoc's men. He, furious at the continuing attacks, drew his sword and, shouting his battle-cry, chased the huge guard from the hall and through a maze of tunnels and passageways which seemed to lead everywhere and nowhere in that strange place.

At length he emerged into a large chamber which was full of armed men. At once they turned upon him and attacked him. Against so many he had little chance and was quickly driven back to the wall. But such was the strength and courage he exhibited that in a while the attackers withdrew to within a few feet and granted him the right to surrender and depart as he willed.

Exhausted by his great efforts, Meriadoc made his way slowly back through the maze of passages until he once again reached the great hall. There he found no one except those of his company who had been felled by the giant. The rest had fled, or been carried off.

Sick at heart, Meriadoc went in search of his horse and those of his companions. The stables were empty, however, and, no longer sure what to do, Meriadoc wandered out of the castle and, alone and on foot, took the road back towards the forest.

For the rest of the day he pursued his way wearily, then just as the sun was setting he heard horses approaching. He waited to see who else was riding in this strange wood and saw a young woman on a palfrey and leading a charger. She was weeping dolefully, and when Meriadoc stepped out into the road she flinched away in fear. Soothing her with gentle words, he asked the reason for her sorrow and she explained that her husband had been killed that day by evil brigands. She herself had been taken prisoner, but had escaped when her captors fell asleep.

'If you will avenge me, this horse is yours,' she said, and to this Meriadoc agreed.

It did not take him long to find the brigands, and he slew them both, dispatching one while he slept and the other as he woke. He did this without mercy, knowing them for evil men. That night he rested at the dead brigands' campsite, then in the morning he and the woman parted company, she to return to her home, which was nearby, and Meriadoc to ride on alone.

There as it chanced he encountered the knight of his own company who had refused to enter the castle and had warned them all against doing so. Meriadoc was glad to see him and begged forgiveness for ignoring his sound advice. The two then rode on together until they saw a large party of armed men on the road ahead. Overtaking them with caution, Meriadoc suddenly recognized Waldomer among the group, and with that he realized that they were indeed his own men! The greeting which then ensued was great indeed, the knights glad to see their commander and he equally glad to see them.

Thus reunited, the company continued on through the forest until they were halted by what seemed to them to be the sounds of battle: cries and the clashing of armour and swords. Quickly Meriadoc dispatched scouts to discover the truth of the matter. Pressing forward under cover of the trees, these men found themselves looking upon the great and terrible battle. Such was the carnage that rivers of blood seemed to flow across the plain that stretched before them, and the dead lay heaped in piles. Seeing a boy crouched in the bushes watching, one of the scouts demanded to know who were the combatants.

'That is the army of the emperor,' said the boy, 'and the other belongs to King Gundebald's brother Guntrannus.'

'How can this be?' asked the scout. 'When last we heard, that battle was taking place many leagues from here.'

'I have heard,' said the boy, wide-eyed, 'that the leader of the emperor's forces vanished into this very forest, and when the rest of the forces went in search of him they met with the army of their enemy. Now it seems they are losing, but for the might of those three mighty knights.'

Looking where the boy pointed, and where the fighting was thickest, the scout saw three men, one in red armour, the other in white and the third in black. Then they knew that these were indeed their own fellows, and the mightiest among them were Meriadoc's three companions.

Returning swiftly to where their leader waited, the scouts told him everything they had seen. Meriadoc almost wept when he heard how their own forces were faring. Then he rallied himself and began to order his thoughts. Gathering the remnants of his own force around him, he gave them words of encouragement, reminding them of their honour and skills and the needs of their beleaguered fellows. Then, dividing his force in two, one under his own command and the other under the command of Waldomer, he ordered charges against the enemy from two sides.

They, thinking a far greater force had come against them, turned at bay, and at this point both the remnant of the emperor's tired army, along with others who had fled to the forest in fear of their lives, turned and fought with renewed vigour. Within a few moments the tide of the battle turned and Meriadoc, reunited with his three great friends, drove the enemy from the field, killing most of them, including King Guntrannus himself.

In the weeks that followed the victorious army of the emperor, led by Meriadoc, passed through and over the lands of the enemy with fire and sword. City after city fell to them, either by force or by willing submission. At the end of this time Meriadoc was able to send word to the emperor that the greater part of King Gundebald's lands were won over and that he, Meriadoc, now sought only one final glory to prove his worth.

The emperor's reply was swift. If Meriadoc could but rescue his daughter from the clutches of Gundebald, then Meriadoc would inherit the emperor's own kingdom and the hand of his daughter in marriage.

Now, unknown to the emperor, his daughter had already heard of Meriadoc's extraordinary prowess and had contrived to send him a message of her own, in which she promised him every aid in her power, and a warm welcome if he should succeed in his undertaking. However, she counselled him to come with only a few supporters, for thus she believed he would fare much better. With this advice in mind, Meriadoc selected only his three friends, the Black, Red and White Knights, to accompany him, and accordingly they set out together for the heart of Gundebald's kingdom.

As fortune would have it, being unfamiliar with the roads, they became lost in a forest, and wandered there for five days without seeing any sign of human habitation. They began to grow very hungry, having consumed their victuals, and were thus more than glad to meet a herd of home-coming cows in the road. Meriadoc at once dispatched the Black Knight to search ahead, for where there were cows there must also be a village or farmstead.

The Black Knight soon returned with news that they had in fact found their way to a city, strongly fortified and heavily defended. It did not take long to discover that this was in fact Gundebald's citadel. All that remained was to find a way to gain entry.

Finally Meriadoc decided upon a bold approach, and the four knights followed the herd of cows through a narrow gate and right up to the main gates to the citadel, where they were challenged by the porter, who opened the postern gate a crack and asked them to identify themselves.

'We are all knights from Britain,' said Meriadoc, 'We have been in service to King Arthur and just recently learned of the need of your king for soldiers in his fight against the emperor. We are here to offer our services.'

'Then you are welcome,' replied the porter, 'for the king has given orders that no one else is to be admitted. He himself has but lately ridden forth to encounter the knights sent daily to rescue the emperor's daughter. Do you go and find lodging in the city and await the king's return.'

'First,' said Meriadoc, 'since the king is not here, I would speak to the prefect of this castle. Go and tell him that four knights stand before his gate awaiting entry.'

'That I shall not do,' answered the porter, beginning to be suspicious. As he spoke he started to close the postern gate. Meriadoc, realizing the porter was alone, kicked the gate open. The blow was so hard that it felled the man, and Meriadoc seized him and threw him into the river which ran past the gate. Then he opened the door and admitted his companions.

Now it happened that the emperor's daughter was housed in a tower which abutted upon the wall close beside the very gate where Meriadoc had just gained entrance. And, as fortune would have it, she was at that moment standing by one of the windows with her two ladies-in-waiting, looking out sorrowfully at the world beyond her prison. Seeing what took place at the gate, she at once guessed that only Meriadoc would be daring enough to attempt such an entry, and at once summoned a messenger she could trust to intercept the four knights and bring them to her.

When they stood before her, all four were overwhelmed by her beauty. She smiled at them all, but her fondest look was for Meriadoc. 'You are very welcome,' she said. 'Now I may perhaps be quit of this place.' She went on to tell them how best they might arrange her escape, pointing out that King Gundebald had treated her with honour, more as a daughter than a prisoner, and that, within the confines of the castle, she was free to come and go at will. Thus she was able to find rooms for all four of her would-be rescuers, and then proceeded to instruct Meriadoc as to how he might secure her release.

'Gundebald is hated by all his people,' she told Meriadoc. 'Thus you will find many here who will support you when the time comes. Here is what you should do. First, make yourself known to the king on his return and tell him that you have come to offer your service to him. It is his custom that he will except a new knight into his ranks only after he has tested their prowess in single combat. He is exceptionally strong, and very proud, and will expect to beat you easily, after which he will admit you to his company.'

'I am confident that I can beat him in a fair fight,' said Meriadoc.

'That may well be,' replied the emperor's daughter, 'but there are conditions to this combat which make it less than fair – unless you are prepared.'

'Tell me everything you can,' said Meriadoc.

'Listen well then,' said the emperor's daughter, and proceeded to tell him that Gundebald would choose to fight on a stretch of country called 'The Land of No Return', from which he received his title. It was a strange and terrible waste, an island in the midst of the land on which nothing grew, and where the very ground consisted of shifting mud banks. Anyone who walked there unprepared was swallowed up at once. At the very centre of this evil place was a great tar pit, surrounding the only patch of solid ground. Gundebald had caused two causeways to be built which connected the only solid earth to the surrounding countryside from four directions. Great timbers sunk in the shifting ooze supported these, enabling a single rider to cross the shifting mud banks and the pits of tar and reach solid ground at the centre, where Gundebald had built himself a splendid palace. Four towers guarded the approaches to this place, each one well guarded.

'Thus has Gundebald managed to defeat so many brave knights,' said the emperor's daughter. 'Only those lucky enough to be felled by him on the road itself have survived. The rest fell into the pit of tar and were consumed. The other thing you should know is that Gundebald possesses a remarkable horse of exceptional strength. You will be certainly overcome without my help, for I have in my possession a steed of equal prowess – in fact, Gundebald gave it to me himself as a gift to make me like him better!' She shuddered and went on, 'I will give you this horse, and also fresh arms and armour. You are my only hope. If you fail, I am destined to remain here for ever.'

'I shall do all within my power,' said Meriadoc.

And thus it was that he came to encounter Gundebald, on one of the causeways which crossed the sea of shifting mud, armed in fresh and brilliant armour, and riding the magnificent Arabian horse which the emperor's daughter provided for him. If the king suspected anything, he gave no sign of it, and agreed, as was his custom, to fight Meriadoc as a test of his skill before admitting him to the ranks of his personal retinue of knights. He also, more in jest than in earnest, promised that if Meriadoc could defeat him then not only was the sanctity of his person assured but, as challenger, in the event of Gundebald's death, he would become heir to the king's lands and titles.

It was only when the day appointed for their battle dawned, and he saw the steed ridden by Meriadoc, that King Gundebald realized he had been tricked. He paled at once when he perceived this, for it had been prophesied to him long since that he would be overcome by a man riding this very horse. Then his colour went from white to red and he screamed in rage that he had been betrayed, and spurred his own mount to meet Meriadoc in the midst of the causeway.

There Meriadoc have him such a buffet with his spear that both king and horse spun away and fell from the causeway. Both were swallowed in a matter of moments by the stinking tar and perished utterly. Meriadoc continued on to the palace, where he was made welcome and, under the terms of Gundebald's own agreement, received the submission of all there.

Word went forth swiftly that Gundebald was dead, and it was not long before the identity of his slayer was also known. This was a cause for great rejoicing, since, just as the emperor's daughter had said, Gundebald had been much hated in his own land, and many rejoiced at the thought of gaining so famous and honourable a lord.

Meriadoc called a council of all the lords who owed allegiance to Gundebald and explained to them that he had acted in the name of the emperor, and that they should prepare themselves to submit to him as their new lord. Many responded by saying that they would take no one but Meriadoc himself as their liege, and it says much for the worthiness of the hero that he sought to dissuade them, until at length they swore that, so long as the emperor kept his word and married his daughter to Meriadoc, they would accept his rule over them.

However, during Meriadoc's absence, matters had altered radically in the emperor's domain. War had broken out on another front, against the King of Gaul, and so hard had this powerful ruler pressed the emperor that he was forced to concede not only many of his lands but also the hand of his daughter – the same maiden whom Meriadoc had but lately set free.

Now the emperor was careful to allow none of the news concerning this to escape, and Meriadoc remained in ignorance of how matters stood. He returned to a hero's welcome, bringing with him a huge force of knights formerly in the service of King Gundebald and now sworn to serve Meriadoc to the death. The emperor at once appointed him regent over the empire; yet, while he smiled and heaped rewards upon the hero of so many battles, in secret the emperor plotted his death.

To aid this he first placed his daughter in a tower where apartments suited to her station had been prepared. Then he set a watch over her, and, having given Meriadoc free access to her, soon revived reports of them whispering and kissing, embracing and making merry together.

At this the emperor smiled and began to plot against his loyal vassal. First he summoned all the nobles of his own land, and then those who had journeyed with Meriadoc from the lands of King Gundebald. Then, with the hero himself seated among them, he addressed them thus.

'My lords, I have called you here to discuss a serious matter which concerns you all. I refer to the question of this Meriadoc whom you all know well. Just who is this mercenary knight whom I took to my service? Just what had he actually achieved? Little, I would say. For was not everything provided by me? Was not the gold to provision the army from my own war chest? And did he not succeed only with my soldiers at his back? As to my daughter, even in this case he was able to rescue her only with her own connivance and support.'

A murmur ran through the crowd, as man looked at man and questioned all they heard. Meriadoc himself sat as though stunned. The emperor continued.

'Despite all of these things, I was ready and willing to reward this man with all the riches and lands at my disposal – had it not been for word of a grave matter which reached my ears just in time. Not content to await the promised betrothal of my daughter to him, he has forced her and, I believe, from the swelling of her belly, left her with child. I put it too you, my lords, is this the proper behaviour of a faithful vassal to his lord? I submit that it is not. What, then, must I do? I ask you all to consider this matter and answer me from your wisdom.'

At this Meriadoc could contain himself no longer. He leapt to his feet and stormed into the centre of the room, ready to challenge the emperor. At this pandemonium broke loose. Armed guards, set there for this purpose by the emperor, entered and took Meriadoc prisoner. At the same time, in other parts of the city, Meriadoc's own loyal followers were rounded up and either killed or confined. The gathering broke up in confusion, no one being certain whether Meriadoc was to be deemed innocent or guilty.

When news of this reached the ears of the emperor's daughter, she was beside herself with anguish, and had to be restrained by her women from doing herself harm. Gradually, as she became calmer, she began to think that Meriadoc would be certain to find a means of rectifying matters. But within a few days of Meriadoc's arrest the king of Gaul arrived with a huge train of wagons and men, expecting to marry the emperor's daughter himself.

When he discovered that she was indeed with child, and at that by Meriadoc, he at once repudiated the treaty he had lately signed with the emperor and swore that he would not rest until the slur to his honour was satisfied. He then withdrew and began once again to ravage the empire.

His plot having gone awry, the emperor was forced now to call up all the soldiers and knights remaining in his service and to prepare again for war. This time he would lead the army himself – though he already regretted making Meriadoc his enemy and placing him under arrest.

Meriadoc himself heard of the new war and prepared to make his escape. He was guarded only lightly now that every available man was required to fight at the emperor's side, and with this in mind he laid his plans with care. Waiting until the imperial army had departed, leaving the city strangely quiet, Meriadoc cut his clothes into strips and, making a rope from them, climbed down from the window of the tower where he was imprisoned and made his way to the house of a knight whom he knew to be sympathetic to him. There he was warmly received, and before his escape was even detected he had been supplied with food and drink, and equipped with armour, weapons and a horse, and he set forth from the city.

Once clear of its walls, Meriadoc rode swiftly after the army. Soon he reached the place where the two forces, that of the emperor and that of the King of Gaul, were drawn up. There he secretly joined the king's troops. Now battle was joined and, riding and fighting like twenty men, Meriadoc cut a swath through the emperor's men. In quick succession he felled the leader of the imperial troops, a duke who was a particular favourite of the emperor, and then the emperor's nephew, who was named as his heir.

When he saw this, the emperor rose in his stirrups and screamed that he would be avenged on this knight who slew the best of his fellows before his eyes. Seizing a spear, he rushed madly towards Meriadoc, who turned to face his adversary and, letting go of his reins, grasped his own spear with both hands and rode with all his might at the emperor. Such a blow he struck that the spear passed though shield and armour alike and pierced the body of the emperor through and through. As the emperor fell dying, Meriadoc called out, 'Thus do I repay the wages you offered me!'

Then he rode swiftly back and joined with the king of Gaul's men, doing his best to lose himself among them. But the king, who had observed everything which occurred, quickly sent for the knight who had performed such astonishing feats of strength and courage, and who had single-handedly rid him of his bitterest foe.

When Meriadoc stood before him, the king recognized him from descriptions he had heard upon every man's lips. Then he smiled and said, 'Surely you are the most worthy man I ever met. Well have you served the emperor for the unjust treatment he gave to you. I know your story, and I swear this, that I shall restore not only your intended bride but as many of the lands of the former emperor as you will promise to rule over in my name.'

To this Meriadoc gave grateful thanks. Shortly after he and the emperor's daughter were married and thereafter they lived out their lives in great harmony. Great estates were given to Meriadoc by the king of Gaul, who now became the new emperor. In time a son was born to Meriadoc and his wife, and of him came many other brave knights and kings. Meriadoc himself returned at last to Britain and there, as one of the greatest of King Arthur's vassals, he ruled long and wisely over his father's kingdom.

6

The Madness of Trystan

THIS story is based on the *Folie Tristan* of Oxford (so called to distinguish it from the *Folie Tristan* of Berne, from which it differs only in detail). It is essentially an episode from a much longer tale which relates the story of the doomed love of Tristan and Iseult (here called, in an older spelling, Trystan and Ysolt). Its author, who remains unknown, was evidently familiar with the story in its entirety and expected his listeners to know as much as he. The abrupt beginning, which I have amended here for the benefit of those who do *not* know the whole story, simply refers to Tristan's sorrow and describes him as 'living in his land', which from internal evidence we may assume to be Brittany, though Tristan himself was from Cornwall. From this we can place the episode within the larger framework of the Tristan romance proper.

Having discovered an undying passion for each other, the two lovers have sought to continue an affair under the nose of Iseult's husband, King Mark of Cornwall (who is also Tristan's uncle). Circumstances make it less and less easy for them to meet, and in order to protect her lover, Iseult feigns coldness towards him. This has the effect of driving him away, and he undertakes a loveless marriage with the ironically named Iseult of Brittany, more out of spite for his mistress than for any better reason. Thus ensconced in Brittany, miserable and bereft of his love, Tristan languishes, and it is here that we first meet him in the *Folie Tristan*.

Tristan is the second great lover of Arthurian romance, the first being Lancelot, but there are few parallels between their stories. Lancelot is a far nobler figure than Tristan, who often behaves both savagely and without conscience. Mark, unlike Arthur, is a bad husband, as well as a bad king. The sly couplings of Tristan and Iseult are very unlike the noble passion of Lancelot and Guinevere, though it must be said that they were probably more popular among an audience whose fascination with courtly love led them to praise adultery while condemning it with the same breath. In more recent times, due largely to the success of Richard Wagner's opera *Tristan and Isolde*, their story has continued to overshadow that of Lancelot and Guinevere.

The *Folie* is essentially designed to rehearse the most important episodes from the saga of Tristan – the excuse to do so being that Iseult is unable, or unwilling, to recognize her lover through his disguise. The fact that he continues to use the false voice of the fool, even when they are alone, has prompted one commentator to remark on his cruelty. It seems almost as though he is driven to draw out the torment of her failure to acknowledge him, but it would be a mistake to apply a modern psychological interpretation to the behaviour of a medieval man whose actions are described and set down by a medieval writer. Whoever composed the story was more interested in the game of words between the lovers, and in the device which enabled him to recall the best bits of the much longer cycle of tales about Tristan and Iseult.

The *Folie Tristan* of Oxford was composed towards the beginning of the thirteenth century, but it is a very different work from the vast, high romantic tale of passion written by Gottfried von

Strassburg *circa* 1210 (*Tristan*, translated by A.T. Hatto, Harmondsworth, Penguin Books, 1960). The shorter poem is a much earthier and more powerful evocation of the lovers' destructive desperation, and as such deserves to be better known. It has been edited a number of times, notably by E. Hoepffner, who also edited the *Folie Tristan* of Berne (Paris, Les Belles Lettres, 1943 and 1949 respectively).

The two versions have each been translated once before, the *Folie* of Berne by Alan S. Frederic, as part of his rendition of Beroul's *The Romance of Tristan* (Harmondsworth, Penguin Books, 1970), and the *Folie* of Oxford by Judith Weiss in her anthology of early medieval texts *The Birth of Romance* (London, Dent, 1992). I have referred to both these versions in preparing my own retelling.

RYSTAN WAS ALONE IN BRITTANY. Parted from his love, wedded to another whom he did not love, his passion for Queen Ysolt was as great as ever, threatening to overwhelm him. What point was there in living when he was separated by so many miles from the place where his heart longed to be? Daily he walked about the palace of King Hoel, avoiding Ysolt White Hands, his wife, doing his best to hide his true feelings from his friend Kaherdin, all the while longing to journey back to Britain and rejoin his love.

He recalled his wounding by the terrible Morholt, and his healing at the hands of the fair Ysolt. Now there seemed no cure for his ills, except to be in her presence again. And thus he began to scheme to find a way that he might fulfil his need. The trouble was that he was too well known in Britain, his fame as a warrior having spread wide throughout the lands ruled over by King Arthur. Therefore he decided to go incognito, on foot rather than on his great war-horse, without armour or weapons save for a dagger.

Once he had made up his mind, Trystan wasted no time. He rose early one morning, stole out of the castle and made his way to a nearby port. There he took ship on a stout merchanter bound for Britain. None recognized the poorly dressed man who paid in gold for his passage and spoke little to anyone during the voyage.

It chanced that they made landfall in Cornwall, indeed at Tintagel itself, where King Mark held court with Queen Ysolt, his wife. Trystan looked upon the castle where his heart dwelled and sighed deeply. It was a mighty building indeed, having been built by giants long ago. Its walls were of great red and blue marble blocks, set so finely that there was scarcely a join. It was said, by the local people, that this was an enchanted place, and that the castle actually disappeared twice every year, once at midwinter and again at midsummer. All around stretched meadows and woodlands full of game, and a bright stream coursed by the walls and fell cascading down to the sea. It was indeed a most powerful place, virtually impregnable from either land or sea, its gates well guarded by soldiers.

Trystan walked into the town and asked for news of the king and queen. Yes, they were certainly there, and a great court with them. People spoke well of King Mark, but commented that as ever Queen Ysolt looked sad. When he heard her name Trystan sighed again, and began to think of ways that he might gain entrance to both the castle and its royal folk, for he knew that neither prowess nor knowledge, skill nor intelligence would gain him admittance to Ysolt. Mark, he knew, hated him above all men and, if he once succeeded in capturing him, would surely order his death.

'Yet,' he murmured, 'what matters it if I am killed? As well be dead and at peace than alive and in torment. I am more than half mad with this love.' As he spoke Trystan began to think. Why not pretend to be mad indeed, play the fool and trick everyone? Who will suspect me? he wondered. Not even Ysolt herself shall recognize me. I shall walk into the castle as free as a bird!

So saying, he set about his plan at once. Waiting until he saw a poor fisherman coming along the road, Trystan offered to exchange his own plain but well-made clothes for the other's ragged hose and stained tunic and hood. The man was well pleased with the exchange and ran off before the stranger could change his mind. Then Trystan stained his face dark with the juice of a certain herb and, taking out a little pair of golden scissors which he always carried since he had been given them by Ysolt, cut a strange tonsure in the shape of a cross on the top of his head. Then, having completed his disguise, he set a rough wooden club on his shoulder, adopted a shambling gait and set off for the castle.

The porter saw him coming and strode out to meet him. 'Who or what are you?' he demanded.

'I'm Urgan the Hairy,' replied Trystan, choosing the name of a giant he had killed long ago. 'I've just been to the wedding of the abbot of Mont St Michel. He wedded the abbess, who was a very fat nun. Every priest and cleric and monk from all around was there. After the wedding they all went down to the pastures below Bel Encumbre and began jumping and playing in the shade. But I had to leave them, because today I am destined to serve the king.'

The porter laughed. 'Well, Urgan the Hairy, you'd better come inside then. I'm sure you'll give us all some fun.'

And so Trystan the fool walked into Tintagel. At once some young men saw him and began to chase him round the courtyard, throwing stones and clods of earth at his head. Trystan dodged as best he might, making sure that some at least struck him. He danced around until he was near enough to the entrance to the hall and ran inside.

King Mark was seated on a dais at the furthest end of the room, and from there he caught sight of the outlandish figure. 'Who is that?' he demanded. 'Have him brought here.'

When the fool stood before him, King Mark looked him up and down and then asked whence he came and who he was.

'Not hard,' said Trystan, disguising his voice to sound like a cracked bell. 'My mother was a whale who dwelt in the sea like a siren. I've no idea where or when I was born. But I was nursed by a tigress, who found me under a stone and thought I was her cub. She gave me milk from her teats. As to why I've come. I have a beautiful sister, even cleverer than me, and I thought I'd like to exchange her for your queen. Come on, my lord, you must be tired of your lady by now – try someone new. It will be a fair exchange, I promise.' He leered at the king, out of one eye, closing the other tight and screwing up his face.

King Mark laughed. 'And what would you do with the queen, if I were to give her up to you?'

'Ah,' replied the fool, 'I have a castle up in the clouds. It's made of glass and the sun shines through the walls every day. That's where I'd take her.'

Everyone who heard laughed aloud, and King Mark nodded and smiled. Only Ysolt sat still and unsmiling at his side.

'Why so sad, lady,' Trystan cried. 'I am Tantris, you know. I love you still!' He capered a bit and leered at the queen, who looked upon him with anger.

'How dare you speak to me thus!' she cried.

Trystan tried to look abashed. 'But I speak the truth,' he whined, 'surely you remember me. Did I not fight the Morholt and get a dreadful wound that would not heal? No one in the world could make me better, and I took to sea in a little boat. Then I came to Ireland, and you, sweet lady, healed me. Remember how I used to play my harp for you?' He made strange gestures like a man playing an invisible harp. Everyone laughed, save Ysolt, who changed colour.

'Tantris was a fine and noble man,' she cried. 'You are misshapen and ugly, and very likely mad. Now be off with you and stop saying these foolish things. I do not care for your jokes – or for you.'

Then Trystan began playing the fool for all he was worth, shouting and waving his hands and driving everyone from the dais. 'Leave us, leave us!' he shouted. 'I have come to court the fair Ysolt, Leave us alone!'

Smiling, Mark asked, 'Come, admit it, you are her lover, are you not?'

'Indeed, I am,' replied Trystan, capering madly.

'Liar!' cried the queen. 'Throw this fool out!'

'But, lady,' said Trystan, 'don't you remember how this great king sent me to Ireland to fetch you? I was much hated for having killed the Morholt, but I did as I was bid. I was a great knight, famed from Scotland to Rome.'

'You, a knight!' Now Ysolt was almost laughing through her anger. 'You are a disgrace to manhood, a congenital idiot! Get out of here.'

'But, lady,' he said, 'surely·you remember how I slew a dragon in your name? Remember how I cut out its tongue and then how the poison affected me so that I lay half dead in the road. You came there with your mother the queen and saved me. That was the second time, surely you remember now?'

'These things are common knowledge,' answered Ysolt. 'You are no hero!'

'But, my lady and my love,' Trystan said, pouting, 'don't you remember how you nearly killed me in the bath when you found out I had killed the Morholt, the guardian of your land? Isn't that true?'

'It is a lie!' shouted Ysolt. 'You went to bed drunk last night and dreamed all this nonsense.'

'It's true I'm drunk,' said Trystan sadly, 'but of this drink I'll never be sober.'

He capered again before Ysolt. 'Surely you must remember the drink we supped together on the ship from Ireland? I did my duty, I brought you home to Cornwall and this noble lord – ' Here he bowed comically to Mark. 'But on the way we drank a drink that sealed our fate. I've been drunk of it ever since.'

Ysolt stood up, drawing her mantle round her and preparing to depart. Mark stayed her, placing his hand on her arm. 'Wait, my dear, let's hear all this folly.' He turned to the fool. 'You said you wished to serve me. How will you do so?'

'I've served many kings and nobles. I can do all sorts of things.'

'Do you know about dogs? Horses?'

'Oh, yes. I teach greyhounds to catch cranes as they fly. I teach leash-hounds to catch swans and geese. I have caught many coots and bitterns.'

The entire court was in uproar with laughter at this. Mark, laughing, said, 'Dear friend, little brother, what do you catch in the marshes?'

'Why, whatever I can,' answered Trystan. 'With my goshawk I catch wolves. With my gerfalcons, roe buck and fallow deer, with the sparrow-hawk foxes, with the merlin hare, with my falcon wild cats, beavers and suchlike. I know everything there is to know about hunting,' he added. 'And I can play the harp and the rote, and sing to any tune you like. I can love a queen, or any woman, better than most men, and I know how to cut chips of wood and float them downstream. Today I'll serve you well – ' and he took his club and began to belabour the courtiers, crying, 'Go home! Haven't you eaten enough of the king's food!'

Laughing, Mark rose and began calling for his horse and hounds – it being his intention to go hunting, as was his custom in the afternoon. He bade the fool find a place to rest his head until later, when he was sure to entertain them all some more. Ysolt, pleading a headache, retired to her chamber, where she poured out her heart to her confidante, Brangane.

'I am filled with misery,' she said. 'A fool has come to court, a monstrous fellow, ugly and misshapen. Yet he seems to know all my life, even things that only you and I and Trystan could possibly know. He even referred to the chips of fresh-cut wood he used to send downstream to warm me that he awaited me in our secret place!'

'How can this be, my lady?' replied Brangane. 'Unless this is really Trystan himself.'

'It could not be!' cried Ysolt. 'This man is hideous, filthy. He has a tonsure like a cross on his head. He behaves like a madman. Curse him, I say. Cursed be his life and cursed be the ship which brought him here.'

'Now, my lady, be at peace!' said Brangane. 'Have you never heard of disguises? Surely you know that Trystan is clever and resourceful. I believe it could well be he.'

Ysolt hesitated. 'Dear Brangane, if only it were true! Go to the fool, I beg you. Try to find out who he really is.'

Brangane hastened into the hall, which she found deserted, save only for the fool. As she approached, he jumped up and welcomed her.

'Fair Brangane, how glad I am to see you!'

'Who are you?' demanded Brangane.

'Before God, I am Trystan. You know me well.'

'That I do not! Trystan never looked like you.'

'Listen, fairest lady. When I came to Ireland the queen herself entrusted Ysolt and you to my keeping. She held you by her left hand, Ysolt by her right. To you she gave a little leather flask. Then, on the ship, when I grew thirsty, a boy fetched me a drink. It was from the flask. He poured it into a golden goblet and offered it to me. I drank, then gave some to Ysolt. That drink was the sweetest poison ever devised! It brought love and pain to your lady and to me. Brangane, do you still not know me!'

Brangane stared at the fool a moment longer, then she rose and beckoned him to follow her to Ysolt's chamber. But when he entered, the queen backed away from him, sweating, her face white. Seeing this, Trystan himself fell back, pressing himself against the wall. There he looked at Ysolt sorrowfully.

'Alas that you should forget me so soon!'

Ysolt was desperate. 'I am not sure. I look at you, but I see nothing of Trystan.'

'My love,' said he, 'what more can I say to help you? Do you remember the seneschal who first denounced us to the king? Or the dwarf who was set to spy on us? He put flour on the floor of your chamber so that when I came to you I left marks that showed where I had been. Remember how my wound bled on your sheets? How Mark found blood on my own linen and banished me because of it? And surely you must remember Petit-Cru, the little dog I sent you as a love gift to remember me by? So many things there are we have shared. So many that you must remember as well as I.'

But still Ysolt looked at the face of the fool and doubt showed in her eyes. 'You could have learned all of these things by magic,' she said. 'You cannot be my Trystan.'

Trystan stared at her. 'Do you remember,' he began 'the tree in the very garden of this castle where we used to meet? One day King Mark climbed into its branches and hid there, hoping to spy on us. As chance would have it, I saw his shadow on the ground, and when you came spoke loudly, asking you to reconcile me with the king, to beg him to let me go from his service. On that occasion we were saved.'

The Story of Meriadoc

The Madness of Trystan

Gawain and Ragnall

The Adventure of Tarn Wathelyn

Desperately he went on. 'There was another occasion when I was disguised. Do you remember? The king ordered you to undergo an ordeal by fire to prove that you were faithful to him. We contrived it that I, disguised as a pilgrim, should help you ashore from the craft that carried you to the testing place. There, as I lifted you, I pretended to stumble. I fell between your legs. Thus you were able to swear that no man save the old pilgrim and the king himself had lain between your thighs!'

Ysolt, showing the fear and anguish she felt in every look and gesture, shook her head. 'How can I betray the memory of my love, when I am so unsure that you are he?'

'Lady,' said Trystan, 'there is but one more proof I can offer, and though I am heart-sick at your disdain, I will speak of it.'

He drew a breath. 'Remember the time when we were banished together, before King Mark's heart turned black with hatred for me. We fled, the two of us, to the forest of Morrois. There we found a beautiful place, a cave hidden behind a rock. The entrance was narrow, but within it was large and dry. There we found rest and shelter and there we lived together as true man and wife. I even trained my dog, Husdent, not to bark so that he could not give us away if someone passed that way. I hunted for us everyday with Husdent and my hawk.

'Dear heart, you must remember this and how we were caught, the king's dwarf leading him to our hiding place. But remember that, as we lay, my sword had fallen between us, and so the king believed us innocent. He even laid his glove across your face to shade you as the sun shone down through a crack in the rocks. When we woke, he awaited us, ready to take us back. It was then I gave you Husdent . . .'

Trystan stopped then, light dawning in his eyes. 'Lady, send for the dog! Do you still have him? He will know me surely, even if you do not.'

Brangane was sent at once to fetch the dog, and as soon as it saw its old master, it leapt at him, whining and licking him for sheer joy.

Ysolt watched in wonder, for the dog permitted no one near him save herself and Brangane.

Trystan held the dog close, stroking him. To Ysolt he said 'See! He remembers me, his master, better than you remember your love!'

Ysolt stared and trembled, not daring, even now, to believe.

Trystan looked at her sadly. 'When last I saw you, you gave me a gold ring as a token.'

'Do you still have it?' asked Ysolt eagerly.

Trystan dug into his tunic and produced the ring. Ysolt took it and looked at it, 'Now, alas,' she said, 'I know that my love is lost. For only in death would he have been parted from this token!'

Trystan looked long at her, then he spoke for the first time in his normal voice.

'My love?'

Ysolt looked up in wonder.

'Now you are the fairest of all women, and I love you all the better for doubting me,' Trystan said. 'Only true faith would keep you so loyal.'

Then Ysolt knew him at last and rushed into his arms. Then Trystan looked at Brangane and asked her to bring him water to wash the colour from his face and arms. The lovers embraced again, laughing and weeping in equal measure. That night, while King Mark remained away from the court, they were happy for a time. And when at last the king returned, Trystan fled once more, escaping with his life, renewed for a time by the few precious hours he had spent with Ysolt.

Few more such meetings were to be granted to them before death made them one – but that is told in another tale, while this one is ended.

7

The Wedding of Gawain and Ragnall

THIS is one of the most famous of the independent Arthurian tales and probably does not deserve the appellation 'lost' or 'forgotten'. It forms the basis for Chaucer's *Wife of Bath's Tale*, and while in that retelling the hero has no name, the setting is still Arthurian. By all accounts it is an extraordinary story which deserves to be better known. It also makes a welcome alternative to the misogynistic tales such as *Arthur and Gorlagon* (see pages 41–51) or *The Vows of King Arthur and His Knights* (see pages 9–19).

Though it has been often retold in recent years, frequently as a kind of feminist parable, I have avoided any interpretation within the story itself and have told it 'straight', very much as it was written by the original anonymous author some time in the middle of the fifteenth century (which makes it one of the few stories retold here which may actually be later than Malory's *Morte D'Arthur*).

There is much within the text which deserves comment. The attitude of the day which saw women as chattels, and linked them to their husbands as status symbols, is challenged throughout. Ragnall makes her own choice of husband, selecting Sir Gawain, the most famous and best-loved knight of the Round Table, with a reputation for courtesy and for his numerous relationships with women. Indeed, this service to all womanhood gained him the reputation of a womanizer, and he is portrayed as such in many of the later romances in which he appears. The reason for this seems to have been that as a Celtic hero Gawain (or, as he is known there, Gwalchmai, the Hawk of May) was a champion of the Goddess and therefore of all women. To the disapproving minds of the medieval chroniclers and romancers, this made him not only a pagan but also dangerous, and their reaction was to systematically blacken his name. I have dealt with this at some length in my book *Gawain, Knight of the Goddess* (London, Thorsons, 1991) and recommend readers to this for a more detailed account.

Ragnall herself is a fascinating character, independent and determined and possessed of an earthy sense of humour, despite her perilous situation. If either Arthur or Gawain had refused her offer, she might have been condemned to perpetual ugliness, but her confidence in their chivalrous natures proves well founded. It is probable, from evidence found elsewhere, that she was, at one point, a faery woman who sought to test the king and his nephew. As is often the way in such cases, the bride later vanishes, returning to faery after a number of years (see *The Story of Lanval*, pages 122–27). In this version of the story she simply dies, having given birth to Gawain's son Guinglain, who is of course the hero of *The Fair Unknown* (see pages 20–40), where he is clearly stated to have been the offspring of Gawain's love for a faery or fay.

The answer to the question, what is it women desire most? is here given as sovereignty. In the text this is elaborated to mean more simply 'power over men', but I have chosen to preserve the older interpretation of the word since this itself links Ragnall to an even older figure, Lady Sovereignty herself. In ancient Celtic myth she is the *genia loci* of the land, a personification of the spiritual presence of the earth. No king could assume rulership of the land until he had encountered her, sometimes being challenged to kiss or sleep with her in hideous form – at which point she turned into a beautiful woman, just as Ragnall does in the story here.

In other versions, particularly the ballad found in Bishop Percy's *Reliques of Ancient English Poetry* (George Routledge, 1857, re-printed in R.J. Stewart, *Celtic Gods, Celtic Goddesses*, London, Blandford Press, 1994), the cause of Ragnall's state and Gromer's animosity towards Arthur is attributed to the arch-villainess of Arthurian tradition, Morgan le Fay. As a woman of faery blood herself and a direct descendant of the Irish battle goddess Morrigan, she has a firmly grounded enmity with both Gawain and Arthur. In the most famous Gawain story, concerning his encounter with the Green Knight, she is again said to be the driving force behind the attack. Here she appears as a hideous old woman, while the Green Knight himself bears more than a little resemblance to Gromer Somer Jour. That both these characters derive from more ancient ancestors than is apparent in the medieval poems is evidenced in both the works. In *Sir Gawain and the Green Knight* the challenger bears a holly bough in his hand and dresses entirely in green, marking him out clearly enough as a type of Winter King. In Gromer's case, though his behaviour in the poem makes him no more than a challenger of a kind frequently encountered in Arthurian literature, his name suggests that he was once much more. Gromer Somer Jour may be translated as meaning 'Man of the Summer's Day', making him the polar opposite of the Green Knight, Summer Lord to the others Winter King.

Behind both stories lies an ancient tale of the struggle of the kings of summer and winter for the hand of the spring maiden – here represented by Ragnall, who, like her ancestor Lady Sovereignty, represents the land in its barren, sleeping, wintry mode, which can be awoken to the beauty of spring by the love and trust of Gawain, who in Celtic tradition is himself a solar hero.

The text of *The Wedding of Gawain and Ragnall* has been edited a number of times, notably by B.J. Whiting in *Sources and Analogues of Chaucer's Canterbury Tales*, edited by W.F. Bryan and G. Dempster (New York, Humanities Press, 1958, pp. 242–64) and by Donald B. Sands in *Middle English Verse Romances* (New York, Holt, Reinhart and Winston, 1966). A 'modern spelling' edition, with useful notes and commentary, by John Witherington was published by the Department of English of Lancaster University in 1991. Variants of the story are to be found in Frederic Madden's *Syr Gawayne* (New York, AMS Press, 1971; original edition, London, Richard and John Taylor, 1839). For a detailed discussion of Ragnall's role in Arthurian legend and tradition, see *The Ladies of the Lake* by Caitlín and John Matthews (London, Thorsons, 1992).

NE DAY KING ARTHUR WENT HUNTING in Inglewood Forest. Their prey was a mighty hart and the king was sitting very still in the underbrush, his bow at the ready, waiting for it to appear. But the hart was aware of them and stayed hidden.

'I will go and see what I can achieve' said the king. 'The rest of you stay here and keep still!' He advanced alone, stalking the deer like a woodsman, following it from thicket to thicket for nearly a mile. At last he had a clear shot, and let fly an arrow, which transfixed the buck and brought it low. The king drew out his hunting knife and began to butcher the meat as was the custom. He was so intent upon his work that he did not hear the figure who came up behind him until it spoke.

'Well met, King Arthur.'

The king turned quickly and saw an extraordinary man, very tall and powerful and with a strange, unchancy look about him.

'You have done me a great wrong, sir king. Now I shall repay you by taking your life.'

'At least tell me what this wrong is that I have done you,' said Arthur calmly. 'You might begin by telling me your name.'

'My name is Gromer Somer Jour,' replied the stranger. 'As to the wrong you have done me, you gave my lands to Sir Gawain. What do you have to say about that, king, since we are alone here?'

'If you are planning to kill me, I would advise you to think again,' said Arthur. 'My friends are close by, and if you kill me without honour you will get nothing good from it. I think you are a knight, then surely you must remember your vows. Give up this foolishness and let us talk. If I have really done you harm, I shall make amends.'

'Fine words,' answered Gromer Somer Jour, 'but I am not so easily gulled. Now I have you at my mercy. If I let you go, you will escape my punishment.' He raised his sword.

'Listen to me,' said the king, 'Killing me will avail you nothing. I have given you my word that I will make reparation for any hurt I may have caused. You will only be defamed if you slay me while you are fully armed and I only in forest green.'

'Fine words,' said Gromer, 'cost nothing.' He hesitated. 'Will you give me your word to meet with me again at this spot one year from now?'

'Willingly,' Arthur replied. 'Here is my hand upon it.'

'Wait. You have not heard my provision. In that year you must find the answer to a question. Swear upon my bright sword that you will discover what thing it is that women love best. And by that I mean both country girls and fine ladies. All women. One year from now you must be here, at this spot, unarmed and alone. Do you swear?'

'Very well,' said King Arthur. 'Though I must tell you truly that I find this distasteful, I give you my word as a king that I shall return here with an answer one year from now.'

'Good!' said Gromer. 'You can go. But see that you don't try to trick me. Remember, your life is at stake.'

With this the king had to be content. Setting his horn to his lips, he blew a long blast, which brought his companions to him. They found the king with the slain deer, but he was silent and spoke little on the journey home, despite the praise they heaped upon him for his successful kill.

In Carlisle matters went on in this way for several weeks, with the king scarcely speaking, until at length Gawain went to his uncle and asked him why he was so sad and withdrawn. At first Arthur would not speak of the matter, but when Gawain pressed him, at length he told the whole story of his meeting with Gromer Somer Jour, and of the promise he had made.

When he had done, Gawain said, 'Sire, do not be downcast. Let us send for our horses and go together into far-off lands. There we shall ask everyone we meet, be they men or women, the answer to this question. We shall take a book with us, and every answer shall be written down. One at least is sure to be the right one.'

Arthur brightened. 'This is good advice, nephew,' he said. 'Let us set out at once.'

So the two men departed, and each rode in a different direction. Everywhere they went they stopped people they met on the way and asked them Gromer's question. They received some interesting answers, you may be sure. Some said that women love to be flattered, others that their best joy is to have a lusty man in their arms. Still others said a new gown, or a sparrowhawk, or a brachet. In short, they got as many different answers as those they asked, and hardly any were the same. They wrote everything in their books and in a short time had hundreds of answers. Both arrived back in Carlisle within days of each other, and sat down to compare notes.

'Surely we cannot fail with all this information,' Gawain said.

'I am not so sure,' Arthur replied. 'In fact, I am going to go into Inglewood Forest again. There is still some time before the date appointed for my meeting with Gromer. I may still find some more answers.'

'As you wish, sire,' said Gawain, and added, 'Have no fear, my lord. You will succeed.'

So King Arthur set forth again and rode throughout the forest as and where the paths led him. There he met more people and added their answers to his book. But it was as he set out to return to Carlisle that he met a strange woman upon the way. She was sitting beside the road on a low hillock from which grew a thorn tree. As he drew near, the king saw that she was the most hideously ugly creature he had ever seen. Her back was crooked, her nose snotty, her mouth wide, her teeth yellow, her eyes rheumy. Her neck was as thick as a tree, her hair was long and matted. As she peered at him, Arthur saw that both her hands and feet were webbed and that the nails grew out like claws.

'Well met, sir king,' she said. Her voice was low and mellow. 'I am glad we have met like this, for I have the means to save you.'

'What do you mean?' demanded Arthur in bewilderment.

'There is a question to which you have been seeking the answer. And let me tell you now that all the answers you and Sir Gawain have collected will avail you nothing. Gromer will have your head.'

'How do you know all this?' asked King Arthur.

'Never mind,' said the hag. 'I am more than dung, you know,' she added. 'Now, make me a promise and I will tell you the answer that will save your life.'

'It seems to me,' said Arthur, 'that when I make promises it always gets me into trouble! What would you have of me, lady?'

The hag peered at him again. 'I want a knight for my husband. Not just any knight either. Sir Gawain is the name of the man I want. Promise me he shall marry me and I will give you the answer you seek.'

'I cannot speak for Sir Gawain,' said Arthur, aghast.

'Then you will lose your life,' said the hag.

'If what you say is true, and you possess the only answer that will suffice, all I can promise is that I will do all in my power to persuade my nephew to agree to your request.'

'Well,' she said, 'go home, then, and speak persuasively to Sir Gawain. I may be ugly, but I have plenty of life in me. It is said that even an owl can choose a mate. And remember, I can save your life.'

'Lady,' asked King Arthur, 'may I know your name?'

'Kind of you to call me lady,' said the hag, 'for I see that you do not think it . . . My name is Ragnall.'

'God speed, Lady Ragnall,' said Arthur.

'God speed, sir king,' said Ragnall. 'I will be waiting.'

Heavy of heart, King Arthur returned to Carlisle. The first person he met was Gawain, who asked him how he had fared.

'Not so well,' replied the king. 'Today I met the ugliest woman I ever saw. She said that she knew the answer to my question, but that she would give it only if she could have you for a husband. Since this is clearly impossible, I am in fear for my life.'

'There's no need to fear, my lord,' replied Gawain cheerfully. 'I will marry this hag, even if she is as ugly as Beelzebub. How could you think otherwise. I am your man and you have honoured me in 100 battles and jousts. Just say the word and I will comply.'

'Now I thank you, Sir Gawain,' said Arthur humbly. 'And I dare say you are the best knight in all my lands. My honour and my life are yours to command for ever.'

So it was agreed between them, and within five days King Arthur set out for his meeting with Gromer Somer Jour. Gawain rode a little of the way with him, until at length Arthur declared that he must ride on alone as he had promised. He had not long left Gawain's company when he saw Ragnall sitting by the roadside as though she had never moved.

'Welcome, sir king. Do you bring Sir Gawain's promise with you?'

Arthur nodded curtly. 'It shall be as you wish. Now tell me the answer that will save my life!'

'Very well,' said Ragnall. 'I shall tell you what it is that women want above all things, no matter what their age or estate or appearance. Our desire is to have sovereignty over men, for thus are we acknowledged and recognized in all things. Now, go your way, sir king, and tell Gromer what I have said. He will be angry when you do, for he will know whence you came by the information. But that matters not. Your life is safe now, of that you may be sure. Go now, I will await your return.'

The king rode hard from that place to the place appointed for his meeting with Gromer. There the fearsome knight waited, a grim look upon his face.

'So,' said he, 'let us see what answers you have for me.'

The king pulled out the two books of answers which he and Gawain had collected and gave them to Gromer. He scarcely looked at them before tossing them aside. 'Not one is the right answer,' he growled. 'Prepare to die, sir king!' and he drew his sword.

'Wait,' said Arthur, 'there is one more answer that I have not given.'

'What, then?' demanded Gromer impatiently.

'It is this,' said the king. 'Above all else, women desire sovereignty over men, the power to be free – just as this answer gives me my freedom.'

'Now, by my faith, I know who gave you that answer!' shouted Gromer Somer Jour furiously. 'And I hope she burns for ever for giving it to you. For that was my sister, Dame Ragnall, that you met upon the way, and she has brought me low through her spite. Alas that ever I saw this day, for now is my plan brought to nothing, and that is a sad song for me!' He stared gloomily at the king. 'I suppose you will be my enemy for ever.'

'No, indeed,' said Arthur. 'Of that you may be sure. For I hope never to see you again.'

'Then I give you good day,' said Gromer.

'Good day, indeed,' answered King Arthur, and, turning his horse, rode back to where Ragnall waited him.

'Well, sir king,' the hag greeted him. 'I am glad you were successful – though, indeed, this is no more than I promised. I trust you will keep your word now that all is well?'

'Lady,' said King Arthur stiffly, 'be sure that I shall keep my word.'

'Still, I shall accompany you back to Carlisle,' said Ragnall. 'I long to meet my husband-to-be.'

Thus King Arthur returned to Carlisle, with Ragnall riding at his side. His discomfort was great to be seen with so hideous a creature, but there was no help for it.

As soon as they entered the great hall, Ragnall called out that Sir Gawain should be brought to her, so that they might plight their troth in front of all the court. Gawain came forth and took the hag's hand in his and swore to honour her for the rest of his life. Then Ragnall was happy and clapped her hands in delight and asked that the wedding be as soon as might be. Queen Guinevere, who felt only sorrow for Sir Gawain, as did all the ladies of the court, did her best to persuade the hag to settle for a quiet wedding, some time early in the day and as secretly as possible. But Ragnall would have none of it.

'Not so, gracious lady,' she said. 'Thus was the agreement made between your husband and myself, that I should marry Sir Gawain all openly. And so I shall. I want there to be announcements made in every part of the land and as many guests as may be entertained here. Indeed,' she added, casting down her eyes, 'I am sorry that I am not more beautiful for the great knight I am to marry, but I am as I am, and I will have my wedding an honourable feast.'

Shuddering, Queen Guinevere agreed, and let post the banns that day. All across the land women wept when they heard of the wedding of Sir Gawain, for he was ever a most popular knight among ladies.

The day for the wedding soon dawned, and many turned out to see the great knight wed the monstrous hag. All were agreed that her wedding dress was the finest they had ever seen, and that her jewellery was the richest, but as to the woman herself – to make short the story, they thought her ugly as a sow.

After the wedding there was a great banquet, to which all the guests were invited. It was one of the finest anyone could remember, but they were all aghast at Ragnall's table manners. She tore her food apart with her long nails and stuffed her big mouth with it as fast as it could be served. She ate more than anyone else – at least three capons, three curlews, several huge baked dishes and God knows what else beside. She finished every scrap of food on the table and went on eating until the servants took away the table-cloth and brought water for everyone to wash their hands. Then, the banquet over, Gawain and Ragnall retired to their chamber.

'Now, my lord and husband,' said Ragnall, 'now that we are wed, I dare say you will show me every kindness, both in bed and without.' And when Gawain did not at once answer, she said, 'At least give me a kiss.'

Gawain, who had been staring into the fire, turned to her. 'I shall do more than kiss you,' he said. Then he stopped in wonderment, for there stood before him the fairest woman he had ever seen in his life.

'Now what is your will?' she asked quietly.

'Who are you, and where is my wife?' demanded Gawain.

'Sir, I am she,' replied the lady.

'Oh, my lady, forgive me,' said Gawain. 'But a moment ago you seemed the most hideous creature I had ever seen, and now . . . how can this be?'

'First, you must kiss me,' laughed Ragnall, and Gawain complied with her wish most willingly.

Then he asked again the meaning of the mystery. Ragnall looked at him heavily. 'My beauty is not constant,' she said. 'You may see me thus fair by day, so that all may admire your wife, but ugly by night to your despite; or you may have me fair by night for your own pleasure, but hideous by day so that all will pity you. You must choose.'

Now Gawain wrung his hands. 'Alas, fair love,' he said at last, 'the choice is hard. To have you fair by night alone would grieve me, since my honour would be hurt by this in the day. Yet to have you ugly at night would bring me less than pleasure. I confess that I cannot decide. You must do as you wish, my lady and my love. I put the choice in your hands. Whatever you decide I shall abide by it. All that I have, body and goods, are yours to command.'

Then Ragnall clapped her hands and cried, 'Oh, you good and courteous knight! Because of this you shall have me fair both day and night! For I was enchanted into that hideous form by my stepmother until such time as the best man in all Britain would marry me, and give me sovereignty over him. And you, fair and courteous Gawain, have done just that! Now come and kiss me and let us have all the joy we may, as is our right.'

Thereto they came together and spent many a joyful hour until the morning, when King Arthur, fearing for the life of his nephew, came in person to call them to dine. Gawain rose and opened the door to his chamber and invited the king to enter. And there Arthur saw the fairest of women standing by the fire in her shift, her red-gold hair falling below her knees, and the light of the morning sun in her eyes.

'Welcome, sire,' said Gawain, 'here is the lady who saved your life, and who has made mine happier than I thought possible.' And he told all that had occurred, and Ragnall spoke of the spell that was upon her and how Gawain had set her free with his love and the gift of sovereignty.

And thus Gawain and Ragnall were joyful together thereafter and in due time the lady bore a son whom they named Guinglain, who was himself a great knight and brought much honour to his father and to the fellowship of the Round Table. But after only five years Ragnall died, and Gawain mourned her greatly. Indeed, it is said that though he loved often, and was married several times after, he never loved another as much as Ragnall. And King Arthur himself remembered her with friendship thereafter, and received her brother, Gromer Somer Jour, at his court with no ill-feeling.

Thus ends the adventure of King Arthur in Inglewood Forest, and the marriage of Sir Gawain and Dame Ragnall, as it is told in the old books of this land.

8

The Adventure at Tarn Wathelyn

WHAT follows is really two stories, loosely connected by thematic resonances and by their setting – the haunted tarn (a small mountain lake) known as Wathelyn. It contains one of several appearances by ghosts to be found in Arthurian literature – these include the grisly phantoms encountered by Sir Lancelot in the Chapel Perilous, and the appearance of the ghost of Sir Gawain himself to Arthur before the battle of Camlan. All are different from the kinds of ghost we are used to reading about today. Modern ghosts are primarily psychological, whereas their medieval counterparts existed as a perfectly natural phenomenon (though they were no less frightening for all that) whose task was to foretell the future and induce a feeling of repentance in the hearts of those to whom they appeared. In this instance the ghost very precisely predicts the final conflict between Arthur and Mordred (the child who will become a man carrying a black shield with a silver saltair upon it) and Gawain's own death amid the rocky landscape of the Cornish coast.

Gawain himself, whom we have already met several times in this volume (see *The Vows of King Arthur and His Knights*, pages 9–19, *The Wedding of Gawain and Ragnall*, pages 99–106) is one of the most renowned of Arthur's knights. He is also one of the oldest of whom we have any knowledge. He appears in Celtic tradition as Gwalchmai (the Hawk of May) and is renowned for his skill and daring. Until the coming of the French knight Sir Lancelot, he was the foremost hero of the Round Table, and, as in this story, the favoured knight of Queen Guinevere. In his later literary career, he was steadily blackened, until by the time Malory wrote his great Arthurian romance, *Le Morte D'Arthur*, Gawain appears as little more than a murderer and womanizer. In this story, as in several others, he appears as the epitome of chivalrous behaviour.

Nothing more is known of the queen's mother, or indeed of the promise she is said to have broken, though it is more than likely that the anonymous poet who penned this romance may have known other stories that have since been lost. There is certainly a good chance that he had read *The Wedding*, since the fact that Arthur has given lands to his favourite nephew is mentioned in both works.

The original text dates from the fifteenth century. It was written in alliterative verse, in a northern dialect of Middle English, and is preserved in four manuscript copies, notably that now found in the library of Lincoln Cathedral. It has been edited three times: by Sir Frederic Madden in his *Syr Gawayne* (London, Richard and John Taylor, 1839); by F.J. Amours in *Scottish Alliterative Poems in Rhyming Stanzas* (Edinburgh, Scottish Text Society, 1897); and by R.J. Gates for the University of Pennsylvania Press in 1969. It was transliterated into modern English by Louis B. Hall in *The Knightly Tales of Sir Gawain* (Chicago, Nelson Hall, 1976). I have looked at all four versions in preparing this retelling, but have relied primarily on that of Dr Hall.

I

NE DAY KING ARTHUR AND QUEEN GUINEVERE rode hunting in the Forest of Inglewood, not far from the city of Carlisle. With them went Sir Gawain, first among the knights of the Round Table, and also Sir Cador of Cornwall and Sir Kay the seneschal. All were dressed in the finest clothing imaginable. Sir Gawain wore green, trimmed with ribbons and gems; Guinevere had on a blue cloak trimmed with fur and laced with precious jewels; King Arthur, most splendid of all, was dressed in scarlet trimmed with ermine.

All that morning they chased a herd of deer through woodland and across open moors, until finally the king blew his horn to summon back men and hounds to rest. Only Gawain, who rode with the queen, failed to answer. They had ridden far through valleys and by woods and glens unknown to them. Now they grew tired and together found a sheltered spot in a green grove shaded by laurel trees and bordered on one side by a dark and solitary tarn.

There they stopped to rest themselves and their horses, and there they witnessed a strange and terrible vision. The sky, which had been fair until that moment, turned suddenly dark as midnight. Rain began to fall heavily, turning swiftly to sleet and then to snow. The queen and Sir Gawain hurried to take what shelter they could beneath the trees, and from there they saw something terrible arise from the waters of the lake.

Human in shape, though bony and wasted. Shreds of clothing, clods of earth and what might have been rotten flesh clung to it. It rose into the air and advanced across the water, shrieking and yammering like one in torment, all the while wringing its hands.

'A curse! A curse!' the vile thing screeched. 'A curse upon the body that bore me! Because of my life, my suffering consumes me.'

It made straight for Gawain and the queen, who backed away from it in fear. Guinevere cried aloud and raised her hands in horror.

'This must be caused by an eclipse of the sun,' Sir Gawain said, hoping thus to calm the queen's fears. 'For I have read that strange things may happen at such times . . . I will speak with this creature and try to find out what it wants. Perhaps I may even calm it.'

Inwardly quaking, Gawain approached the edge of the tarn, where the creature now hung stationary. It seemed confused, staring madly before it. Its eyes were like hollow pits, red and glowing, and as he approached, Gawain saw with revulsion that a toad crouched in the hollow of the thing's throat and that snakes crawled around its wasted body.

Gawain drew his sword and demanded to know what business the spectre had with them. The ghost's jaw and all its body began to shake as though it would fall apart. Gawain called upon Christ to protect him and again demanded to know what the fell being wanted and who or what it was.

Gradually the shaking and shivering ceased. The red eyes turned upon the face of Gawain. 'Once I was the fairest of women,' it said, in a low and grating voice. 'Kings were among my ancestors . . . Now I am come to this. And so I have come to speak to your queen, for once I was a queen myself, more fair than Queen Iseult or Brangane her fair serving maid. All the treasure and beauty of the world was mine, and I had power over vast lands . . . But now I am lost, exiled in eternal cold. Pain entraps me, and I lie at night in a bed of coldest clay. See, then, what death has done for me, sir knight, and bring me to your lady that I may speak with her.'

Moved to pity by this fearful account, Gawain returned to where the queen stood, shivering with cold and fear.

'Lady,' he said, 'the spirit would speak with you. I believe it means us no harm.'

Drawing her cloak about her, Guinevere advanced at Gawain's side to the edge of the tarn and looked with horror upon the spirit.

'Welcome, Guinevere,' the apparition said in its low and earthy voice. 'Look what death has done to your mother. Once I had roses in my cheeks, and skin soft as the lily. How easily I laughed. Now I am brought down to this, tied to this spot with invisible chains. And, for all the youth and loveliness and power you now possess, in time you also shall become as I am. As shall every king and queen now living. Death will bring you to this, have no doubt.'

Guinevere, with tears in her eyes, answered, 'Are you truly my mother?' To which the spirit replied grimly, 'Aye, I am she that bore you. And by this shall you know it. Once I broke a vow, which only you and I knew of.'

'This chills my very blood,' said the Queen. 'How may I help you? Are there Masses to be said, or prayers to be offered that will help you find rest?'

'All the wealth in the world goes away at last,' intoned the spirit dolefully. 'Perhaps if enough Masses are said I shall indeed find rest. But more important than this are the deeds you can do while you are yet living. Offer mercy to all who need it, give food to the needy. These things alone will help me, as it will help you in time to come. Remember, life is brief.'

Gawain, silent all this while, now spoke up. 'May I ask,' said he, 'what destiny awaits those who, like myself, must fight in battles and warfare, who invade lands not rightfully theirs, and may even massacre those who deserve to live?'

The ghost turned its red eyes upon him. 'Your king is greedy. All the lands he reaches out towards fall to his hand. King Frollo and King Feraunt are dead, and many of the peers of France with them. In times to come even Rome itself shall bow the knee to Arthur. Yet his end shall come soon. At the height of his powers he shall be laid low on the shore of the sea. Fortune, that fickle goddess, shall turn her wheel against him.' The ghost paused, and seemed to be seeking new strength to continue. Gawain had grown pale at the words it spoke. Now it addressed him further.

'I tell you this, Sir Gawain. You should leave Britain now. One is coming who shall be made knight at Carlisle. He will bring great sorrow and strife to Britain. While you are away, you will hear of this and hasten to return. But it will be too late. You yourself, Sir Gawain, shall die in a steep valley. Arthur himself shall fall in Cornwall, slain by one who carries a shield of sable with a saltair, engrailed in silver upon it. Now he is but a child, playing at ball, but he shall grow to manhood and shall conquer all. On that day all the knights of the Round Table shall perish and the dream of Camelot shall end for ever. This is all that I can say. Remember me . . .'

The spirit's voice trailed away mournfully and a terrible silence fell. Then, even as Guinevere and Gawain watched, the ghost began to withdraw, floating away across the lake and dissolving amid the trees like so much smoke. At once the sky began to clear, the rain and wind ceased, and the sun shone again. The sound of the king's horn winding came to their ears and they realized that they were but a short distance from the rest of the hunt.

Thither they returned and told all that had occurred, and many were the grim looks shared between that company on that day, and especially Guinevere looked upon her lord with new eyes, and thought perhaps what might come of her love for Sir Lancelot. But if Gawain wondered at his death-day in a steep valley, or the king at the knight with the sable shield, neither spoke of these things aloud.

II

 UT THIS WAS NOT THE END of the adventures, for that night, as the company were seated at supper in the hall of Randalholme, whither they had withdrawn to rest from the exertions of the day, there came a commotion at the entrance to the hall, and into the presence of the king and queen and the knights came a strange procession. First came two musicians, playing on cittern and cymbal; next came a lady mounted upon a palfrey leading a knight in full armour with visor lowered.

All eyes were upon the lady, for they thought her the most beautiful creature they had ever seen. Her gown was of grass-green silk, her white cloak embroidered with colourful birds, her hair caught up in a net of precious stones, over which she wore a coronet of brightest gold. The knight too was magnificently clad, in mail so polished that the torchlight illuminating the hall was reflected back from it. His shield was of silver, with the arms of three black boars' heads, fierce and challenging.

Right up to the dais on which the royal party were seated rode these two, and all the while the musicians continued to play. Then they fell silent, and the lady addressed the king thus, 'My Lord, here is a wandering knight in search of honour and adventure. Will you receive him as befits your reputation?'

'Fairest lady,' answered the king with his customary courtesy, 'I bid you both a warm welcome. Whence come you and what is your purpose here?'

Then the knight lifted his visor and spoke haughtily. 'I am Sir Galeron of Galloway and I come in search of recompense for the hurts you have done me, King Arthur!'

'What hurts are these?' asked Arthur. 'Do I know you?'

'As to that,' answered Sir Galeron, 'I neither know nor care. Once I held lands in Cumnock, in Cunninghame and Kyle, in Lomond and Lennox and the burnished hills of Lothian. All these lands are now given over to Sir Gawain – by you, lord king. Thus am I come to challenge any knight here to stand against me for the right of this matter. For never shall Sir Gawain hold my lands while I live unless he or his champion stand against me in single combat!'

'Well,' said King Arthur coolly, 'it shall be as you desire. Come, dismount now and rest here tonight. On the morrow we shall be glad to find someone to fight you.'

Sir Gawain himself came forward to lead the knight and his lady and their retinue to take their rest in a splendid pavilion which had been set up outside. Tables were placed within and rich food and drink in fine glasses brought and set before the couple. Then Gawain withdrew. Never once were words spoken between the two knights, save only courtesies, politely uttered.

Then, having seen to the needs of their guests, Gawain returned to the hall, and there Arthur addressed the knights who were present.

'Who shall accept this challenge?' he asked.

'None should do so but I,' Sir Gawain answered. 'The matter is between him and me.'

'Well, then, so be it,' Arthur said. 'But do not take the matter too lightly. Remember that my honour as well as yours is at stake.'

'I shall not forget, sire,' answered Sir Gawain. 'God shall be my guide and my guard in this matter. If this arrogant knight escapes without scathe, it shall be no fault of mine.'

Next morning the two champions prepared to do battle. They heard Mass and ate breakfast and then made their way to the lists which had been set up overnight.

Both were clad in shining mail, decorated with gold. They saluted King Arthur and, setting spurs to their eager mounts, charged together and broke their spears upon each other's shields. Then, drawing their longswords, they fell to hacking at each other with all their strength.

In one pass Gawain missed his stroke, and quick as light Sir Galeron struck, cutting through shield and mail and biting deep into Gawain's collarbone. Gawain groaned aloud and staggered. Sir Galeron's lady cheered him on, while Arthur and Guinevere looked askance.

Angry, hurt and dazed, Gawain regathered his strength and struck back. Such was the power of his blow that he broke his opponent's sword, while his own blade pierced Sir Galeron's side. Maddened by the pain, Galeron swung wildly. The blow missed its mark and cleft the head of Gawain's steed half off. The beast fell dead and Gawain was thrown from its back.

'Ah, brave Grisselle!' cried Sir Gawain, weeping. 'You were the strongest and best steed ever to carry me. As God is my witness, I will have revenge for this!'

Like wild beasts the two knights came together again. Their shields were dented and their armour shiny with blood. Gawain lunged beneath his opponent's guard and the blade cut through the mail and opened a wound in Galeron's belly.

The shock of the hurt made him stagger and for a moment he stood as still as a stone. Then, summoning up his remaining strength, he aimed a blow at Gawain's head which cut away part of his helm.

For a while longer the two knights continued to swing at each other, missing more often now as they grew more and more weak. Finally they clung to each other, too weak almost to raise their heavy swords.

Then Sir Galeron's lady cried out to the queen, 'Lady, I beg you now to have mercy on this brave knight who has suffered so greatly.' And Guinevere knelt before the king and asked him to make peace between the two men.

But already Sir Galeron was speaking to his opponent. 'Sir, I never knew there could be a knight as strong and as brave as you. I willingly give up all rights to my lands and I will freely do homage to your king.'

Then King Arthur arose and commanded them to leave off fighting. Other lords came forward to support them and to help them stand before the king.

To Gawain he said, 'As a reward for your bravery I give you lands in Ireland and Burgundy. In return I ask you to relinquish all claims upon this knight's lands, which I gave you unknowing of his existence.'

To this Gawain readily agreed, and to his opponent he said, 'So brave a knight as you should sit at the Round Table. If it be my lord's will, stay here a while and learn to know us better.'

Sir Galeron gave thanks to the king and to Sir Gawain, and promised to give his finest Frisian steed to recompense his opponent for the death of his own mount. Thus they were accorded, and taken to the surgeons to have their wounds searched and dressed.

The whole company now returned home to Carlisle, where Sir Gawain and Sir Galeron rested from their battle. There, in a while, the latter married his lady, and Queen Guinevere, mindful of her encounter at Tarn Wathelyn, ordered Masses to be said for the repose of her mother's soul.

Thus ended the adventure of Tarn Wathelyn and the Forest of Inglewood, which were ever after known as places where adventure was sure to be found.

9

The Story of Grisandole

THE story which follows is found in two versions. The first, on which this retelling is based, is contained within the *English Prose Merlin*, first edited by Henry B. Wheatley between 1865 and 1899 (*Merlin or the Early History of King Arthur*, four volumes, Early English Text Society, London, Kegan Paul, Trench, Tubner; reprinted New York, Greenwood Press, New York, 1969). The second, more elaborate version appears within the thirteenth-century Arthurian romance of *Silence*, which has been recently translated by Sara Roche-Mahdi (East Lansing, Colleagues Press, 1992). The latter is by far the longest version, but I have opted for the *English Merlin* version on the grounds that it reads better, is shorter (thus enabling the inclusion of longer romances in this volume) and requires less knowledge of events previous to the beginning of the story. None the less, I would strongly recommend a reading of *Silence*, since this is a powerful and charming romance which could be considered one of the first feminist novels. Its author, who is named Heldris of Cornwall in the manuscript, may in fact have been a woman, despite referring to 'himself' as 'Master' Heldris throughout. The story, which tells of a woman brought up as a boy, includes some wonderful scenes, and a long and fascinating discussion between the allegorical figures 'Nature' and 'Nurture' as to whether the forming of a character depends on the natural gender of the child or its nurturing or upbringing. The character of Silence herself, who is called Avenable or Grisandole in the English text, is that of a strong-minded individual who carves out a career in a man's world through her skill, strength and native wit.

The other very interesting aspect of this story is the part dealing with Merlin. The stories of his laughter, capture and his ability to transform himself into a stag are all drawn from much earlier Celtic material, including some early poems attributed to Merlin himself, and Geoffrey of Monmouth's famous *Vita Merlini*.

The only surviving version of the *English Merlin* is now in Cambridge University Library (FF.III.ii). As well as Wheatley's edition, from which I have worked in my own retelling, there is an extract which includes the Grisandole story in *The Romance of Merlin*, edited by Peter Goodrich (London and New York, Garland Press, 1990). I have myself included the Wheatley text in full in both my *Arthurian Reader* (London, Thorsons, 1991) and *Merlin Through the Ages*, edited by myself and R.J. Stewart (London, Blandford Press, 1994). A freer version, written by myself from the point of view of Merlin, appeared in the anthology *Merlin and Woman*, edited by R.J. Stewart (London, Blandford Press, 1988).

N THE TIME OF KING ARTHUR, the emperor of Rome had a wife of great beauty who was also most lecherous. For, unknown to her husband, she had twelve young men disguised as women among her servants. They wore their hair long, in tresses down their backs, and used a special ointment to stop their beards growing. Whenever the emperor was away, she used to lie with them all, one after the other.

Now the emperor had in his service a certain lord named Matan, who was duke of Almayne, and it fell out that this noble lord was disinherited and driven from his lands by a duke named Frolle. But Matan had a daughter, Avenable, who was as spirited as she was fair, and, seeing her father thus vilely treated, she devised a plan to help him regain his lands and titles. To this end she disguised herself as a squire and made her way to Rome. Calling herself by the name Grisandole, she deported herself so well that she came to attention of the emperor himself, who made her first of all his personal squire and, when she had so served him for a year, knighted him, along with other young squires, on the Feast of St John.

A great festival accompanied the celebrations, and the new-made knights set up lists and began to joust with each other. Grisandole fared so well that she defeated everyone who rode against her, and ended by carrying off the prize. The emperor was so impressed by this that he promoted the new-made knight to be his steward.

Soon after this the emperor had a dream. In it he saw a great sow, the biggest he had ever seen, crashing through his palace, pursued by twelve young lions who, when they caught her, mated with her one after the other. As the dream ended, the emperor noticed that the sow wore a circlet of gold like a crown on its head.

Much disturbed by this dream, the emperor rose and went to Mass and then afterwards to dine. But still troubled by his vision, he sat at the table sunk so deep in thought that the best part of two hours passed, and all who were present were forced to sit silent also, and refrain from eating.

Now at this time Merlin came to the forest near Rome, for he knew well the nature of the emperor's dream, and its meaning, and he wished to set matters right. And so he took upon him, by way of his deep magic, the shape of a white hart of seven tines, and then he ran through the streets of the city until he came into the emperor's palace and thence into the very hall where the emperor sat. Everywhere there was uproar. People chased the great beast through the streets and into the palace. In the hall pots and pans went crashing, and food and drink fell to the floor. The stag halted before the emperor and knelt down upon its front legs and laid its mighty head to the ground. Then – wonder of wonders! – it spoke.

'Leave your studying, for it will not avail you,' said the stag. 'You shall never understand your dream until you capture the wild man who lives in the forest outside this city. He alone can tell you what it means.'

Having said this, the stag leapt away through one of the windows, while all the shutters and doors in the room except this one banged shut. By the time they could be opened, the stag had vanished, leaving a trail of bewildered guards and citizens behind it.

The emperor was so infuriated by this that he cried out that whoever brought him either the stag or the wild man should have his daughter to wed, and, if he were nobly born, half his kingdom then and the rest on his death. At once a number of nobles and knights called for their steeds and weapons and set forth on this strange quest. Among them went Grisandole, and though most of the seekers gave up within a few days when they could find neither sight nor word of either the hart or the wild man, she kept on searching, wending her way, now forward and now back, throughout the length and breadth of the forest.

At length, as she took her ease beneath a great oak tree, the hart appeared and said to her, 'Avenable, you waste your time searching, for you cannot succeed unless you do what I say.'

'What shall I do?' asked the startled girl, wondering how the stag knew her true name.

'I shall tell you,' answered the stag. 'Get fresh meat and salt, milk and honey, and hot bread newly baked. Then bring with you four strong men, and a boy to turn a roasting spit. Make a camp in the heart of the forest, where it is wildest, and set up a table with a linen cloth on it. Then roast the meat and set out the table with milk and bread and honey, and hide among the bushes until the wild man comes, for I promise you he shall come.'

Then the hart leapt away at a great speed, leaving Grisandole to wonder if this was some evil trick being played upon her. Neverthelesss, she decided to follow the stag's advice, and made her way to a nearby town, where she obtained all that the hart had asked of her, and hired the services of four men and a boy. Then they repaired to the forest and, finding a clearing amid the depths of the trees, set up camp beneath a huge oak tree and there laid a fire and set the meat to roast. Soon the savour of the cooking spread through the forest on every side, and Grisandole and her companions hid themselves in the bushes.

They did not have long to wait, for soon there came in sight a wild-looking man, clad in animal skins, with long, matted hair and beard. As he came he struck the trunks of the trees on either side with a great staff. When the spit-boy saw him, he was so frightened that he fled, half out of his wits. The wild man, seeing the fire and the table spread with good food, began to sniff and snort and finally sidled up and snatching the meat in his hands and tore at it furiously, dipping it in the milk and honey and slavering like a mad dog.

After a time, when he had eaten his fill and was stuffed near to bursting, the wild man lay down by the fire and fell fast asleep. At this Grisandole and her four companions stole out of the bushes and bound the wild man fast. Then, as he awoke and began to bellow and cry, they put him upon a horse and tied him to it. Then one of the men sat behind him in the saddle and set forth to return to Rome.

As they rode, the wild man looked at Grisandole and began suddenly to laugh. When questioned, he was at first silent, then at length he said, 'Creature formed of nature changed into another form, hold your peace, for nothing more will I say until we stand before the emperor himself.'

With this Grisandole had to be content, and the company rode in silence for a time, until they happened to pass by an abbey, where there were many poor folk gathered to beg for alms. At sight of this the wild man began to laugh again.

'Why do you laugh so?' demanded Grisandole, but the wild man only looked at her sideways and said, 'Image impaired and disnatured from its kind, hold your peace. Ask me nothing more until I stand before the emperor of Rome.'

And so they continued on their way, until they came to a wayside chapel where a priest was saying Mass for a knight and his squire. There they paused to rest and to make their prayers, and as they knelt before the altar the squire, who was standing at the back of the room, suddenly rushed forward and slapped his master on the right cheek so that all might hear the crack. At this, the wild man whom they had pushed and pulled into the chapel began to laugh loudly and uncouthly. Everyone stared at him and the priest faltered in his orisons. At which the squire came forward again and again struck his master, this time on the other cheek.

The knight, who had looked abashed before, now looked even more out of face, but still he said nothing. The wild man, meanwhile, was beside himself with laughter. Then, as everyone there stared, the squire got up from his place and came yet again and struck the knight a third time in the face, causing the wild man to laugh even louder.

Mass ended in confusion and everyone left the chapel. Outside the squire came and asked Grisandole who the bound man was, and Grisandole told him they were taking him to the emperor to answer a riddle. Then, turning to the knight, she asked why he allowed the squire to strike him and yet said nothing.

'That I was about to ask myself,' said he, and called the squire to him.

'Why did you strike me?' he demanded. 'There had better be a good reason.'

But the youth only shook his head. Crimson-faced, he swore that the urge had come over him for no reason and that he could not resist it.

'And have you this desire now?' asked his master.

The squire shook his head.

'Perhaps the answer may be had from this wild man,' suggested Grisandole. 'Why not come with us to the emperor's court and see what we can learn there?'

To this the knight agreed, and the company rode on for a time. Finally Grisandole could no longer keep from asking the wild man why he had laughed again. He looked at her and said 'Semblance of a creature to whom the dance of love is nothing, hold your peace. Nothing will I tell you until I stand before the emperor.'

When she heard this, Grisandole looked askance, for she feared greatly that the wild man knew her secret, since love was indeed forbidden her in her guise as a man. She fell silent then and spoke no more to the wild man until they came to the gates of Rome.

As soon as the citizens saw Grisandole with her prize, they flocked into the streets and followed the company all the way to the emperor's palace. He, hearing the noise, came out to see what was happening and, seeing Grisandole with her prisoner, came out to meet them.

'Sir,' said Grisandole, 'here is the wild man you have been wanting to question. I give him to you and wish you joy of him, for to me has given nothing but trouble.'

Then the emperor promised to reward his faithful knight, and sent for a smith to put the wild man in chains. But he, standing up straight, said that there was no need, for he would not try to escape.

'How can I be sure of this?' the emperor asked.

'I swear it by Christ himself,' said the wild man.

'Are you then Christian?'

'That I am,' said he.

'But how were you baptized, living all wild in the forest?' asked the emperor.

'That shall I tell you,' said the wild man, looking less wild with each passing moment. 'One day as my mother was returning from the town she entered the Forest of Broceliande. There she became lost and had to spend the night under the trees, and there a wild man came and lay by her, and begot me upon her, for she was no match for his strength. And next day my mother went home, and in a while found she was with child. Thus she carried me a full term and so bore me and had me baptized. But as soon as I might, I left her and returned to the forest, for such was the way of my father and I could do nothing else.'

'Well' said the emperor, stroking his chin, 'I will not put you in irons as long as you promise to help me and promise not to go hence without leave.'

To this the wild man gave his word. Then Grisandole spoke up and told how he had been captured and then relayed all that had occurred upon the road, including her prisoner's strange laughter. 'And he said that he would no wise speak of these things until he stood before you.'

'Is this true?' demanded the emperor.

The wild man nodded.

'Then speak.'

But the wild man shook his head. 'Not until you have called your lords and nobles before you. For I have much to say that they will wish to hear also.'

And so the emperor sent for his privy counsellors and his lords and nobles, so that it took fully eight days for them to assemble. Meanwhile, the wild man made himself at home and ate and drank well and washed and dressed himself in clean clothes so that he no longer seemed so much like a wild man at all. And when at last the court was all assembled, the emperor demanded that he speak. But still the wild man refused, until the empress and her twelve maidens were also present. So they were sent for and the empress seated herself next to the emperor and they all looked at the wild man.

He, in turn, looked at the empress, at her ladies, and at Grisandole, turning his head from one to the other in some amusement. Then he began to laugh as he had done before.

'Enough of this,' said the emperor. 'Speak!'

Then the wild man stood up and said before them all, 'Now as you are a true emperor, give me your word that no harm will come to me whatsoever I say – and that when I have done, I may depart of my own free will.'

'It shall be as you ask,' the emperor said. 'Now, speak, and tell me the meaning of my dream.'

'First, let me remind you of that vision,' said the wild man. 'Remember that you saw a great sow, crowned with a golden crown; and that as you watched, you saw twelve lions come and lie with her, one after the other. Is this the truth?'

The emperor nodded. 'Then hear the meaning of your dream. The sow that you saw signified the empress, your wife, who is here, and the twelve lions who lay with her signify her twelve handmaidens – who are no women at all, but men disguised, that lie with her when you are away.'

There was a stunned silence at this, and the empress grew so white that it seemed she might swoon. The emperor spoke no word for a while, then he turned to Grisandole and said quietly, 'I would know the truth of this. Do you despoil these women of their garments that all may see the truth.'

Grisandole came forward, signalling to the guards to surround the 'women'. They were quickly stripped of their clothes and it was soon clear to everyone that they were indeed men. Then the emperor was so angry that he could not speak for a time. Indeed, the only sound was the sobbing of the empress and the groans of the twelve men. At last the emperor asked of his counsellors and all the nobles who were gathered there what sentence he should carry out against those who had done him wrong, and with one accord they declared that the felons should all be burned to death.

Then the emperor rose up and commanded that this be done and done swiftly. The empress and her lovers were taken hence and a great fire piled up in the courtyard of the palace. Then were they all burned to death in that place and so paid for their crimes.

Then the emperor turned again to the wild man and thanked him for his wisdom. 'And though I know not how you came by this knowledge, yet I am glad of it, though it shames me deeply.' After a moment's silence, he then said, 'Now I would ask you to tell why you laughed upon the road here, first at the people before the abbey, then again at the chapel when the squire struck his master, and again when you looked at the empress and at Grisandole.'

'As to that,' said the wild man, 'the answer is simple in every case. The first time I laughed at the poor people before the abbey was because they stood upon earth where there was buried the greatest treasure, worth more than all of them, and the monks, and the abbey itself. The second time I laughed was not because of the three blows the squire gave his master, but because they brought to mind the evils of the world that cause some to rule over others, and they that have nought to borrow from they who have too much, and they who go to lawyers for their rights when they could as easily win them on their own. It was for this reason that I laughed, for I saw the servant behave like the master, though he knew not why he did so.'

The wild man paused and looked at Grisandole. 'And the third reason I laughed, when I saw the empress and her false women, was that I knew this brave knight to be no man but a woman, and nobly born at that, and as brave and true as any man here.'

The emperor turned to Grisandole and said, 'Is this true? Speak now, for I am in no mood to be gainsaid.'

Silently, Grisandole nodded.

'Then,' said the emperor, 'I bid you go from here and put off your men's clothing and dress yourself as befits a woman. Then we shall speak further.' To his servants he said, 'Go, and dig in the place described by the wild man, and bring me word of what you find.'

In a while Grisandole returned and everyone gaped in astonishment when they saw what a fair and gentle maiden she was. And they learned then that her true name was Avenable, and that her father was the Duke Matan that had been driven away by the Duke Frolle. All these things the emperor considered, then he turned to the wild man.

'Now what shall I do?' he asked, 'for I have promised the hand of my daughter to the one who brought you before me. Yet I can scarcely marry her to another maiden!'

At this the wild man smiled and said. 'Sir, this is my advice. The lady Avenable's father and mother, and her brother who is a good and brave youth named Patrick, having been driven into exile for no better reason than the greed of your duke, are now in Provence in a town called Montpellier. It would be a good thing if you were to send for them and restore them to their proper estate, for they are truer to you and have served you well in the past and will do so again. As to the matter of your promise, that is simply set right. You are in need of a new empress. Why not take the fair maiden Avenable to your wife. I dare say she would not object.'

The emperor looked at Avenable and saw from the colour that suffused her cheeks that she was indeed not averse to the notion. He turned again to the wild man, who said, 'I might add that if you are looking for a husband for your fair daughter, you need look no further than Avenable's brother. But that I leave to your own good judgement.'

Then the emperor, looking long and searchingly at the wild man, asked, 'Who are you that know so much of the affairs in my empire?'

'That I will not say, for there is no need for you to know,' replied the wild man. And with that he prepared to take his leave, nodding first to Avenable, then to the emperor, then bowing to the rest of the assembly. No one attempted to stop him as he walked from the palace. But at the entrance he paused, and raised a finger to the lintel of the door. As he did so, letters grew there that were engraved deep in the stone. This is what they said:

KNOW YOU THAT THE WILD MAN WHO INTERPRETED THE EMPEROR'S DREAM WAS MERLIN OF NORTHUMBERLAND, COUNSELLOR TO KING ARTHUR OF BRITAIN, AND THAT THE STAG WHO ENTERED THIS PALACE AND WHO SPOKE TO THE MAIDEN IN THE FOREST WAS MERLIN ALSO.

With that the wild man was gone, no one knew where. And the emperor did as he had advised and married Avenable. Also he restored her father to his lands and rewarded him greatly for the suffering he had known. Indeed he gave him the best part of the treasure which was found exactly where the wild man had prophesied. And last of all he married his daughter to the duke's son, Patrick. After that the emperor lived long and happily, as did his daughter and her husband. But Merlin was never more seen in that land again, having returned to Britain, where King Arthur had need of him and where there were many great deeds and magical acts to be achieved.

10

The Story of Lanval

LANVAL is one of a series of *Lais* (stories) written by the twelfth-century poet who wrote under the name Marie de France. Her work is characterized by a mixture of the romantic and the down-to-earth, of magic and human passion, which far outstrips the confines of the courtly love ethic from which she was nominally writing. Her stories are all of love, and were written for a courtly audience in both France and England. She was highly literate in a time when learning was not encouraged among women. Nothing more is known of her than that she apparently lived in England and may have dedicated her collection of stories to Henry II. Apart from the *Lais*, she also composed a group of fables and a version of the legend of St Patrick. The only complete text of the *Lais* is found in a manuscript preserved in London (BL Harley 978).

The story of Lanval belongs to a group of tales which deal with the theme of the faery lover. Typically, a mysterious woman appears, forms a liaison with a mortal, then vanishes again, often stipulating that no one must know about her on pain of losing her. Similar stories are frequently told of Gawain. In common with most of the stories in Marie de France's collection, the origins are in Celtic myth. She seems to have either heard the stories being recited by wandering Breton story-tellers or had access to an earlier group of such tales which she chose to turn into verse.

Somewhat unusual is the portrayal of Guinevere as an unfaithful wife. Elsewhere, of course, her affair with Lancelot was well known, but in most versions where this is mentioned, it is stated that other than this both were faithful to each other. In *Lanval* Guinevere not only propositions the hero but, when he refuses her, acts in a thoroughly unpleasant manner, suggesting that he had approached her and accusing him of insulting her.

The way in which Lanval extricates himself from this decidedly awkward situation is powerfully portrayed, and his last-minute rescue makes a fitting conclusion to this brief but fascinating tale.

The *Lais* have been often edited but rarely translated until recent times, when several new versions have appeared. The best of these is the translation by Glyn Burgess and Keith Busby, *The Lais of Marie de France* (Harmondsworth, Penguin Books, 1986), which I have used for my own retelling. Earlier versions are by Eugene Mason, *French Medieval Romances from the Lays of Marie de France* (London and New York, Dent/Dutton, 1911), which gives a less accurate account, and *The Lais of Marie de France*, translated in verse by Robert Hanning and Joan Ferrante (New York, Dutton, 1978).

NE DAY KING ARTHUR HELD COURT at Carlisle, whence he had gone to make war on the Picts and Scots, who had been ravaging the countryside and raiding deep into Logres itself.

At Pentecost Arthur rewarded all those who had aided him with lands and rich wives. All save one, that is: Lanval. This knight, who was as brave as he was courteous, was not well liked. Many were jealous of him and for this reason spoke no good words to Arthur on his behalf. Arthur himself forgot him, and, despite the fact that he belonged to the king's household, he possessed almost nothing save his horse and arms.

One day he went for a ride. His course took him through the woods below Carlisle, along the bank of a stream, until he came to a broad meadow. There he stopped, and, since the day was warm, he took off his horse's saddle and let it roll in the grass and drink from the stream. Then, having folded his cloak and placed it beneath his head, he lay down in the sun and gave thought to his troubles.

He was so disconsolate that he was scarcely aware of two girls coming along the river bank towards him until they were almost at his side. Then he jumped up and greeted them politely. One, he saw, carried a golden bowl, and the other had a towel draped over her arm.

'Sir Lanval,' said one of the maidens, 'our mistress, who is nearby, has sent us to fetch you to her. Look, her tent is very near.'

Looking across the meadow, Lanval could indeed see a magnificent tent set up in the shade of the trees. He allowed the two maidens to escort him thither. They ushered him into the cool interior of the tent and retired discreetly.

Within was a great bed, the cover of which alone was worth a castle. On it lay a woman of such surpassing beauty that it almost caused Lanval's heart to cease beating. She lay stretched out under a mantle of white ermine, trimmed with Alexandrian purple. Her face and neck, one arm and part of one white flank were uncovered. As Lanval entered, she stirred and sat up.

'Sir Lanval, I have come on a long journey from my own lands in search of you. I love you deeply, and if you are as fair and courteous as I have heard, then I will offer you all the joy you could desire.'

Lanval gazed upon the lady with all his heart in his eyes. The spark of love woke in him. 'Lady,' he replied, 'if it gives you pleasure to love me, be assured that my own pleasure is the greater for knowing this. I shall forsake all others from this moment, for the sake of the love I feel for you.'

And at this the lady held out her arms to him, and he lay with her in deep delight. Later, as they lay together on the great bed, the lady said to him, 'Beloved, I must ask that you do not reveal this love to anyone. Let it be our secret, and all will be well. But if you ever forget and speak openly of our love, you will certainly lose me.'

To this Lanval gave his word, and the two remained there as lovers will throughout the day. When it was time for supper, they rose and the two maidens brought Lanval fresh clothing – far superior to the old clothes he had worn before. They also gave him a purse of gold, and told him that his horse, which had been well cared for, had a new saddle and another harness. Then they brought in wine in golden goblets and food on golden plates.

When they had eaten, the lady turned to Lanval and said, 'My love, the time has come for us to part. This must be our understanding. Whenever you have need of me I shall come to you, no matter where it may be. You will have all that you need by way of goods, money and other riches – sufficient to proclaim you a wealthy man. No man save you will see me or hear my voice. Our secret is for no other to share.'

Thus it was agreed between them, and Lanval returned to Carlisle a happy man. There he found that his servants were clad in fresh attire, and that all his goods were renewed and his fortunes completely restored.

Thereafter Lanval's life changed. He gave gifts. He clothed and fed poor folk. He ransomed prisoners. There was no one, friend or stranger, who did not owe something to his generosity. And, whenever he wished it, there was his lady by his side, ready to comfort and love him.

That same year, round about St John's Day, several of the Round Table knights had gathered in the garden which lay beneath the windows of the Queen's lodging. Sir Gawain was there, and his cousin Yvain, as well as maybe twenty others. Gawain said, 'My friends, we do ill by our companion Lanval. Is there anyone here who had not benefited from his generosity, yet we have not included him in our company today. Let us go and fetch him at once.'

The other knights agreed and dispatched some of their number to find Lanval and bring him back. Now it happened that Queen Guinevere was sitting in the window, chatting with two of her ladies, and, seeing the company gathered below, summoned more of her women to accompany her to the garden, where they might spend time with the knights and make merry. The knights were delighted and made the women welcome – all save Lanval, who had joined them willingly enough, but at the sight of the knights walking arm in arm with the ladies of their choice felt nothing but a desire to see his own love.

The queen, seeing where Lanval had drawn to one side and was standing alone, went to him and begged him to sit with her. Once they were settled, she leaned close to him and said, 'Ah, Sir Lanval, I am so happy to be with you and to have this opportunity to speak with you. I have been watching you for a long time, and I dare say I have never seen a more handsome, charming man.' As Lanval stammered his thanks, the queen moved closer to him. 'If you wish, we may spend more time together, alone that is. I will give you all my love if it pleases you.'

Lanval drew away in alarm. 'Madam,' he said, 'what you say does not please me at all. I have served the king faithfully for years. I will not break that faith now.'

At this Guinevere became angry. 'I swear you love boys more than women!' she cried. 'When I think of it, I have never seen you with a lady of your own.'

Lanval rose angrily. 'I assure you you are wrong. Furthermore, I love and am loved by a lady whose poorest serving wench is worth more than you, in beauty, wisdom and honesty!'

At this the queen fled to her chamber in tears. She took to her bed and swore that she would never get up again unless the king heard her complaint and saw that justice was done.

The king, meanwhile, returned from a pleasant day hunting in the woods. He entered the queen's chamber and, when she saw him, Guinevere fell at his feet, weeping and demanding justice for the insult done her by Lanval. 'For I was with him in the garden, and thought he appeared lonely, but when I approached him he demanded my love. Then, when I refused, he said that he had a love who was so much more beautiful than I that even her chambermaid was worth more than me.'

At this the king became extremely angry and declared that he would have Lanval brought before him at once, and that if he were unable to answer for his words he should be hanged or put to the flame.

Lanval, meanwhile, had returned home and was in great distress. He knew that he had lost the love of his lady by speaking of her to the queen. Still, he sat in his chamber and called out to her repeatedly, but to no avail. When the king's men arrived to take him into custody, he made no attempt to resist them, and would indeed have been quite happy if they had slain him.

He came before the king in a sad state, subdued and unspeaking. Arthur demanded to know the reasons for the slanderous attack he had made upon the queen. 'You have been my good vassal these many years. Now you return my favour in this way. Answer me! Why do you do this!'

Lanval said little, however, merely swearing that he had not asked the queen to betray her lord, and that in speaking of his own love he had lost her for ever. Arthur, frowning, heard him in silence. Then he said that he would take no action, but rather would await the return of the whole court in a few weeks' time, and then ask them all for a judgement that would be unbiased. Meanwhile, he asked for sureties that Lanval would not flee, under which condition he could remain at liberty.

At first no one would come forward to stand surety for him, but at length Gawain offered to make good his bail, and several of the knights followed suit, for in truth they thought well of Lanval and were more than a little ashamed of their earlier treatment of him. The king accepted their guarantee against all the lands and fiefs they held from him. Lanval then returned to his lodging, where he stayed, very miserably, awaiting the day appointed for his judgement. Gawain and the rest came daily to visit him, afraid that he might do himself harm.

The weeks passed, and the barons returned to Carlisle, where Arthur demanded that they sit in judgement on Lanval. Many were reluctant to do so, knowing him for a good and faithful man, but Arthur insisted and pressed them hard for a verdict. At length, after much deliberation, it was decided that since only the Queen was witness to the things that Lanval had said, he should be given the chance to prove his innocence. 'Let him produce this lady that he spoke of so foolishly and boldly. If she comes, then we shall make our judgement accordingly. If not, then we shall order him to be banished.'

Lanval shook his head when this was conveyed to him, and said that no help would come from that quarter. The barons therefore prepared to make their judgement. But at that moment there appeared two maidens of surpassing beauty, richly clad, riding on twin white mares.

'Is one of these your love?' demanded Arthur, but Lanval shook his head. The two maidens rode up to the dais on which Arthur was seated and dismounted. 'My lord,' said one of them, 'we beg that you prepare the best room you have for our mistress, for she wishes to stay here this night.'

Courteously Arthur called two of his knights to show them to the best chambers in the castle. Then he turned again to the judges and angrily demanded that they reach a verdict. As they again spoke together, two more maidens, as fair or fairer than the others had been, were seen approaching, richly dressed and riding two white mules. Again they approached the king and requested lodging for their lady, who would appear shortly.

Yvain, seeing their beauty and richness, went quickly to Lanval and said, 'Surely you are saved. One of these must be your love!' But he only shook his head and answered that he neither knew nor loved either of them.

At this Arthur demanded that the barons reach a verdict at once, for the queen had waited all day and like him was becoming angry. Just as they were about to comply, a woman came riding into the town on a white palfrey. There was not a person there who thought her any less than the most beautiful woman they had ever seen. Her skin was white as the whitest clouds, her lips red, and her hair tawny gold. Her figure and deportment made her the envy of every woman there, but the brightness of her eyes and the gentleness of her looks won everyone's heart. On her wrist she carried a fierce and splendid sparrowhawk. Behind her mount trotted the finest hunting dog anyone had ever seen.

Several of the knights hurried up to Lanval and said, 'Surely, the woman who will rescue you is even now approaching. Her hair is gold, her lips are red and she is by far the most beautiful creature we have ever seen.'

When he heard this, Lanval turned first white, then red. He rushed to a window from which he could see the street, and when he caught sight of the lady a cry escaped him. 'It is my beloved! Now is my fate sealed, for if she will not forgive me for breaking my promise to her, I am as good as dead.'

The lady rode right up to the place where King Arthur sat and addressed him thus, 'Sire. I have loved and been loved by one of your vassals. Lanval is his name and he is a worthy knight. Because I wish him to come to no harm, I have come to defend him. You should know that your queen is wrong, and that he never demanded her love. Though none but she can show this to be true, I at least will stand by my love and hope that my presence will help prove him innocent.'

Then the judges looked at one another and with one accord declared that Lanval was innocent. For they were all agreed that there could be no other as fair in all the land, and if Lanval's honesty was proved in this, it were as well to believe all that he said.

Once she had heard the verdict, the lady turned about and rode away from the castle – nor would she turn back, even though Arthur begged her to stay. As she passed through the gates of the city, she passed a great block of stone which was used as mounting block. There Lanval was waiting, and sprang on to the back of the horse and kissed her lips before the sight of all.

The white horse bore them both away, and after that time no one ever saw Lanval or his lady again. Some say they went to the island of Avalon, which was the lady's true home. More than this I cannot say, for I have not heard any more.

11

The Mule without a Bridle

THE story of *La Mule sans Frien* (*The Mule without a Bridle*) was written in Old French, and is attributed to one Paien or Pagan de Maisières, which is sometimes assumed to be a pseudonym parodying the name of the great French Arthurian poet Chrétien de Troyes. It exists in a single manuscript which also contains another, somewhat similar romance, *Le Chevalier à l'Épee* (*The Knight of the Sword*). Both are brief and have a satirical tone which pokes fun at the more serious chivalric romances of Chrétien and his followers.

Yet despite its frivolous-seeming story, it in fact hides a more serious theme, that of sovereignty over the land – an important theme in Arthurian romance which dates back to Celtic times. Essentially it revolves around the relationship between the king and the land, seen in Celtic tradition as an almost symbiotic connection between the ruler and the spirit of the place over which he rules. Only kings who are perfect in body can rule. Thus when the Irish king Nuadhu loses a hand, which is replaced by a silver one, he can no longer rule. Gawain, who is Arthur's nephew, and often his representative (*tanaiste*, in Irish tradition), is here depicted as securing a bridle which gives him the right to rule over the lands owned by the girl with the mule, and which also gives him power over animals. (This is discussed at greater length in my book *Gawain, Knight of the Goddess*, London, Thorsons, 1991.)

The setting of the adventure itself is very clearly otherworldly. The valley with the wild beasts, the place of scorpions and finally the castle itself with its revolving walls and strange inhabitants – the churl who offers to play the beading game with Gawain, the lions and dragons and the obviously faery lady – all make this apparent. The beheading episode is of particular interest as it marks a very different account of this ancient theme, best known from the version found in *Sir Gawain and the Green Knight* but in all probability derived from an ancient Celtic text, *Bricriu's Feast*, in which a remarkably similar event takes place, the protagonists being the great Irish hero Cuchulainn, and the trickster (*bachlach*) Bricriu. A full account of this and other analogies will be found in Elizbeth Brewer's book on the subject (see below).

In its present form, the story ends rather abruptly and perhaps even unsatisfactorily. One feels that Gawain ought to have married either the girl with the mule or her mistress, but since both are faery beings and Gawain is known to have had liaisons with several other such magical women, this might be the explanation. In any case, Gawain is depicted in his most heroic guise, contrasted, as so often, with the foolish and cowardly Kay (see *The Vows of King Arthur and His Knights*, pages 9–19).

The whole story has a great deal of mystery about it. Nothing is explained, and the departure of the girl is just as mysterious and sudden as her arrival. This may be simply because the author was retelling a story which he himself understood imperfectly. There is a strong chance that this is, in fact, the earliest record of the beheading game in medieval literature, and that it preserves a fuller account than even that found in *Sir Gawain*

The Story of Grisandole

The Mule Without a Bridle

The Knight of the Parrot

The Perilous Castle

and the Green Knight. The mysterious churl could well be an earlier version of the Green Knight, and harks back to the *bachlach* in *Bricriu's Feast.* It seems evident that he is the real master of the otherworldly goings-on at the castle, since he controls the beasts with which Gawain does battle (despite the fact that the lady of the castle complains that Gawain has killed her beasts) and is able to stop the castle revolving.

The episode of the people who suddenly appear rejoicing in the streets at the end is reminiscent of the Grail story, where the land and people are healed by the achieving of the Grail adventure. One may also compare it with Lancelot's visit to the home of the Grail king in Malory's tale of the Grail quest, where the knight rescues a woman from a boiling bath and emerges to a tumultuous reception. In addition, there is the curious fact that both the knight with whom Gawain fights – and who is apparently healed by his efforts – and the lady of the castle are discovered lying in bed. This recalls the wounded king episode in the Grail romances, where the king also lies on a bed and is only healed when the Grail winners ask the famous 'question' which releases the spell that has both king and land in thrall.

The text has been edited twice. Once by B. Orlowski (*La Damoiselle à la Mule*, Paris, 1910) and again in *Two Old French Gauvain Romances* by R.C. Johnston and D.D.R. Owen (Edinburgh and London, Scottish Academic Press, 1972). It was translated into rather curious verse form by M. Le Grand in *Fabliaux or Tales Abridged from French Manuscripts* (London, 1815) and more recently in prose form by Elizabeth Brewer in *Sir Gawain and the Green Knight: Sources and Analogues* (Cambridge, D.S. Brewer, 1992).

NE PENTECOST KING ARTHUR HELD COURT at Carlisle. Knights and their ladies came from all over the country, and the queen was there with her court, which consisted chiefly of beautiful girls. After supper the knights retired to the rooms which were above the dining hall, where they sat talking and laughing. Then one of their number, who happened to be looking out of a window, called the others to join him. They saw a young and pretty girl riding a mule which came at a fast pace across the meadow below the castle. As it approached, they saw that the mule had no bridle, only a halter of rope, which made it very hard for the girl to steer it properly, which seemed to be causing her some distress.

The knights wondered much at this and Sir Gawain, who thought the girl especially pleasing, said to Sir Kay, 'Go and welcome her, and tell the king he should come here at once to find out what she wants.'

Kay hurried off to where Arthur and Guinevere were sitting talking and told them what Gawain had said.

'Bring the girl here,' said Arthur.

Several of the knights, including Gawain, had already gone outside and, having helped her to bring the mule to a halt, spoke kindly to the girl and made her welcome. She, however, made it clear that she had no time to exchange pleasantries, and asked to be taken to the king immediately.

When she stood before Arthur and Guinevere, she said, 'Sire, you can see how distracted I am. I shall be like this until I get back the bridle belonging to my mule. It has been wrongfully taken from me, and until I have it again I cannot inherit the lands which should be rightfully mine. So if there is any knight here who will do what he can to get it back for me, I promise that I shall give him everything he could possibly desire. I shall be entirely his to love and cherish once he has succeeded.'

Arthur smiled and answered, 'I am certain there is one here who will do what you ask. Tell us how he shall find the way to the place where the bridle is kept.'

'Sire, that is simple. My mule knows the way. All that is required is to climb upon its back and it will take you right to my castle. But I warn you, the winning of the prize will not be easy.'

Now all this while Kay had been looking at the girl with hunger in his eyes. He said, 'I will undertake this task. But first, I would like a kiss.'

'That you shall not have, until you find my bridle,' the girl answered angrily. 'Then you shall have as many kisses as you want, and my castle to boot.'

'Very well, then,' said Sir Kay, 'I shall leave at once.'

'Be sure and let the mule have its head, for it knows the way.'

Kay strode off and was mounted upon the beast's back as soon as he might be. He did not even stop to call for his armour and weapons, but took only the sword he was already wearing. When she heard this, the girl began to weep. 'He will never succeed,' she cried. 'I shall never have my bridle again!'

Well, all that day Kay road along on the mule, giving it its head. Soon after midday they entered a deep forest, and as they plunged deeper into it, Kay began to hear the sounds of wild beasts all around him. He began to feel anxious about this, and when he saw several lions, tigers and even a leopard draw near, his discomfort turned to terror and he called out to them that he had come that way only because the mule had brought him there. But when the animals saw the mule, they stopped snarling and growling and bowed low before it, out of deference to the lady who had but lately ridden upon it, and who allowed them all to live there in the forest in peace.

Sweating a little, Kay rode on, and soon came to a narrow, unfrequented path which led out of the forest and into a deep valley with sheer sides over which hung a pall of darkness. Such a breath of cold came from every side that it seemed like winter there. Then, as the mule picked its way onwards, Kay became aware of a terrible smell, the worst he had ever known or was ever to know. When he saw from whence it came, his terror knew no bounds, for on every side of the valley were snakes, and scorpions, and serpents, larger than any he had ever seen. They all breathed fire and smoke from their mouths and it was this that created the terrible stink.

Somehow, holding his hand over his mouth, Kay managed to stay on the mule's back until it passed through the dreadful valley and came out on a flat plain. In the distance he saw where a spring of very pure water bubbled out of the earth. It was surrounded with flowers, and bushes gave shelter and shade. Kay dismounted and took off the mule's saddle, then he allowed it to drink, and splashed the cool water on his face and drank his fill also. Then, much refreshed, he saddled the mule and rode on once more, wondering how much further he must go to reach the castle and obtain the bridle.

Soon after he reached a wide stretch of water which ran fast and furiously between steep banks. Kay looked at it in dismay, seeing neither barge nor crossing place nor bridge in either direction. Turning the mule to the left, he began searching for somewhere to cross, and finally found a place where a narrow iron plank stretched across to the other bank. It looked strong enough to bear him, but it was certainly a perilous place, and as he looked at it Kay began to grow angry.

'All this way through that forest and that hideous valley and now this! I'll be damned if I'll go any further. And all for a stupid bridle.'

So saying, he turned the mule around and set its head in the direction of Carlisle. Back though the poisonous valley and the dark wood he rode, as fast as he could make the mule go, and very glad he was to see the walls of Carlisle in the distance.

As he rode across the meadow, Gawain, Gareth and Griflet came out to meet him, while others went to find the girl. 'Come,' they cried, 'Sir Kay is back already. You will soon have your bridle.'

'I shall not,' said she. 'If he has returned this soon, he cannot possibly have got it!' And she began to weep loudly.

When he saw that she spoke the truth, Gawain said cheerfully, 'Lady, will you grant me a boon?'

'What boon?'

'That you will cease weeping and go inside to supper. I will undertake to retrieve your bridle.'

'How can I be sure you will succeed any better than your companion?'

'I promise that I shall not rest until I have succeeded, or die in the attempt,' said Gawain solemnly. And at this the girl dried her tears and looked happier than she had been from the start, for she knew of Gawain's fame and prowess, and had greater faith in him than in Sir Kay.

Then, while Kay himself retired to his lodgings, shamed by his failure and reluctant to speak of it, Gawain requested of the King that he be allowed to ride in quest of the lady's bridle. To this Arthur and Guinevere both acceded willingly, and gave Gawain their blessing.

Without wasting any time, Gawain prepared to depart at once. Before he did so the girl came forward and, flinging her arms around his neck, gave him a kiss. Thus encouraged, Gawain set forth on his way. He soon came to the forest and as before the wild animals came racing towards him. Then, when they saw the mule, they stopped and bowed low. Thus Gawain continued on his way, and came at length to the dark and dismal valley, through which he passed, not without a shudder, and emerged safely in the meadows beyond.

There, as Kay had done, he rested the mule and drank some of the pure water which flowed from the spring. After that he rode on until, like Kay, he was stopped by the rough and furious river. Following its banks he arrived at the iron platform and, after hesitating and studying it for a time, drove the mule on to it. The plank quivered and shook, and for much of the time one or other of the mule's hoofs was off the edge, but Gawain pressed onward and at length came to the further bank. There he looked across a wide meadow to where a fair and well-appointed castle stood gleaming in the sun.

All around the walls stretched a wide moat, while around that, forming another ring of defence, was a palisade of sharpened stakes. As he drew nearer, Gawain saw that each of them bore a human head upon it – a grisly indication of the fate of those who had ventured here before. To make matters worse, the outer walls of the castle revolved continuously, like a giant spinning top, so that as he watched, the gate passed by again and again.

Undaunted, Gawain pressed forward until he found a level spot outside the walls. There he waited until he saw the gate coming towards him again. Then, at the moment it came level, he spurred the mule forward. The poor beast jumped like a hare, and they passed through the gate in a flash, leaving part of the mule's tail behind! Gawain praised his steed as he looked around him, seeing to his consternation that the place seemed deserted.

Slowly he rode on through the streets, until he drew near to the castle keep. There, suddenly, he espied a dwarf hurrying to meet him. As the small man came abreast, Gawain called a greeting, which the dwarf answered. But he did not stop, hurrying on as though on urgent business.

Puzzled, Gawain got down from the mule's back and advanced towards the keep. He saw a wide archway set in the side, which opened on to a vast, deep cellar, going down into darkness. Gawain hesitated, thinking to himself that this place might be worth exploring. At that moment a figure emerged from the shadows: a huge churl, very hairy and wide as a corn-stook, with a great sharp-looking axe resting on one shoulder.

'I give you greeting and hope you have good luck,' the churl said.

'Why, thank you,' answered Gawain. 'Do I have need of it?'

'Aye, that you do,' said the churl. 'So does any man that comes here. Anyway, you have wasted your time. The bridle you seek is in a safe place, and very well guarded. You would need to be a hero indeed to overcome them.'

'Well, I shall try anyway,' said Gawain.

The churl shrugged and beckoned him to follow. He led the way away from the keep to a house where lodgings were already prepared. Setting aside his axe, the churl brought clean towels and a bowl of water in which Gawain could wash. Then he served the knight from the plentiful viands already set out on the table. Then, when Gawain had eaten, the churl led him to a room with a fine bed and a bright fire made up in the grate.

Gawain prepared to lie down, but before he could do so, the churl spoke again. 'Sir Gawain, I know you for a man of courage and honour. Before you go to your rest – and I promise you shall lie in comfort and with no threat to your safety – I ask that you undertake a test that I shall set for you.'

'I will gladly do so,' said Gawain steadily, for he was not afraid of the man, for all his ill-looks and rough way of speaking. 'What is this test? Am I to know?'

'That you shall,' said the churl. 'It's this. Cut my head off tonight with my axe, and in the morrow let me cut off yours.'

Gawain did not hesitate. 'Very well. Though I'd be a fool if I didn't realize there was more to this than you are telling me.'

The churl made no answer, but handed his axe to Gawain and then stretched his neck on a block close at hand. Gawain took the fearsome weapon and, hefting it high above his head, delivered a blow which sent the churl's head flying. No blood came out of his body, however, and in a moment it stood up and went to retrieve the head. Carrying the grisly object, the churl's body left the room. Gawain went to bed, and slept well.

Next day, at first light, Gawain arose. He saw the churl coming, with his head back on his shoulders as though it had never been off. 'Gawain,' he said, 'I hope you haven't forgotten our bargain?'

'Not at all,' replied the knight. 'I am ready.' And he lowered himself down until his neck was stretched on the block where the churl himself had knelt the night before. 'I wish I could be as certain as you that the blow would do me no harm,' he said. 'But, strike anyway.'

The churl raised the axe on high, and brought it down – but the blade thudded harmlessly into the wood by Gawain's ear, and the churl praised him for his courage.

Gawain got up – a little shakily – and asked where the bridle was to be found.

The churl laughed and said, 'There will be enough time for that soon, and enough fighting for you, Gawain. For you must fight two fierce and terrible lions who are sent to guard the bridle. Now you should eat, for you will need all your strength to overcome them.'

'I need nothing,' Gawain said, 'but it would be useful to have some armour and weapons, for as you see I have only my sword.'

'Come, then,' said the churl, 'there is plenty of gear in the castle, and a good horse which no one has ridden for months. But first let me show you the lions, so that have an idea of what awaits you.'

'There is no need for that,' Gawain said. 'But I should be glad if you would arm me right away.'

The churl led him into a room in the castle where many suits of armour lay about – doubtless having belonged to those whose heads now decorated the stakes outside the castle – and there he armed Gawain well, and then took him to where a fine horse was stabled. Gawain mounted and went outside.

At once the churl let out the first lion, a huge and fearsome creature with a shaggy mane and tough hide. It sprang with a roar at the knight and with its first blow knocked away his shield. Gawain struck back and succeeded only in blunting his sword, for its hide was hard and tough. The churl threw him a second shield, but he soon lost that, and two more like it, in the flurry of blows he exchanged with the lion.

'You're slow,' commented the churl.

Gawain gritted his teeth and with a huge effort drove his sword into the beast's jaws and pierced its heart. He stood panting for a moment, then cried, 'Let loose the next beast.'

The churl obeyed and the second lion sprang forth. Already angry, it became savage when it saw that its fellow lay dead. Hurling itself at Gawain, it tore his mail down to the ventail with a single blow of its great clawed forefoot. The knight struck back with all his might, and split the beast's head in twain. He stood there breathing heavily, with blood running down from a dozen slashes in his flesh.

'Now fetch me the bridle,' he said, through gritted teeth.

'Not yet,' the churl said. 'You need food and rest. This is not over yet.'

He led Gawain into the keep and though a maze of corridors and passages to a room where there was a bed. On it lay a huge knight whose bloody condition spoke of many wounds. Yet when he saw Gawain, he cried, 'Welcome, sir knight. Your bravery has healed me. Now let us fight! For everyone who comes in search of the bridle must do so, and if you lose, your head will join those that already adorn my house.'

Wearily Gawain drew his sword, and prepared to do battle. But the churl took him outside and showed him the place where they would fight. And he explained that Gawain must beware, because even if he won, the only prize he would get would be to have his head on one of the spikes – unless he could slay the knight of the castle.

The two men mounted their horses and prepared to fight. In their first course they broke their spears, and were both almost unseated. They descended to the earth and baring their swords fell to with a will, neither giving an inch of ground. Like blacksmiths, they struck sparks from each other, until at last Gawain struck a blow which cut through his adversary's helm and left him stunned. Gawain raised his sword to finish the fight once and for all, but before he could strike the knight begged for mercy. 'I was wrong to fight you, Sir Gawain. Until now I thought there was not another man in the world who could best me. Now I see the foolishness of such a thing, and I beg you not to kill me!'

Disgusted, Gawain turned and strode away. The churl followed him, and Gawain said bitterly, 'Now may I get the bridle?'

But the churl shook his head. 'Shall I tell you what you have to do yet?'

Wearily Gawain nodded.

'There are two dragons, very fierce and terrible, that squirt hot blood and breathe fire. You must defeat both of them to win the bridle. No one has ever succeeded. If you do, there are no more trials.'

'Then go and fetch them,' Gawain said.

'First let me get you water and a fresh harness,' said the churl. 'The one you wear now will not avail you against these creatures.'

As good as his word, he found a fresh hauberk and bright mail to put over it. He also brought a new shield, which was especially large. Then Gawain said, 'Go, then, bring out these creatures.'

The dragons were terrible indeed. Black and red scales covered their bodies, and noisome smoke and flame belched out of their mouths. Hot black blood spurted from their nostrils, and where it fell the ground smoked. Gawain was glad of the wide shield, which protected him somewhat from their fiery breath, but it was soon afire, and he was forced to drop it. Then, gathering all his strength, he dodged in beneath the jaws of one of the beasts and with a great blow cut off its head. The other dragon roared and attacked with even greater force, beating the knight back almost against the walls of the castle. There he turned at bay, and, leaping high in the air, slashed the beast's neck half through. As it roared in agony, he leapt upon its head and stabbed downward into its brain with his sword. The beast fell dead, and Gawain slumped to the earth, spattered with blood and filth.

With surprising gentleness, the churl came forward and helped him unarm, then washed his wounds. As he finished, the dwarf whom Gawain had first seen as he entered the castle appeared from somewhere and greeted him politely. 'Sir, on behalf of my lady, I greet you and ask that you come with me and eat at her table. After that you shall have, without further hindrance, the thing which you seek.'

Gawain looked down at the small man. 'I will go only if this churl accompanies me,' he said, 'for I have greater trust in him than in any other man here.'

The churl led him once again through a maze of passages to a room in which the lady of the castle lay abed. As Gawain entered, she sat up and smilingly beckoned him forward. 'Welcome, Sir Gawain. Though it is a cause of grief to me that you have slain my pets, yet I acknowledge that you are the greatest knight ever to enter this castle. Let us eat together and talk for a while, then you shall have the bridle.'

So saying, she bade Gawain sit on the bed beside her, and the churl served them with food and fine wine. When they had dined, the lady turned to Sir Gawain.

'Sir,' she said, 'you have done well, and now you must be rewarded. I will tell you that she whom you have helped in this way is my sister, and by coming here you have done her, and me, great service. If you are willing, I will take you for my lord and give over not only this castle but five others as well.'

Gawain bowed politely. 'Lady,' he said, 'I thank you, but must refuse. I am already overlate for my return to King Arthur, and besides, the lady, your sister, must be worried that I have failed in my task.' He looked directly at the lady and said again, 'May I now have the bridle?'

'Take it, Sir Gawain, for you surely deserve it.' And she pointed to where the bridle, a rich thing encrusted with many jewels, hung from a silver nail on the wall, though Gawain had not noticed it there before. He took it now and, giving thanks to the lady, went outside, where the churl had brought the mule. There he put the bridle on the beast and saddled it. Then he prepared to depart.

The lady had given instructions that no one was to hinder his departure, and ordered the churl to stop the walls of the castle turning. At the gate Gawain paused to take his leave of the churl, and as he looked back he saw that the streets around the castle were suddenly filled with people, who danced and made merry as though they had been released from some terrible imprisonment.

'What is the meaning of this?' he asked the churl.

'These are the people of the castle,' said he. 'They were forced to take refuge in the cellars while the creatures whom you slew were at large. Now they are free, and they are all thanking you in their own language for what you have done for them.'

Thus Gawain left the castle, and in a while crossed the narrow bridge and passed through the valley and into the woods beyond. There the beasts came as before, but now they accompanied him, pressing right up to him and rubbing themselves against his legs and feet and the sides of the mule. Only at the edge of the forest did they leave him, after which he made swift passage to Carlisle.

There the King and Queen and all the knights came out to greet him, and of course the girl who had come in search of help was there also. She rushed right up to Gawain, and when she saw the bridle on the mule she embraced the knight and kissed him 100 times. 'Sir,' she said, 'you have done more than you can ever know for me and my people. Not one other knight of more than 100 who came to the castle succeeded where you have triumphed so greatly. I give you my thanks and promise that anything I can ever do for you I shall do.'

Then they all went inside and Gawain told the whole story of his adventures. At the end of his recital, Queen Guinevere turned to the girl and asked if she would now stay there at the court. But she only shook her head. 'Would that I might, but l am not free to do so. Now that I have the bridle, I must return from where I came.'

No persuasion would serve to change her mind, and next morning she set off, alone as she had come, riding the mule with its bridle glittering in the sun. The court watched her go from sight, and after that they saw her no more.

12

The Knight of the
Parrot

L E Chevalier du Papegau (*The Knight of the Parrot*) is that rare thing, an Arthurian satire. Others do exist, such as the thirteenth-century Gawain romance *Hunbaut*, but by and large the writers of these stories took their subject matter seriously. The anonymous author of the story retold here takes the opportunity to poke occasional fun at the concept of chivalry. Not that he was altogether against the institution, as we can see from Arthur's early remarks on the subject to the Merciless Lion. This is balanced by his later behaviour when he strikes the Lady of the Blonde Hair for causing him to lose face in the tournament. The excuse – You asked me to behave like a bad knight! Well, I'm still doing it! – is a thin one by medieval or modern standards, but reflects the attitude towards women at the time. The parrot itself, indeed, seems to have offered a device through which the author could put a more rational and ironic point of view.

The story is unusual on two further counts: it takes place at the beginning of Arthur's reign and it features him as a hero. Generally the best-known stories of this genre tend to focus on later periods, and they very seldom feature Arthur as anything other than a figurehead who sets the ball rolling by sending forth one of his knights in response to the usual call from a distressed damsel. Here, however, Arthur takes the lead from the beginning, and shows himself to be every bit as worthy a knight as any of the great Round Table fellowship.

Despite the comic passages – mostly provided by the parrot – the story is in fact archetypal.

Arthur faces a whole range of tests and trials, ranging from serpents to wild women, to sword bridges and crushing wheels. He also encounters a helpful ghost, one of the few in Arthurian tradition (for another, see *The Adventure at Tarn Wathelyn*, pages 107–13). He overcomes them all with the usual amount of sweat, bravery and occasional magical help. A succession of distressed damsels is on hand to keep him busy and on the whole he fares well and provides readers with enough to keep them entertained throughout a lengthy text.

I have made two abridgements to the story. First, I have omitted Arthur's encounter with two giants, in part to save space but also because this episode holds up the action a little too much; it occurs between Arthur's initial fight outside the Amorous Castle and his continuing mission to find the Perilous Castle and defeat the marshal. The second cut comes near to the end, when, after he has successfully overcome all opposition and reached the Perilous Castle, a further series of adventures take place which adds little to the story. I have generally tidied up the ending also, to give a tighter and more fitting resolution to the story. For those who wish to read either the omitted passages or the ending given by the original story-teller, I recommend Thomas Vesce's translation (see below).

A word about the names. These are all symbolic, serving to identify characters by type. Thus we find Arthur's mistress is called the Lady of the Blonde Hair, and he encounters the Amorous Knight of the Savage Castle, and the Count of the Amorous City. These are all part and parcel of the medieval story-teller's art, and I have retained them in translation rather than putting them back into the original Old French.

The romance exists in a single manuscript in the National Library of Paris (BN, Fr.2154) This is a text copied in the fifteenth or sixteenth century, but both its recent translator, Thomas Vesce, and its only editor, Ferdinand Heuckenkamp, agree that the original version of the story dates from the late thirteenth century. It certainly suggests a knowledge of several of the romances of Chrétien de Troyes, including *Erec and Enide*, *Lancelot* and *Perceval*, from which several episodes in *Le Chevalier* appear to have been borrowed. However, there is a freshness and an originality about the romance which mark out its author as having a mind of his own and a very independent viewpoint.

The edition by Ferdinand Heuckenkamp was published in Halle by M. Niemeyer in 1896, and the work has only recently been translated by Thomas E. Vesce as *The Knight of the Parrot* (New York and London, Garland Press, 1986). I have used this text throughout and am indebted to Professor Vesce for his work in making this story available in English.

HE DAY OF KING ARTHUR'S CROWNING fell on Pentecost, and there was much rejoicing and holiday in the city of Camelot. At the height of the feast a damsel appeared and greeted the young king with these words.

'My lord, the best and fairest lady in all this land sends me to you to ask for your help. An evil knight comes daily to raid her lands. He has already killed some sixty of her best knights, and now she feels that she can do no more. And so am I sent to ask if there is some brave knight you can send to help her.'

And King Arthur answered that he would most certainly give thought to her request, and that meanwhile she was to be treated as an honoured guest at his court. And thus she was taken to the house of a rich lord and cared for with the utmost respect until the ceremony and celebration for King Arthur's crowning were over, at which point the damsel came again before the young king and reminded him of her quest.

'My lady,' said Arthur, 'I have not forgotten your request. Indeed, I intend to undertake this adventure myself, for yours was the first such request to be made of me and I would in no wise let any other man undertake it.' And though his lords protested that one of them should go in his place, King Arthur refused to be moved, and that very day prepared to depart, having made King Lot of Orkney his regent and bade his court to obey him as they would the king himself.

Then, armed with lance and sword, and clad in plain armour, the king set forth with the damsel at this side. They had not gone far before they entered the Forest of Camelot, and as they rode along, chatting as the mood took them, suddenly they heard a woman's voice crying out for help. Then they saw where a well-dressed lady rode full-tilt towards them, pursued by a knight with drawn sword. As she drew level with them, the lady called upon King Arthur to help her against the knight, who had already slain her companion. Arthur, setting his spear in the rest, called upon the man to hold hard and face him. 'For surely you will get no honour from killing women!'

At this the knight put away his sword and retreated a suitable distance to couch his own lance. Then the two knights charged towards each other and met with a great crash. King Arthur received his opponent's spear on the shield, which broke in half; his own blow struck the man so mightily that he was knocked clean out of the saddle and fell stunned to the earth. As he came to, he saw King Arthur standing over him with drawn sword, and at once begged for mercy.

'I shall spare you on one condition,' said the king. 'That you place yourself in the service of this lady whom you lately pursued.'

At this the knight changed colour. 'I would as soon be dead as in her service,' he cried.

'Why should this be so?' demanded Arthur.

'Sir, I will tell you,' answered the knight, sitting up. 'You can see how beautiful she is, and in truth her beauty is like a naked sword against my neck. I have loved her this long while, but she loves another, and it was for this reason that I desired to slay her, for if I cannot have her then neither shall he.'

Shocked by these words, the king asked the knight his name and learned that he was known as the Knight of the Wasteland. 'Well, sir,' said Arthur, 'you must put yourself at this lady's mercy or I will be forced to kill you.'

'Sire, I have no trust in any lady's mercy,' said the knight, 'but I will do as you ask, for the sake of your chivalry and honour.'

By then the lady herself spoke up, saying that she had no wish to have the man commit himself to her. 'Do what you will with him,' she told King Arthur. 'Kill him or imprison him as you will.'

Then Arthur made the knight swear on his honour to return to Camelot and there to place himself under the recognizance of King Lot, and to say that he was sent by the young knight who had but lately departed with the damsel. Then, when he had departed, the king asked the lady which way she wished to go and whether she needed company on the road.

'Sir,' said she, 'I would as soon lead you to a court which is close by. It is the finest court in all the world, and many of the finest knights and ladies dwell there. Until recently it was the happiest place, where every year the knights joust together in friendly sport for the prize of a far-famed parrot which is able to discourse on many matters. But alas, recently a knight has come there who has proved himself stronger than the rest, and he has made himself the lord of that place through strength of arms. Now he forces us to serve him and to pay homage to his lady, who is the most hideous damsel you ever saw. Every month we must all assemble at Clausel Field and swear allegiance to this knight and declare that his lady is the most beautiful ever seen.'

'Madam, this is a terrible thing you tell me,' said King Arthur. 'Surely there is something you can do.'

'There is, indeed,' said the lady quickly. 'I would ask of you that you accompany me and help us to overcome this evil knight. If we join together and you become my knight, you may claim that I am fairer than his companion.'

'That would certainly be true,' said Arthur with a smile. He turned to the damsel. 'Will you permit me to turn aside from the path for a while so that I may help this lady?'

The damsel shrugged. 'It is not me you serve, but my lady. If you wish to turn aside, I will certainly not stop you.'

Thus accorded, the three turned their mounts towards the lady's court, which was no great distance away. As they approached they saw tents set up in the meadows below the castle, and there many knights and ladies disported themselves, singing and dancing and making much noise. When they saw the party approaching, they ceased from their games and began instead to call out to Arthur, telling him that he was foolish to come there and would best be served by leaving again at once. Arthur suffered their gibes in silence for a time, then reproved them with all the seriousness of youth.

At this moment there came in sight the knight of whom the lady had spoken. He was fully armed and accompanied by his companion, whose hideous appearance could not be disguised by her fine apparel. Before them came a dwarf, who was goading a palfrey on whose back was a golden cage containing the parrot of which you have heard tell.

As soon as the knight saw Arthur he at once shouted for everyone to clear the way, then without so much as a word of warning, he charged straight upon the young king with all his might.

The battle which ensued was long and furious, and for a long time neither knight had the upper hand. Then the knight struck a blow which cut through King Arthur's helmet and wounded him in the face so that he bore the scar ever after. The pain and anger this caused were such that Arthur fought back, half blinded by the blood from his wound, with even greater force, until he struck a blow which severed the sword-arm and hand of his adversary.

The knight fell to the earth with a scream and begged for mercy. King Arthur stood over him and demanded to know his name. 'Sir,' gasped the wounded man, 'I am known as the Merciless Lion for all the knights I have overcome.'

'And how have you treated those foes?' demanded the king.

'Those who died I took all their lands and possessions, their women and children. Those who lived I took half their goods and made them come before me every month and swear their allegiance.'

'And for how long have you done these things?'

'Sir, for fifteen years I have been supreme. Until today I never met a knight who could overcome me.'

'You have not acted according to the laws of chivalry,' said Arthur sternly. 'But I will not slay you.' He thought for a moment, then continued, 'This is what I will have you do. First, restore everything you have taken from the people you have subdued wherever you still have it, and right any other wrongs you can against them. Then you shall remain here, at his place, and build a charterhouse. There, every month, until King Arthur of Britain shall summon you to his court, you shall have all those whom you once forced to pay you homage come and visit you. Then, when King Arthur shall summon you, you must journey to Camelot in a cart, as knights must who cannot ride. And all those who until now served you of their own free will shall go with you, and all shall seek forgiveness of the king. Do you understand this?'

Groaning with the pain of his severed arm, the Merciless Lion agreed to everything King Arthur asked. Only then did surgeons rush forward to attend him, and general rejoicing broke out upon every side, save only that the hideous damsel stole away quietly and full of hate for the young knight who had felled her lover. As to the lady who had brought them there, she was overjoyed at the outcome and gave great thanks to the king.

At this moment the parrot, who had watched all of this, began to call out to the dwarf to lead it closer. 'For this is surely the best knight in all the world,' cried the bird, 'and I would see him who has won me fairly and squarely.'

And when the dwarf obeyed, the wise and astonishing bird looked long at King Arthur and uttered these words, 'Now I see that this is the very man of whom Merlin spoke when he said that one day a son of an ewe should subdue a lion without mercy!' And having said this, the remarkable bird began to tell all the deeds of Merlin until that time – a recital which would undoubtedly have taken a long time had not Arthur called for silence!

Then he took formal possession of the bird, along with the dwarf who cared for it and the horse on which its cage rested, and prepared to take his leave of the lady and her people. Before he departed, they begged to know by what name he was called, and the king, thinking for a moment, answered, 'You may call me the Knight of the Parrot, for such I am now.'

And so the king and the damsel rode on their way, accompanied by the dwarf and the parrot. And as they rode Arthur glanced often at the maiden, who was of great beauty. The parrot, noticing this, was moved to comment that they would make a fine couple – he so handsome and strong, she so fair and well born. At this the maiden looked in wonder at the parrot and said, 'How do you know about my lineage?'

'Lady,' replied the parrot, 'do you not remember when you were a child receiving instruction from the lady of the Castle of Love? I was there, though I did not have so much to say then.'

While the damsel marvelled at this, the parrot addressed King Arthur. 'Sire, would you not like to know the name of this lady with whom you are riding?'

'I would well,' replied the king.

'She is named Beauty without Villainy, and she is the daughter of the noble Count of Valsin.'

King Arthur was pleased indeed to hear this, and the little company rode on pleasantly together until the time of vespers, when it began to grow cold. The parrot demanded of the dwarf that his cage be covered and then fell silent as they continued on their way. Soon they sighted a fine castle and sought shelter there for the night, which they were readily granted by its lord.

In the morning King Arthur was woken by the voice of the parrot calling him to get up, for this was a day in which he would receive great honour. So, having dined with the lord of the castle, the company set forth again, and had not gone far before they heard a great commotion ahead of them, and saw people running away on every side. A knight came in view, raging and waving his sword, and with a cry the damsel identified him as the very knight she had brought King Arthur to fight.

As the knight came thundering towards them, they saw that he was huge beyond mortal size and mounted upon a horse the size of a small elephant. When they saw this, the damsel and the dwarf both fled and the parrot, left behind, began to cry out to King Arthur to open his cage and let him fly free. But to this Arthur merely laughed and reminded the bird of the song it had but lately sung to him concerning honour. Then he prepared to defend himself against the huge knight.

That was to be a mighty battle, as you may well expect, for the giant knight was a terrible foe and King Arthur was still young and untried. But he fought bravely and with skill, and youth was on his side, so that he began to force the huge creature back before him and to inflict several great wounds upon him. And it amazed the king that, whenever he struck the knight, no matter if it was upon the shield or the helm or the leg, blood gushed forth as from a far deeper wound. Finally he struck several blows which brought the huge fellow to his knees and then with all the force in his body King Arthur cut off the man's right arm, which still held his sword.

Then the knight gave forth a great roar and staggered back and forth, crying out and fountaining blood everywhere. And Arthur could not help noticing that wherever the blood fell the earth smoked as if it were burning. The giant smashed through several trees, and began to flail about with his good arm, which now somehow held an axe, though he had not seemed to possess one a moment before.

Arthur stood in awe at the giant's death throes, which felled several trees and gouged great trenches in the earth. But at last he lay still and the king approached to examine the body. There he found a most marvellous and terrible thing. For when he tried to remove the fallen knight's helm, he found it to be all of a piece with the body, and indeed everything – armour, helm, even the axe he carried – was of flesh and bone. And the flesh was hot to the touch, though beginning to cool, and hard and dry like a snake's.

Then Arthur knew that he had fought no mortal man, but some kind of demon, and he marvelled greatly where this frightful creature had come from. Then he heard the parrot singing close by, praising him for his great deed in defeating the inhuman creature.

So after he had rested a while, King Arthur set off to follow the path he believed the damsel to have taken, and as he rode he was met by four knights whom she had dispatched to find if he lived and to offer him any help they might. They were much amazed to find him still living, and asked to be taken to where the body of the great knight lay. Then they rejoiced exceedingly to see that he was finally slain, and praised the Knight of the Parrot greatly for his prowess. Then they set off for the castle where the damsel was waiting for them, sending one of their number ahead with the good tidings.

When they came in sight of the city, a great procession came forth to greet them. Everyone wanted to touch or thank the Knight of the Parrot for setting them free. The damsel herself, Beauty without Villainy, came forth to meet them. She begged forgiveness of King Arthur for fleeing and this he willingly granted. Then they went inside to supper, and Arthur's wounds were dressed and fresh clothing put upon him and he was altogether treated as a hero should be.

All this while the parrot complained bitterly about the dwarf, who had left him behind in the forest and fled. So loudly did he cry and squawk that in the end Arthur sent a squire to bring him to his own room, at which the bird became quieter, though it continued to sing his praises and accuse the dwarf of leaving it to die. Arthur was at length able to calm it down and to bring about a reconciliation between the bird and its servant, after which he went down into the great hall and supped well among those who could not cease from praising him.

Meanwhile, the damsel had rejoined her mistress, and had told her all that had occurred on the journey. The lady of the castle, who was known as the Lady of the Blonde Hair, and who was herself not unskilled in magic, had already looked upon the face of King Arthur, and had evinced a great love for him, of which she spoke not a word at this time.

So when supper was ended, the ladies came into the hall and joined the knights, and then for the first time the lady of the castle met her saviour, and as she looked longingly upon him, her colour changed and she began to speak of love and the service which all knights owed to their ladies. And she asked the Knight of the Parrot if he had a lady, and upon hearing that he did not, expressed great astonishment that so fine a hero should be thus lacking. The parrot, hearing all of this and seeing which way the wind blew, began to sing a romantic song, so that both the king and the lady stopped talking and listened.

After this wine was brought and then all retired to bed. A place had been made up in the hall for the Knight of the Parrot, and the bird kept him entertained until he fell asleep by telling him a story about a lady who was wrongly imprisoned.

In the morning after they had all dined, they went forth to view the body of the dead knight and, like King Arthur himself, they marvelled to find that man and armour were all of a piece. Then the Lady of the Blonde Hair ordered her seneschal to skin the creature, which was clearly not human, but must be likened to other creatures of this kind which are mentioned in the book *Mappa Mundi*, which lists many such strange and unlikely creatures that dwell in far-off places in the world.

As the company was returning to the castle a damsel appeared, riding hot-foot towards them. She was crying bitterly and wringing her hands, and when she was near enough for them to hear, they heard that she was calling out for the Knight of the Parrot. Arthur at once rode forward and asked her what was amiss, but when she saw him she fell fainting from her horse. Leaping down, Arthur lifted her head and supported her until her senses returned. Then he asked again what he could do for her.

'Ah, fair sweet sir,' she said, 'I have come from the Lady Flor de Mont, daughter of the late King Belnain of Ile Fort. After he was killed in a tournament, his lands were given into the care of his marshal, who had served him well in his life. But now this man grew greedy and, having won the barons over to his side, proposed to marry my lady, who has no love at all for him. Now he has imprisoned both my lady and her mother the queen in a castle, which they are stoutly defending against him as he has laid siege to it. Sir, I have ridden far and through great danger to find you. Will you not return with me and set free these noble ladies?'

'I shall do everything in my power to aid you,' replied King Arthur, and at once made preparations to return to the city before departing on this new adventure. Everyone was ready to cheer him on his way save the Lady of the Blonde Hair, who was much angered at his willingness to depart with another damsel. Concealing her thoughts, she rode in silence back to the city. Once they were there, however, she announced that there was to be a tournament eight days hence, the winner of which would win a kiss from her and her promise of friendship for at least a year. Then she begged the Knight of the Parrot to take part and pressed the damsel from the Ile Fort so hard that she eventually gave her consent, though with great unwillingness. Thus King Arthur himself could not refuse and so matters stood as preparations went forward to set up the lists and pavilions and send forth messages to all the knights of that land.

In the days that followed, the Knight of the Parrot and the Lady of the Blonde Hair were much in each other's company. Finally, on the evening of the day before the tournament was to begin the lady summoned King Arthur to a magnificent chamber which he had not seen before. It had in it a great bed over which was set a wonderful carving of a hawk. They sat together on the bed and spoke of many things, and all the while the lady looked upon the Knight of the Parrot with great desire, until at last he could no longer resist her looks but took her in his arms. It is likely, indeed, that they would have lain upon the bed and made love had not the lady heard one of her damsels approaching and disengaged herself from the king's embrace. But now she looked upon him and asked him where his heart truly lay.

'I think you know that, lady,' said he. But the Lady of the Blonde Hair was not satisfied with this. Instead, she pointed to the carving of the hawk and asked him to read what was written around the base.

'It says,' Arthur said, 'Sir Knight, you who sit here with a lady, give to her whatever she will ask of you.'

'Just so,' said the lady. 'Will you do what is asked of you, for me?'

'If it is within my power,' replied the king.

'Then I ask that when you fight in the tournament tomorrow, you will quit yourself as poorly as possible.'

Arthur looked at her in astonishment.

'Surely you mean as well as possible?'

'That is not what I said,' answered the lady. 'Will you keep your word now?'

Pale and trembling, the young king bowed his head. 'Since I have given my word to you, I will keep it. But I had far rather prove myself the best knight than the worst in your sight.'

He left the chamber at once and returned to the hall. There he pretended to be light-hearted and content, though within he felt angry and confused. The parrot, noticing this, sang a little song about the lover who turned anger to honour. And when he heard this, Arthur smiled in truth and that night he slept well despite all his fears for the outcome of the tournament.

Next day the games began with a great show of arms and a mighty splintering of spears. Everyone watched the Knight of the Parrot to see how he would perform and all were amazed to see him easily overcome – sometimes seeming to fall from his horse without being touched. At the end of the day, everyone was speculating how he could possibly have killed the monstrous knight, and assumed he must have used magic. But, if he had the power of magic on his side, how could he be so easily defeated? The overall winner on that first day was one Count Doldays of the Castle of Love, and he was soon boasting that he would be the recipient of a kiss from the Lady of the Blonde Hair. The Knight of the Parrot, overhearing this, exclaimed in the hearing of all that he would prove otherwise on the morrow. At which everyone laughed, thinking him quite the poorest knight they had ever seen.

Meanwhile, the Lady of the Blonde Hair, who had overheard this argument, came to join them. She upbraided Count Doldays for speaking so rashly and foolishly of the hero who had slain the monster knight when he could not. Then she turned to the Knight of the Parrot and asked him who he would serve in the lists tomorrow.

'Why, you, my lady,' he replied.

At this the parrot, who had been listening to all this, broke out in loud cries, swearing that his knight would do much better at the tournament tomorrow since he would be free to prove himself. King

Arthur and everyone else looked in wonder at the bird and asked what it meant.

'Why,' said the bird, 'since today my knight was in prison, he could hardly do well.'

'What do you mean?' demanded the Lady of the Blonde Hair. 'Surely he was present today.'

'Not so,' said the parrot.

'Then tell us where this prison you speak of is to be found.'

'Right here,' answered the bird.

'How can this be?' replied the lady. 'I myself saw him riding about the field all day.'

'I swear he was in the worst prison ever devised, for it stripped him of his courage and made him seem a fool.'

'Who placed him in this prison you speak of?'

'That I will not say,' answered the parrot.

'If you do not,' said the Lady of the Blonde Hair, 'I swear I shall have you killed if your knight does not do better tomorrow.'

'Well, be that as it may. I believe he will do as well as any man in fair combat.'

Thus matters stood, and they all returned to the castle. There the Lady of the Blonde Hair retired to her room in great agitation. She knew that the Knight of the Parrot had proved himself more than worthy, and that she could never recompense him for the dishonour he had borne in the lists that day. Nor could she think of any way to make up for the promise she had forced from him. Finally she went in search of the knight and with great humility offered herself to him as a reward for all that he had suffered.

King Arthur, angry and hurt to the core by the slights and dishonour he had been forced to undergo that day, looked at her and wondered how he could have thought her fair. Then angrily he struck her to the floor and told her, 'Since you made me swear to behave in the worst way I could today, see how I continue to obey you!' And he struck her again, and left the chamber.

The lady, weeping bitterly, was even more torn than before. On the one hand, she reviled the Knight of the Parrot – a man whose true name she did not even know – for striking her; while on the other, she knew in her heart that he had been more sorely pressed because of her actions than any man had the right to be, and she imagined what her people would say if the matter ever came out – as well it might – that she should so harshly deal with the brave and valiant hero who had saved them all from the evil knight!

Thus she did her best to restore her appearance and to conceal the blows she had received. Then she sent for the marshal of the lists and told him that she suspected the Count of Doldays might try to ambush the Knight of the Parrot and kill him, and that therefore the marshal was to arrange that a number of her own knights should surround him at all times and protect him to the best of their abilities.

Indeed, the Lady of the Blonde Hair need not have worried. Next day the Knight of the Parrot rode everywhere like a whirlwind. Wherever he rode, he left behind heaps of unhorsed and bleeding men, so that soon no one dared face him but did everything they could to avoid him.

The parrot, who had asked to be carried to the lists and placed in his cage near the Lady of the Blonde Hair, spoke to her thus, 'Now you see my master is no longer in prison, and that he is showing his true worth. I believe this will release me from the promise I made to you.'

The Lady looked on blankly as the Knight of the Parrot proceeded to chase everyone from the field. Finally there was only Count Doldays and he remaining, the Knight of the Parrot having made certain to avoid him until this moment. Now they faced each other and everyone else retreated from the lists to give them room. With lances in rest, they charged together and, thanks to the anger which now consumed the count, he struck such a blow that it pierced the Knight of the Parrot's side and made a great wound there. He, in turn, struck the count such a blow that he was unhorsed and sorely wounded. As he lay on the ground, the Knight of the Parrot came and stood over him with drawn sword.

At that the count begged for mercy, and his opponent granted it on condition that he place himself for ever at the mercy of the Lady of the Blonde Hair, whom he had so recently boasted of conquering.

Thus the tournament ended with the Knight of the Parrot the undoubted victor. All those who had slighted and mocked him yesterday now praised and honoured him, and it was as if the previous events had not happened. The hero went up to the Lady of the Blonde Hair and there before all the company kissed her and held her to him as the best knight in the tournament. And whether it was for the anguish he saw in her eyes, or from courtesy, he forbore to speak of the promise she had forced from him.

And so the whole company returned in joyous mood to the court, and both the Count Doldays and the Knight of the Parrot were taken to be healed of their wounds.

That night, after the feasting held in celebration of the games was over, the Lady of the Blonde Hair and the Knight of the Parrot retired each to their beds. But it was not long before the knight rose again and went in search of the lady. Nor was she slow to receive him, for this was her heart's desire. And so they spent the night in the pursuit of love and each had much joy of the other, and for several nights after that they came together to explore the pleasure that each gave the other. Then the morning dawned when the damsel of Flor de Mont came before them and reminded the Knight of the Parrot of his promise to help her own lady. He, abashed by her reminder, at once begged leave of the Lady of the Blonde Hair to go, and though she was reluctant indeed to see him depart, none the less she saw that there was no help for it and so gave her blessing.

The knight prepared to leave at once and the Lady of the Blonde Hair and many of her courtiers rode out with him part of the morning. When the time came for them to turn back, the lady drew King Arthur to one side and asked him, in a low voice, if she would ever see him again.

'If God grants it, I shall return to you soon,' he replied.

Thus they parted and the Knight of the Parrot, accompanied by the dwarf carrying the bird in its golden cage and the damsel, set out upon the next part of his adventure.

When they had ridden for several days, they arrived at a castle of one of the knights in service of the Lady Flor de Mont. This man, whose name was Andois, had remained neutral in the quarrel between the lady and her marshal, and when the Knight of the Parrot and his companions arrived, he made them welcome. Sitting with him later in a splendid garden, King Arthur put to him the question as to why he had failed to serve his lady in her hour of need.

'I will tell you,' said Andois. 'When I was younger, I served the Lady Flor de Mont's father, King Belnain, in a war against two other lords. They proved to be far stronger than he, and he was losing the war. In the end I gathered a force which consisted of my own men and various foreign mercenaries. With their help we drove the two lords out of my master's lands and re-established him. In return he gave lands and money to the foreigners, but to myself and my men he gave nothing. When I questioned him about this, he said that I was his vassal anyway and therefore it was my duty, and that if I had been less rich already, he would have got better service from me far sooner. Thus when he died at last, he gave his daughter into the keeping of the marshal, as you know. I swore then that I would never help her, but yet she remains my lady to whom I owe fealty and therefore neither will I help the marshal against her.'

Now, when he heard this, King Arthur spoke at length to the noble knight and called upon him in the name of his honour to help the lady who was rightfully his suzerain. Indeed, so eloquently did he plead that in the end Andois agreed to offer whatever help he could.

Next morning the Knight of the Parrot and his companions rose early and set out for the castle of the Lady Flor de Mont. The only way into the Ile Fort was through a narrow pass which was heavily guarded by the marshal's best knights. They had been warned to expect the coming of the Knight of the Parrot, word of whose fame had begun to spread, and had arrived there well before him. Thus it was that when Arthur rode up to the entrance to the pass, a knight challenged him at once.

'Sir,' said the Knight of the Parrot, 'I have come a long way to this place and I intend to go further. Either get out of my way or accept my challenge.'

'Who may you be?' demanded the guardian of the pass.

'I am the Knight of the Parrot,' Arthur replied.

Then the guardian laughed and looked upon him with pity, thinking him mad, for he did not notice the parrot in its cage, and did not believe that one so young could possibly be the mighty knight of whom he had heard to many stories.

'Laugh if you will,' said Arthur, 'but I will pass.'

And so saying, he set his spear in rest and covered himself with his shield and charged the guardian. He, surprised but in no wise afraid, rode to meet him. The two met in the midst of the way and the Knight of the Parrot easily overcame his opponent. The guardian of the passage at once rose and, with great respect and humility, acknowledged him to be whom he said. Then he offered shelter to the knight and the damsel, the dwarf and the parrot that night. This King Arthur accepted gladly and the companions spent a comfortable night in the lodgings of the defeated knight.

Next morning they rose early and continued upon their way. As they drew nearer to the castle where the lady and her mother were imprisoned, the damsel began to weep. When King Arthur enquired why she did this, she pointed to a nearby hill from which flew a scarlet pennant. 'There waits the most powerful knight in the world. He is the marshal's champion and he will surely kill you.'

'As to that,' said Arthur, 'what will be will be.'

So saying, he turned his mount towards the hill and saw coming towards him a tall figure who, having spied him coming from afar, and realizing his identity, waited no longer but spurred his horse to full gallop against the young king. Arthur met him unswervingly and there ensued a furious combat which, both men having been unhorsed, continued on the ground with swords.

After they had been fighting for some time, Arthur drew back and said, panting, 'Sir, never did I encounter a better opponent. Let us continue this fight before the castle of those whom I have come to rescue, so that they may see both he who defends them and he who comes to their aid.'

'Agreed,' said the knight, 'for in you also I own a better fighter than any I have ever encountered.'

So the two adjourned to the meadow below the castle walls, and there, in full sight of the Lady Flor de Mont, they continued their battle, until the Knight of the Parrot finally delivered such a blow to his adversary's helm that it split in twain and the man fell down upon the earth stunned. When he recovered his senses and saw the Knight of the Parrot standing over him, he at once cried for mercy and this King Arthur granted him on condition that he promised to serve the lady of the castle.

At this moment the lady herself, accompanied by her damsels, approached. She gave thanks to the Knight of the Parrot and praised him for his courage and strength. Then they all went up into the castle, where they were royally entertained. The parrot began to sing songs about his master, telling some of his great deeds, and he sang so sweetly that he was soon surrounded by the lady's damsels, who hung upon every word and applauded the parrot for his remarkable skills.

On to this scene of rejoicing came the Queen of Ile Fort, a sad-faced lady whose presence commanded respect and quiet. She greeted the Knight of the Parrot and asked him from which country he hailed.

'From Britain, my lady,' he replied.

'Then you are acquainted with King Arthur?'

'Indeed, he is well known to me,' replied the king, smiling.

'Your fame has flown before you,' said the queen. 'We are eternally in gratitude to you for coming.'

'My thanks to you, my lady,' replied Arthur. 'I pray you, tell me where I may find this marshal who has dared to hold you and your daughter prisoner against your wills.'

'It is too soon for that,' said the queen gently. 'First you must rest. I know something of what you have accomplished already.'

'Madam, I did not come here to rest,' said the king.

'Very well, then,' said the queen with a sigh, remembering other young knights who had been just as eager as this. 'Stay here tonight and I promise that tomorrow one will come to show you the way.'

And so King Arthur rested there that night, and was well housed and fed. Then, in the middle of the night, the queen came to the chamber where he was sleeping and woke him. 'Sir knight,' she said, 'the one who is to lead you into even greater danger has arrived.'

The Knight of the Parrot rose and dressed quickly, then he followed the queen out into the meadow before the castle. There his horse awaited him, freshly groomed and with supplies of food and wine hanging at the saddle-bow. There the Lady Flor de Mont awaited him, and when several squires had helped arm him, she handed him his helmet herself. On it she had fastened a silken scarf which she had embroidered.

'Wear this for me,' she said softly.

Then the queen led him to a nearby tree, beneath which stood the strangest creature he had ever seen. It was about the size of a young bull, but with a long, slender neck like a dragon and a small head like a deer with two white horns sprouting forth. Its fur was reddish and gleamed in the light of the moon. When it saw the knight, it bowed before him. The queen, tears in her eyes, said, 'This beast will lead you to your destiny. Only once every three months it appears, but it has not done so in over a year. From this I gauge that this is a moment of great import. Take care, sir knight,' she added, sighing, 'and come back to us safely.'

King Arthur looked at the creature and it gazed back at him with a look that seemed to say it would speak if it might. Then it turned away and began to lead him.

They went by a long road which led through forest and field and valley, until they reached a castle that had once been a fair and mighty hold, but which was now in ruins, thanks to the ravages of the marshal. Here the beast made known by gesture that it needed to rest, then it vanished into the ruins. The Knight of the Parrot tied his horse to a tall and shady tree and sat down beneath it to rest himself. After a while, he became aware of a most beautiful scent, and as he rose to his feet he saw coming towards him an old man, dressed entirely in white.

'Greetings, king of Britain,' he said.

Arthur greeted him in return and asked him how he knew his true identity.

'Fear not,' replied the old man, 'I am he by whom you are set forth upon the greatest of adventures. I am the beast who has led you all this day.'

'How can this be?' asked King Arthur in astonishment.

'I am,' said the old man, 'that same King Belnain whose wife and daughter you but recently met. Though dead I am permitted to walk the earth for a time in the shape you have seen, until such time as the marshal to whom I entrusted my lands is brought to book for his evil deeds.'

King Arthur, filled with wonder, asked, 'What place do you inhabit when you are not either in the form of the strange beast or in your present form?'

'I may not speak of this,' said King Belnain, 'save only to say that it is a most beautiful place, and that I shall remain there until a prophecy made by Merlin is fulfilled. After that I shall go to a place of even greater glory, such as God promises all who serve him.'

Then the old king looked at him for a long while and said, 'I bid you to remain here this night and to rest beneath this tree from which you shall take a flower and place it within your bosom. I shall tell you why. This very night you shall see a great company of knights and ladies come into this place, and there they will hold a most splendid tournament. Many of the knights will ride up to you and ask, "Where is the Knight of the Parrot? Will he not join us in our sports?" On no account must you do so, for then you will die as surely as the sun is bound to rise on the morrow. Take care to remain beneath the tree, for as long as it endures, and the scent of its flowers surrounds you, no harm can come to you.'

Then the old king bade him farewell and prepared to depart. 'I shall not see you again, I believe, but I wish you well. Do not fail me.'

With that he was gone, and King Arthur prepared for the long night ahead. He drew his horse closer and pulled a flower from the tree, breathing in its heady scent. So peaceful and quieting was its effect that he needed neither food nor drink nor sleep. He was alert to every noise, however, and soon heard the sound of muffled hoofbeats announcing the arrival of a great company. Varlets and sergeants came first, setting up pavilions and lists in the meadow before the ruined castle. Then came the knights and their ladies, squires and damsels, in great numbers, and the tournament commenced just as the old king had said. Many mighty encounters took place, and the Knight of the Parrot was hard pressed not to join in – especially when men from one side of the general mêlée came and begged him to save them by fighting upon their side. Indeed, it was at this point that he was prepared to forget the old man's warning and even rose and made ready to fight. Then he heard a bell ring out somewhere beyond the ruins and at this the entire company – tents, varlets, squires, knights and damsels – vanished away as though they had never been, nor could the Knight of the Parrot see where they went.

Soon after, dawn broke and Arthur rode on his way, wondering greatly over the events of the night. Soon he came to a crossing of the ways, where a great boulder stood. On one side were carved letters which read:

THREE MISADVENTURES THERE ARE IN THE WORLD. THE FIRST CONCERNS HE WHO KNOWS THE GOOD BUT CHOOSES TO LEARN NOTHING MORE OF IT. THE SECOND CONCERNS HE WHO KNOWS WHAT IS GOOD BUT FAILS TO FOLLOW ITS WAY. THE THIRD CONCERNS HE WHO KNOWS WHAT IS GOOD BUT WHO CHASTISES OTHERS FOR NOT FOLLOWING IT WHILE HE HIMSELF DOES ONLY EVIL.

On the far side of the boulder were more letters. These said:

WHOEVER SEEKS A MARVELLOUS ADVENTURE LET HIM FOLLOW THE PATH TO THE RIGHT AND WAIT HERE NO LONGER.

Musing on this, the Knight of the Parrot chose to follow the path to the right. All day he followed it until he heard a voice calling out to him, 'Alas, my friend, get away from here, for I cannot help you.'

He looked around and saw a damsel coming towards him from the top of a hill. Her face was smeared with tears and her clothing was torn. At once Arthur demanded to know what had happened.

'Alas, Sir Knight, a terrible serpent has carried off the Amorous Knight of the Savage Castle, with whom I was riding. I fear for his life – and for yours if you do not flee.'

'Where is this creature?' asked the knight.

The damsel pointed towards a nearby lake and he at once made his way there. The serpent was indeed a fierce and terrible creature, and what was more it still had the Amorous Knight in its jaws, only his armour preventing it from crushing him. As soon as the Knight of the Parrot saw the evil worm, he spurred his mount towards it. His lance pierced its breast and heart in one and it dropped the wounded knight and fell thrashing to the ground. So mighty, indeed, were its death throes that its tail struck the Knight of the Parrot a terrible blow, knocking both he and his horse into the lake. Though sorely wounded and in danger of drowning, it was yet the water which saved him, since it washed away some of the poison the glancing blow from the serpent had inflicted upon him.

Staggering forth from the water, King Arthur found his horse wandering in a dazed fashion close by. He mounted with difficulty and rode in what he thought was the right direction. He had not gone far before the poison overcame him and he fell senseless to the ground.

The wounded knight, meanwhile, who had been dropped from the very jaws of the serpent, recovered his senses and found his way back to the damsel, who was overjoyed to see him. They both wondered what could have happened to the knight who had so bravely attacked the serpent, and concluded sadly that he must have perished.

They made their way home to the Savage Castle and were preparing for bed when they overheard a local fisherman and his wife talking outside their window. 'I think he still lives,' said the man. 'Glory! Look at the armour on him. How it shines!'

'Aye,' replied his wife. 'Thank God we came by when we did!'

Hearing this, the Amorous Knight leaned out of the window and called down to them. 'Ho! You there! What are you about?'

The fisherman, sounding fearful, called back, 'Nothing, my lord!'

'Villain!' shouted the knight, 'I do not believe you!' And he sent his soldiers to investigate. They found the fisherman and his wife crouching over a figure who lay in the bottom of their boat. He was barely conscious and seemed paralysed and unable to speak. The soldiers carried him carefully back to the knight's castle and laid him in a bed where his wounds were tended and warm covers placed over him. When they removed his armour, they found a strange flower caught in his bosom, which gave off a powerful and pleasing scent. The Amorous Knight and his lady, realizing that this was the very man to whom they owed their lives, they watched over him anxiously.

For several hours he neither moved nor spoke, then shortly before midnight he opened his eyes and asked to know where he was. The knight told him and explained how they had found him. Then they gave him water to drink and in a while he asked for food. From there on he made rapid progress, so that within three days he was as hale and strong as he had been before encountering the serpent. Meanwhile, he told the whole story of his adventures to his host and hostess, who, on hearing that he was on his way to the castle of the marshal, were able to tell him something of the dangers he would have to face.

'In three days' time you will reach the place,' said the Amorous Knight. 'It is called the Perilous Castle, and not without good reason. It is set upon a steep hill, which is surrounded by water. There is but one way to enter, and that is across a bridge so narrow that only one man may pass it on foot. In the centre of the bridge is a great wheel turned by magic. No one I know of who had gone there has ever returned, they have all been crushed by the wheel. However . . .' He paused and looked at the Knight of the Parrot. 'Though I serve the marshal, you have saved my life. I will help you to save yours. Know that when you reach the wheel you will see two marble pillars, coloured red as blood, on either side. On each of these is written a message: "You who seek to cross come close to me." On no account take any notice of this. If you do, you will die. Instead, look closely at the pillar on which is the inscription and you will see a small hole there. Inside you will see all manner of wheels and gears turning. Sever these with your sword and you will stop the wheel from turning. Thus you will have at least a chance of surviving, though after you pass the wheel I cannot say what dangers you will have to face.'

With this sound advice in mind, the Knight of the Parrot prepared to set forth. The Amorous Knight rode part of the way with him, then turned back, wishing him Godspeed. The road was steep and stony, but he made good progress that day, and most of the next. This found him in country of wild heathland, and as he rode through it, he was suddenly attacked by a naked wild woman, who leapt out of the bushes and on to the back of his horse behind him. She set her long and powerful arms around him and began to squeeze. If he had not been wearing his armour, he would certainly have been crushed to death. As it was, his horse, startled by the sudden extra weight on his back, began to buck and threw the wild woman to the ground. Drawing his sword swiftly, the Knight of the Parrot clubbed her about the head and then rode on before she could regain her senses.

Thus he passed the second day and night, and on the morning of the third day, just as the Amorous Knight had told him, he came in sight of the Perilous Castle. It was, if possible, even more forbidding than he had been led to believe. The moat was deep and dark and filled with black, swift-flowing water. The bridge was not only narrow but sharp, being made of fine-honed metal, which trembled whenever anyone set foot upon it. As to the wheel, the Amorous Knight's words had not prepared him for its terrible aspect. It too was made of metal, sharpened to the keenness of a sword, and it whirled so fast that it could scarcely be seen. Beyond it, on the further side of the bridge, was a tower of marble which looked as forbidding as did the great pile of the castle itself, where it rose, grim and forbidding, beyond the bridge.

The Knight of the Parrot looked at the task before him and his heart quailed. Yet he knew that only by facing this peril would his task be complete. Therefore, he prepared himself as best he might and, tying his horse to a boulder at the edge of the bridge, began to make his way slowly across.

At once the bridge began to tremble so much that Arthur was forced to get down on his hands and knees and crawl. The sharpness of the bridge was muffled by his mail leggings and gloves, but the trembling of the narrow way was as terrifying as anything he had ever endured.

At last he reached the whirling wheel and saw, as the Amorous Knight had told him, the writing on the pillars and the small hole through which he could make out the whirling of machinery. Drawing his sword and dragging himself into an upright position, he hugged the pillar and pushed his sword point into the hole. At once there was a loud screeching of tortured metal and the wheel slowed to a stop. Withdrawing his sword, which despite its tempered steel was battered and chipped, the Knight of the Parrot made his way onward across the rest of the bridge, which had now almost completely ceased from shaking.

Entering the tower, he found himself face to face with two powerful knights, who at once drew their swords and prepared to attack him. Wearily, Arthur raised his own weapon, but spoke to them thus, 'Alas, must every knight who crosses the bridge successfully still die?'

The two men looked at one another, then one of them abruptly lowered his sword and said, 'We have killed a great many brave knights. I for one am sick of it. You have little chance against the foes who await you within. I say you shall go without challenge or scathe from us.' The second knight, after a moment's hesitation, put away his sword also. 'Aye. I agree. Go in peace,' he said.

Arthur gave them thanks and, passing down from the tower, entered the Perilous Castle at last. By now the sun had set, and within the castle all was dark. Then, as the Knight of the Parrot entered a great hall, he saw first one, then another damsel enter from a side chamber. Every one of them was dressed alike, in purple and red, and every one carried a torch, so that by the time as many as fifty of them had come in, the hall was lit almost as bright as day.

Then there came in another figure, that of the marshal himself, clad in red armour. When he saw King Arthur, he gave a roar of fury and attacked with all his might. Defending himself, the king began a battle which lasted until well past midnight and in which neither opponent gained any ground or inflicted any serious wound.

Then the marshal became even more enraged, and swung his sword with such force that it cut through Arthur's helm and into his head. Had not his mail been of the finest steel, he might have received his death wound there and then. As it was, when he felt the blood run hot into his eyes, he grew so enraged that he rose up and struck a single blow which split the marshal's head in twain to the jaw, so that he fell dead in a single moment.

Then all the damsels who had stood by, and beheld this in silence, placed their torches in silver holders around the hall and came and thanked the Knight of the Parrot profusely, hugging and kissing him until he felt more dizzy from their thanks than from his wounds.

Then four of the damsels went up into the tower and rang a bell that had not been rung since the death of King Belnain, so that all who heard it knew that the marshal was dead and that they were free. Everywhere bells began to peal out, taking up the carillon of joy, and by the time dawn broke many knights and ladies had assembled before the Perilous Castle to thank the Knight of the Parrot for his courage and chivalry and to do homage to him.

There the young king addressed them, calling upon them to go with him to the queen and her daughter and there to rejoice and swear their fealty again to she who was still their lady. All were glad indeed to hear this, and once the Knight of the Parrot had rested and bathed his wounds and been dressed in fair clothes, they all set out, in a mood of great rejoicing, for the Fearless Keep, where the queen and her daughter, Flor de Mont, awaited them. There they met a strong force of knights led by the lord Andois, who had kept his word and brought his men to the service of the queen.

Then began a time of celebration and rejoicing for all the people of that land. And no one was more glad to see the Knight of the Parrot than the bird itself. For it had waited patiently for the return of its master, and had entertained the count with its songs and tales of honour. Indeed, when the bird saw Arthur approaching, he fell down into the bottom of his cage like one dead. But the knight rode up to him and said, 'Ho! Sir Parrot! Do not leave me yet!' At which the bird sat up and began to sing as gaily as ever, to everyone's delight. Then King Arthur revealed to them his true identity, at which they marvelled greatly and swore to serve him all their days.

And so the Knight of the Parrot remained at the Fearless Keep for a time, until he felt the need to return home. And so he took ship from the nearby harbour and returned swiftly along the coastline to his own lands. On the way, you may be sure that he had further adventures, though I will not speak of these here. But at length he landed in the country belonging to the Lady of the Blonde Hair. It was almost Pentecost again, and a full year had passed since he had departed on his great adventure. He sent word to the Knight of the Merciless Lion, reminding him that he should go to King Arthur, who would hold court that Pentecost at Vindesores.

And so he remained for a few days with the Lady of the Blonde Hair, and the two found as much joy in each other as they had previously. And the parrot sang sweetly as ever to them, songs of love no doubt, for that was a time of love. And the next day King Arthur returned to the court at Vindesores and was made welcome by all his fellows, who had heard nothing of his deeds and had almost begun to believe him dead. King Lot had proved a good and faithful steward in the king's absence, and revived his reward as was fitting.

The day of Pentecost dawned and there were celebrations throughout the day. The Knight of the Merciless Lion arrived at midday and was received by King Arthur in the great hall. When he discovered that it was the king whom he had fought, the knight bowed his head in humility, but Arthur raised him up and made him a knight of the Round Table, where he served loyally to the end of his days. In the evening at the feasting the parrot sat in the midst of the hall and sang his songs and told all of the adventures of the Knight of the Parrot. Everyone there was astonished and delighted to learn that the knight was their own lord, and all praised King Arthur for his courage and chivalry.

The parrot remained there in the court until its death, at a good age, when it was mourned by everyone, not least King Arthur himself, who remembered when he was the Knight of the Parrot long years after the adventures told here.

Index